"WHOEVER SHEDS MAN'S BLOOD,
BY MAN SHALL HIS BLOOD BE SHED. . . ."

THE COPS WERE ALREADY THERE, the white one with his gun extended, the black cop down on one knee, uselessly pressing a kerchief against the throat. The material had already turned scarlet. Gerald stepped over the scattered groceries as he approached. He felt absurdly calm.

The black guy looked up at his partner. "He won't make it," he said.

Funny, he thought, *why don't they ask me? I'm the doctor.*

"What'd you say?" the white cop called out, swinging around. The streetlight gleamed on his outstretched gun.

Had he said something? Funny, he hadn't realized he had spoken.

Very slowly, he pointed to the gun in his pocket. He stood still, motionless, until the cop—his face grim—had pulled out the revolver. Only then did he look down at Martin. Prone now. Quiet. No longer laughing. Would never hurt anyone's daughter again.

"An eye for an eye," Gerald Braun said clearly. "A life for a life."

By the same author

The Unorthodox Murder of Rabbi Wahl
The Final Analysis of Dr. Stark
The Nine Questions People Ask About Judaism
Why the Jews?
Jewish Literacy

AN EYE

FOR

AN EYE

JOSEPH TELUSHKIN

BANTAM BOOKS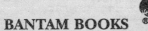

NEW YORK TORONTO LONDON SYDNEY AUCKLAND

This edition contains the complete text of the original hardcover edition.
NO ONE WORD HAS BEEN OMITTED

AN EYE FOR AN EYE

A Bantam Crime Line Book / published in association with Doubleday

PUBLISHING HISTORY
Doubleday edition published October 1991
Bantam edition / October 1992

CRIME LINE and the portrayal of a boxed "cl" are trademarks of Bantam Books, a division of Bantam Doubleday Dell Publishing Group, Inc.

ISBN 0-553-29620-5

Published simultaneously in the United States and Canada

Bantam Books are published by Bantam Books, a division of Bantam Doubleday Dell Publishing Group, Inc. Its trademark, consisting of the words "Bantam Books" and the portrayal of a rooster, is Registered in U.S. Patent and Trademark Office and in other countries. Marca Registrada. Bantam Books, 666 Fifth Avenue, New York, New York 10103.

PRINTED IN THE UNITED STATES OF AMERICA

RAD   0 9 8 7 6 5 4 3 2 1

Acknowledgments

It is very gratifying to have the opportunity to publicly thank those who have helped me during the writing of this book.

Several good friends read the manuscript in progress and made suggestions which greatly strengthened it: Shira Wolosky and Ari Weiss, Dennis Prager, and Judge Nicholas Figueroa. Parnell Hall stepped in at a difficult moment, and offered advice so effortlessly that I felt very grateful to have a friend and fellow mystery writer as my neighbor. And, as always, I am grateful for the friendship, encouragement, suggestions, and extraordinary skill of my agent, Richard Pine.

Several people helped me in the editing of this book. *An Eye for an Eye* is the fourth book on which I've worked with Linda **Kachani,** and her editorial suggestions were invaluable. I was likewise aided by the editorial advice of Stephanie St. Pierre. This is the first book on which I've worked from its inception with my beloved wife, Dvorah, and the experience of working with her so closely and intensely has been undiluted joy. And, of course, I feel the deepest sense of gratitude to my editor, Kate Miciak, who has been an inspiration, a relentless taskmaster, and a mentor. I would also like to thank Michelle Rapkin.

In addition, there are a number of writers whose works have influenced my thinking, but whom it was impossible to footnote in a work of fiction. Among them are Ernest van den Haag, who has done perhaps the most provocative and creative writing on the issue of crime and capital punishment in America; William Tucker, whose book, *Vigilante,* chronicles very precisely the devastating impact violent crime is having on our country; Rabbi Irving "Yitz" Greenberg, and his essay,

"Will There Be One Jewish People in the Year 2000?";
and Saul Bellow and his quote, "A man is only as good
as what he loves." The prologue to the book was
largely shaped by a story told by the late Rabbi Abraham Joshua Heschel, and which I heard from Rabbi
Wolfe Kelman. The section in which Daniel Winter
speculates on differences in Jewish and Christian atti-
tudes on forgiveness and punishment was influenced
by the essays of a man who has been my closest friend
for more than twenty-five years, Dennis Prager. His
writings are regularly published in his extraordinary
journal, *Ultimate Issues.*

My final acknowledgments are made with equal
gratitude but with great somberness. The issues of
crime, justice, and punishment have long obsessed me,
and I was in large part motivated to write this book by
the horrendous experiences recorded in "Justice: A
Father's Account of the Trial of His Daughter's Killer,"
by Dominick Dunne, published in his book, *Fatal
Charm.* In it, Dunne recounts the story of his daughter
Dominique's murder, and the legal farce that ensued,
which culminated in her murderer serving less than
three years in prison. I was likewise permanently af-
fected by Dr. Willard Gaylin's *The Killing of Bonnie Gar-
land,* and by living in New York City during the time of
the murder of Jennifer Levin. While writing this book,
Death of a Jewish American Princess by Shirley Frondorff
was published, chronicling the murder of Elana Stein-
berg, and the resultant nonpunishment of her killer.
That all of these injustices occurred in a society in
which I am an active participant makes me very angry,
very ashamed, and very sad. "For these things," the
Book of Lamentations declares, "do I weep. My eyes,
my eyes, flow with tears."

AN EYE
FOR AN EYE

1

Prologue

The beverage cart had just passed Rabbi Daniel Winter's row when the stocky man in the seat beside him summoned the stewardess back.

"Give me another scotch," he ordered. Smiling pleasantly, the stewardess pulled out a miniature whiskey bottle and collected the man's three dollars.

"And don't go running off like that again," the man said brusquely, "until I'm sure what I want."

"You had ordered a bottle, sir," the pony-tailed woman said. "I thought you had finished."

"Next time count six before thinking." Color flamed in the stewardess's cheeks. The man quickly uncapped the bottle and gulped the liquid down in one long swallow.

"You were rather hard on that woman," Daniel said after the stewardess retreated.

The man leaned back in his seat and laughed. "Think so? The way I see it, if you put a little fear in them, it pays. Next time I say jump, she'll jump." His hand reached up and pressed the call button. Within seconds the flight attendant reappeared.

"Another scotch," he ordered.

"Excuse me, sir," the woman said, her lips a tight line, "I have other passengers I'm serving."

The man squinted up at her name tag. "Are you really anxious, Miss Marian T., for the president of this airline to get a special letter all about you on my business stationery?"

Marian T. glared down at him, brought the bottle over and set it down hard on his serving tray, and quickly departed.

The man clapped Daniel on the back. "Ever hear about that marriage custom in Greece? Right after the ceremony, the bride and groom rush to step on each other's feet. Whoever does it first, rules the roost. I kid you not, my friend, I even think Aristotle Onassis tried to do it to Jackie." The man chortled. It was not, Daniel thought, a pleasant sound. "Step on their feet first," he went on, his thumb gesturing back towards the offended stewardess, "and they'll treat you like royalty. Otherwise, they treat you like crap."

"I hadn't noticed," Daniel said. His hand rose to adjust the black beret that kept slipping to the back of his head, then he anxiously returned to the article in front of him, "Some Postulates of Criminal Law in the Bible." The previous evening, Daniel had delivered a keynote paper at the Association of Jewish Scholarship's annual convention. His subject, *"Lex talionis*—An Eye for an Eye—Some Twentieth-Century Reflections," had stirred an unprecedented ninety-minute question-and-answer session. Then, a few hours ago, as he was starting out for the airport, an old yeshiva roommate had stuffed the photostated article into his attaché case. "There are some contrasting Babylonian and Hittite laws that you completely missed," he'd explained to Daniel.

"Want a drink?" The man next to him was eyeing him possessively. Clearly he had decided to take Daniel under his wing.

"No, thank you."

Back to the article. Minutes later, his concentration was shattered by the riffling of a card deck. Daniel tried to ignore the sound, but his seatmate seemed an addicted shuffler.

"Could you possibly stop that?"

"Sure," the man said. "Want to play a little gin?"

"No, thank you."

"You're not very friendly," the man protested.

"I'm sorry, but I'm very caught up in this article I'm reading."

The man seemed not to have heard him. "Marvin Golden," he said, extending a hand.

Daniel cringed. Obnoxious people bothered him. Obnoxious Jews bothered him more. They made him ashamed.

"Daniel Winter," he answered.

"I shouldn't even be here," Golden persisted, ignoring the fact that Daniel had not shaken his hand. "Marvin Golden only travels first class. But they were totally filled up today. Can you believe that?"

Daniel could. From the look of it, there appeared to be not a single seat available on the New York–Los Angeles flight.

"First class," Golden continued sourly, "they treat

you right. Drinks on the house. Stewardesses fawning over you.'' He slipped a tiny bottle from his suit pocket and took a swig. ''Here you're just another *asshole.*''

Speak for yourself, Daniel felt like answering. Instead, he silently returned to his article, vainly hoping that Golden might grant him at least a twenty-minute reprieve before the next interruption.

Less than ten minutes later the call button rang out again. The pony-tailed flight attendant returned.

''Yes, sir,'' she said wearily to Golden.

''Two more scotches.''

''I'm sorry. I can't bring you any more.''

''And why not?''

''I've already served you ten drinks on this flight.''

''Who are you—my mother? Last time I flew cross-country I took thirteen. Now bring me those drinks.''

She sighed softly, clearly summoning all of her training to deal with a situation that was rapidly becoming explosive. ''Airline regulations forbid us from serving drinks to passengers who have already drunk too much.''

''Miss Marian T.,'' Golden said, ''bring me that scotch right away or by God you'll regret it.''

Behind them a baby began to wail, frightened perhaps by the ferocity of Golden's tone.

Daniel had had enough. ''Stop threatening this woman!'' he snapped.

Golden's face became rigid with fury. Turning in the narrow confines of the seat, he slapped down his deck of cards and glared at Daniel. ''Shut your goddamned mouth, buster. I've had as much crap from you as I'm going to take.''

Daniel drew a card out from his wallet. ''This is my business card,'' he told the flight attendant, ignoring Golden's snort of disgust. ''If this man causes you any unpleasantness, please be in touch with me. I can confirm your version of the events." Marian's face brightened gratefully as she took the card.

Golden slammed his palm down on his tray. "You self-righteous jackass—"

Daniel carefully scanned the interior of the aircraft. He would gladly have plopped himself down next to a convention of cigar smokers who hadn't bathed in three months. But there was not a seat available. He finally turned back to Golden.

"I'm sure you don't like sitting next to me," he said, "any more than I enjoy being here by you. But we're stuck, Mr. Golden. So why don't we both just finish the flight quietly?"

"Screw you, big shot," the man snapped.

Daniel returned to his article. Or at least pretended to.

Forty minutes later, the plane glided into LAX airport. Daniel quickly gathered his things and started off.

"Thank you very much," Marian told him, as he started out the cabin door. He nodded and hurried on.

Daniel wished he hadn't told Brenda not to bother picking him up. He yearned for a loving face. Sighing, he shouldered his bag and headed inside the terminal.

Streams of people were jostling and rushing past one another. Eager to get home, Daniel strode through the bustling crowd.

"Rabbi—" The slightly accented voice startled him. Daniel spun around, in time for Sam Bornstein—his congregation's chairman of the board—to enfold him in a crushing bear hug. The stench from Sam's cigar was overwhelming.

Daniel hadn't expected anyone to greet him. His

first anxious thought was of Brenda. "Is anything wrong?"

Bornstein laughed heartily and thumped him affectionately on the shoulder. "Not at all. I'm not here for you, Rabbi. This one's strictly business. A big real estate guy from New York is coming in to bid on the Samborn development." During the three years Daniel had known Bornstein, the businessman had been semi-obsessed with this project. "It's going to make the difference," he had once told Daniel, "between my being just another comfortable Joe and my having real *money*." For a man who had spent his teen years scrounging for stale bread and little else in concentration camps, the distinction was an important one.

"Good luck, Sam. I really hope it works out." He was just starting off, when Bornstein called out. "Here he comes."

Automatically Daniel pivoted, just in time to come face to face with Marvin Golden.

"Marvin," Bornstein announced, pumping the newcomer's hand. "I'm so happy you're here. It's good to see you at last. Was your trip okay?"

"Fine," the man said in a clipped tone, but he didn't look at Bornstein. His eyes glared pugnaciously at Daniel.

Sam, oblivious, went on cheerfully. "Funny thing, Marvin, a very dear friend of mine was also on the flight. I'd like you to meet him, Rabbi Daniel Winter."

Marvin Golden's very red face suddenly looked in danger of turning green.

"I had no idea," he stammered, "that you were—"

"A rabbi?" Bornstein roared. A woman carrying a tiny baby turned to stare. "The greatest rabbi in LA, for my money. I always tell people, Auschwitz alienated me from God, and Daniel Winter brought me back to Him.''

"Eh, Rabbi,'' Golden said, "could I speak to you privately for a moment?''

"But—'' a baffled Sam Bornstein began.

Daniel waited until the announcement of a flight to Dallas died away. "Certainly,'' he said to Marvin Golden. The two stepped away from Sam Bornstein, who watched them in speechless astonishment, and moved towards the terminal's large windows.

Golden leaned toward Daniel. "I just want you to know, Rabbi, that if I had had any idea who was sitting next to me, I would never have acted like that.'' He thrust his hand out. "Please forgive me.''

Daniel's deep blue eyes sought out the man's. "I would very much like to forgive you, Mr. Golden, but I really am afraid I can't.'' He shook the man's still out-stretched hand. "Good day, sir,'' he said, and walked off.

"You're not going to believe what's inside the letter that was just delivered here,'' Daniel's secretary, Pat Hastings, greeted him the next morning.

"A request from the governor to enroll in my class on basic Judaism.''

Pat laughed merrily. "Not quite. But almost as strange.'' She held out a neatly opened envelope to him.

Inside was a check made out to Congregation B'nai Zion, dated the previous day, and signed by Marvin Golden. The only thing missing was the sum. Daniel went to his desk and quickly scanned the handwritten note accompanying the check. The note was written on Beverly Hilton Hotel stationery.

Dear Rabbi Winter,

I again ask your pardon for my inexcusable behavior yesterday afternoon. I was up in my room half the night, unable to sleep. Please fill in this check for any amount you deem appropriate. Only I must know you forgive me.

Sincerely yours,
Marvin Golden

Daniel leaned back in his chair and studied the ceiling for a long time. Then he picked up the check, tore it into three pieces and deposited the pieces in the wastebasket. He wrote a reply on the same sheet.

Believe me, Mr. Golden, I would very much like to forgive you, but I cannot.

Daniel Winter

He messengered the note back to the Beverly Hilton.

Daniel had just turned from the Talmudic text to Rashi's commentary on the side of the page, when Pat Hastings's buzzer sounded. "Mr. Bornstein is here," she said in a low voice, "with another gentleman."

"Send them in, Pat."

Bornstein ushered Marvin Golden to the levered armchair opposite Daniel. He flicked the ashes off his thick cigar and then took the seat alongside him.

"There seems to be a mix-up, Rabbi," Bornstein began, looking uncomfortable.

Daniel regarded him quizzically.

"Marvin tells me a story that I frankly find unbelievable," Bornstein said. "That the two of you had some sort of run-in on the plane, and that he's apologized twice already, but that you've refused to accept his apologies. I assured Marvin that you're a kind and forgiving man.''

"Sam," Daniel said, "you also don't understand. The reason I can't forgive this man is because he never insulted me.''

Golden started out of his chair. His cheeks flamed. "What the dickens!"

"Had he had any idea," Daniel went on, "it was a rabbi sitting next to him, he would never have dared act as he did. He wants forgiveness? Let him go find a poor anonymous soul sitting on an airplane trying to study a book and ask *him* for forgiveness.''

Bornstein, who was about to object, closed his mouth speechlessly. The room was quiet.

"I think I understand," Marvin Golden finally said.

"By the way," Daniel said, "did you ask forgiveness from the stewardess?''

Golden cleared his throat.

"What stewardess?" Bornstein asked.

"Marian was really afraid you might cause her trouble," Daniel said to Golden. "Think you might want to write her a letter of apology? I'm sure the airline will forward it to her.''

The man coughed.

"I really think it would be appropriate," Daniel said.

"I'll do it, Rabbi, only if you forgive me.''

"I personally have no grievance with you.''

"Then you'll accept my contribution to the synagogue?''

"This has nothing to do with money," Daniel said.

"You think so?''

"Most definitely.''

The man's big hand gripped Daniel's. "I'll write

that letter as soon as I get back to my hotel." He turned to Sam Bornstein. *"This man is a rabbi."*

"I'll drink to that," Bornstein said.

Daniel laughed. "No more drinking."

The two men stood to leave, and Daniel returned to the open Talmud in front of him. From just outside the door, he heard Sam Bornstein's penetrating voice. "Who the *hell* is Marian?"

2

From the *Los Angeles Daily Post*, Monday,
October 23:

COED STRANGLED IN
WESTWOOD APARTMENT
by Richard Brock

Twenty-four-year-old UCLA law student
Donna Braun was found strangled in her
apartment at 1120 Westwood Boulevard early
today. Braun's body was discovered at just after seven this morning by Enid Gurney, a
friend of the murdered woman, who was planning to meet Braun for a daily jogging date.
When repeated rings of Braun's doorbell
brought no response, Gurney became
alarmed and alerted building superintendent

Jesús García who opened the door. The fully clothed body of the dead woman was found on the couch in the living room. Aside from an overturned chair nearby, there was little evidence of physical struggle. Lieutenant Joseph Cerezzi of the LAPD homicide division announced that a special hotline has been set up on the Braun slaying and appealed to anyone with relevant information to contact his office at 555-6850.

From the *Los Angeles Daily Post*, Tuesday, October 24:

MURDERER WALKS IN WITH HIS CONFESSOR
by Richard Brock

Celebrity photographer Ron Martin confessed late yesterday afternoon to the strangulation murder of beautiful law coed Donna Braun. According to a highly-placed source inside the LAPD, the thirty-one-year-old Martin told police that he had gone to Braun's apartment late Sunday night in an attempt to rekindle a relationship the young woman had ended three weeks before. Martin claimed that Braun spurned his efforts at reconciliation, bragged about another man she was already seeing, and then ordered him out of the apartment. He added that she kicked him, at which point he grabbed her from behind in an attempt to protect himself. But Braun, he said, then reached for a scissors on a nearby coffee table. Martin locked his upper arm around her throat, and, as he explained, "I was so petrified and shocked that I held on longer than I should have." Martin said: "All I wanted was to marry her."

Accompanying Martin to homicide headquarters was a very tall middle-aged man dressed in suit and tie whom the suspect was heard to address as "father," and who remained closeted with the killer throughout the session in Lieutenant Joseph Cerezzi's office. But in a shocking twist, when the two emerged later, the "father" was recognized as Father Michael O'Brien, of Our Lady of Mercy Roman Catholic Church, in West Los Angeles.

According to the same LAPD source, after the killing—which occurred about 2 a.m. Monday, according to police—Martin drove aimlessly around West LA and Santa Monica, stopping in at several all-night coffee shops. Sometime around 7:30 a.m., the alleged murderer drove past Our Lady of Mercy and saw a light on in the church rectory. Martin entered the church seeking a priest. When he found Father O'Brien, Martin told him that he had attacked his girlfriend and that he was afraid he had hurt her. Father O'Brien then called the police anonymously, telling them to send medical personnel and an ambulance to Ms. Braun's Westwood apartment. But, of course, the dead girl's body had already been discovered.

The source also reports that when Martin later heard the murder reported on the news, he told the priest he knew he should go to the police but was afraid—at which point Father O'Brien offered to contact a lawyer. But it was Martin who insisted, "I want you."

From the *Los Angeles Tribune*, Wednesday, November 22:

GOODE SUBPOENAS BRAUN'S "SEX" DIARY
by Cynthia Owens

Defense attorney Leonard Goode appealed this morning to Judge Samuel Feld to order murdered law student Donna Braun's diary turned over to the defense. "That diary will show," Goode told this reporter outside the courtroom, "that even while Donna Braun was supposedly in love with my client—for months, even wearing a ring he had given her —she was aggressively pursuing other sexual relationships. When Ron heard rumors about these affairs and confronted her about them, she taunted him, and read him entries from her diary mockingly comparing his sexual performance to other men with whom she'd been intimate. When my client attempted to wrest the diary from Ms. Braun in order to stop her cruel verbal attack, she became physically abusive, kicking Mr. Martin in the testicles, then attempting to stab him with a scissors. It was my client's attempt to protect himself from this attack which culminated in Ms. Braun's tragic and unfortunate death."

When Goode was asked if he planned to enter a plea of self-defense on behalf of his client, despite Martin's confession to the killing, the diminutive, chain-smoking lawyer, who seems to thrive on controversy, responded: "Any other plea would be a lie."

Meanwhile, inside the courtroom, the dead girl's father, Gerald Braun, a prominent cardiologist affiliated with the Sinai Medical Center, furiously denied the existence of any sex diary and accused Goode of "calling my daughter a whore, and a would-be killer, in a vile attempt to turn a cold-blooded murder into some sort of self-defense killing."

At the conclusion of the highly emotional hearing, Judge Feld ordered Braun to turn over to the court any diaries of his daughter in his possession. Feld announced that he would personally read through them, and reserve judgment until that time on Goode's request.

Outside the courthouse, fifteen women and two men, led by Enid Gurney, close friend of the slain woman and the person who discovered her body, picketed, demanding, "Justice for Donna." One of their signs read, "If you love the Nazis and the Mob, you'll love Leonard Goode," an obvious reference to the controversial appeal Goode brought earlier this year for the American First Amendment Union on behalf of the Los Angeles Nazi Party. The Nazis were seeking to overturn a mayoral ban on their right to march through the heavily Jewish area of Fairfax in their annual "Pro-Final-Solution-to-the-Jewish-Problem Parade." Goode's appeal was successful, though the rally did not subsequently materialize. The other allusion in the sign was, of course, to Goode's defense of more than twenty well-known LA mob figures—though his string of incredible courtroom successes suffered a stunning setback three months ago when his client John "the Gent" Vieto was given a twenty-five-year sentence for heading a West Coast-based heroin distribution network.

When this reporter confronted the pickets outside the court with Goode's allegation that Donna had kicked Ron Martin in the groin, and pointed out that, if true, how much such an attack must have hurt, Enid Gurney, a vivacious brunette in her mid-twenties, snapped: "Not as much as being strangled to death."

Feature story from the West LA *Tribune*, Tuesday, January 9:

PASSION SLAYER DONATING TALENTS
TO OUR LADY OF MERCY
by Cynthia Owens

For the last five weeks, Father Michael O'Brien has had a most unusual volunteer at his bustling Westside church, and according to the priest, "If we could attract a few hundred more lay workers with talents and dedication like his, Catholicism in America would be enjoying an extraordinary renaissance."

Since December 7, confessed killer Ron Martin has been living at the rectory with Father O'Brien, spending his days and most evenings preparing a photographic exhibit on "The Church in Daily Life." Prior to Martin's arrest on October 23 in the passion slaying of Donna Braun, he was ranked as one of the finest new talents in the Hollywood photography scene. His acclaimed spread on actress Mona Six appeared last October in *People*, and in the months before, his work was featured in both *Life* and *Playboy*. But, for the moment, Ron Martin is through with cheesecake, and what he's most apt to see through his lens now are Masses, baptisms, Christmas celebrations, and hospital visits.

While Martin declined to answer any questions relating to the murder case, Father O'Brien was more forthcoming. "When Leonard Goode [Martin's attorney] and I first approached Judge Feld, Ron was rotting—and that's not too strong a word—in jail. That's when I guaranteed the court that I would personally supervise him, and Judge Feld finally set a bond which Ron's parents could afford. But the first day Ron came here, he didn't even leave his room: we had to send food in to him. It was terrible to watch, he was so overwhelmed by shame and despair. He felt in the core of his soul that what he had done was awful, and he didn't feel he could go on functioning. And I told him, 'Ron, Donna is dead, and she's not coming back. Now, I can forgive you, and everyone here can forgive you. But it's up to you to do the hardest thing of all: learn how to forgive yourself.' "

When asked about church members who have expressed displeasure at the photographer's presence in their midst, Father O'Brien produced the following statement issued this week on church stationery. "While we all mourn the tragic death of Donna Braun," it read, "it is vital that, having lost one young life, we do all that we can to salvage another."

"What's the point," Father O'Brien challenged, "of calling a church Our Lady of Mercy and then showing a hard heart to those most in need of it?"

From the *Los Angeles Bulletin*, Thursday, February 22:

WHAT MURDER LEAVES BEHIND
by Thelma Dickens

The white-coated physician at Sinai Medical Center was dispensing his own brand of prescriptions yesterday: "Liberals have been saying for years that no killer has ever been deterred by capital punishment. Fine. Let's find out once and for all if that's true. For the next three years let's have capital punishment only for murders committed on Monday, Wednesday, and Friday. Then we'll see if homicide rates go down on those days, or if, as the bleeding hearts tell us, it won't make a bit of difference."

The speaker, Dr. Gerald Braun, is a bitter man and makes no effort to hide it. This past October his beautiful young daughter Donna was strangled by her estranged boyfriend, celebrity photographer Ron Martin. Braun told me that in the immediate aftermath of the slaying, he and his wife Roberta were treated to an enormous outpouring of sympathy, but that more recently a lot of that sympathy has been shifting to the killer. "Roberta and I took a one-two punch to the heart from two heavyweights," Braun told me. "First, that lawyer [Leonard] Goode manufactured those disgusting charges about Donna's so-called sex diary. We turned everything over to Judge Feld, who ruled that there was nothing in Donna's diary to justify the defense subpoenaing it. But do you think his ruling did any good?'' With trembling hands, Braun lifted up a thick folder of newspaper and magazine articles about the killing and pulled out a *Santa Monica Telegram* of December 3. A banner headline dominated the tabloid's front page: WAS DONNA CHEATING WITH SOMEONE ELSE? "Goode gave everyone free rein to write whatever trash they wanted about my daughter.''

On the wall of Braun's medical office, alongside his diplomas, is a college graduation photograph of Donna, a winsome blonde with deep blue eyes and a shy smile. "Femme fatale,'' her father snorted, "that's what another one of the papers has been calling her —a manipulative, rich Beverly Hills brat who didn't treat this wonderful man who murdered her nicely. But it's a lie. Donna was the sweetest . . . a naïve girl who was under the spell of an obsessive man. We saw it, all of us . . . I only wish we'd tried harder to make her see it, because by the end she was desperate to extricate herself from his clutches. But nobody hears about that now. And then that saint over at Our Lady of *Misery,* he's the one who gave us the second punch. I'd like someone—anyone—to explain to me how this Father, who undoubtedly thinks it's the most heinous thing in the world to abort a fetus, can tell a man who's snuffed out a twenty-four-year-old girl's life that 'you have to do the hardest thing of all: learn how to forgive yourself.' ''

Braun's colleagues at Sinai speak of him as one of the most devoted doctors on the hospital's staff. But they also add that since his daughter's murder, he has become obsessed, one even hinted a trifle unbalanced. "I feel for the guy,'' one doctor confided to me anonymously, "how could I not, but enough's enough. There is just a limit to how much ha-

tred and anger I can listen to from him and
then be expected to share in.''

Since the killing, Braun's wife, Roberta,
has become an active member of Compassionate Friends, an organization of bereaved parents. Despite her husband's complaints about
a drying up of sympathy, the petite Mrs. Braun
explained in their elegant two-story house on
Camden Drive that Congregation B'nai Zion,
where Dr. Braun is on the board of directors,
has been a fount of support since the killing.
"Our rabbi, Daniel Winter, must have been
over here every day for the first two weeks,
and even since then he calls or visits once or
twice a week." It is true, the bereaved mother
concedes, that some friends have drawn back,
but she doesn't attribute it to a lack of sympathy. "It just frightens some people to be with
me, makes them more afraid it could happen
to them. A few people I know treat me like a
Holocaust victim, very sympathetic, but afraid
I'm going to start telling them my story.
That's the saving grace of Compassionate
Friends. They're not sympathetic outsiders,
they're empathetic insiders, and that makes
for an environment where you can talk. And
that's what we need most.''

Ron Martin's murder trial is scheduled to
start in ten days, on March 5.

**From the *Los Angeles Daily Post*, Tuesday,
March 13:**

JUDGE KEEPS JURY AND BATTERED
EX-GIRLFRIEND APART

HER TESTIMONY SHOCKS COURTROOM

Prosecution witness Mona Lance rocked the
Braun murder trial this morning with revela-
tions that during her two-year relationship
with Ron Martin she was beaten by the defen-

dant on seven separate occasions. These stunning disclosures were made during a hearing in the jury's absence. After declaring a recess, Judge Samuel Feld ruled this afternoon that Lance's testimony would have an unfair, prejudicial effect on the jury and therefore could not be used by the prosecution as evidence.

In her shocking testimony, the attractive, stylishly-dressed Lance revealed that, in the worst episode, Martin broke her nose, two ribs, and punctured an eardrum, injuries which led to her hospitalization for five days. A few weeks later, when she tried to permanently end their relationship, Martin cut up and destroyed every dress in her closet and used a hammer to smash an antique chair.

Seeking to impeach her credibility, defense lawyer Leonard Goode subjected Lance to a withering cross examination, referring to an old arrest on a drug charge. "Are you not concealing from this court that Ron Martin's rage was brought on by his discovery that you were bringing drugs into his home?" Later, when Lance described an incident at Ma Maison restaurant, claiming Martin had slapped her across the face Goode interrupted to demand: "You were drunk at the time, weren't you?" Lance steadfastly denied Goode's accusations and didn't veer from her story.

The hushed, packed courtroom hung on to Lance's every word, except, of course, for the twelve jurors, who spent the hour and a half reading newspapers and old magazines in a jury room in another part of the courthouse.

This afternoon, Judge Feld gave his ruling, stating that Lance's allegations would make it extremely difficult, if not impossible, for the jury to give defendant Martin a fair trial on the current charges. In addition, he noted the difficulties in ascertaining the truth of Lance's allegations, since the events occurred five years ago. He also pointed to the "peculiar fact that despite the severity of her allegations against the defendant,'' Lance never contacted the police or brought criminal charges against him. He therefore concluded that ''the extreme prejudicial effect of Ms. Lance's testimony on the jury would far outweigh its probative value, and that, in the final analysis, such incidents must be regarded as remote to the issues in the case before us.''

When the jury returned to the courtroom, Feld announced that as of this evening they will be sequestered until the end of the trial, and their reading material monitored to exclude all media references to it.

Courtroom observers see Feld's ruling as a serious blow to prosecutor Ira Nessim, who contended that Martin's assault and killing of Donna Braun was merely the final, depraved act in a continued history of violence and abuse against women. This, of course, sharply contrasts with defense counsel Leonard Goode's contention that the death of Donna Braun was the tragic, unintentional result of a fight that erupted when the unfaithful young woman jilted Martin and subsequently attacked him with a scissors.

With the dismissal of Lance's testimony, the case shifts tomorrow to the defense. Goode announced that his first witness will be Fr. Michael O'Brien, the West LA priest to whom Martin fled after the killing.

3

Wednesday
Morning

Rabbi Nachum Czernow, white hair half-hidden under an enormous black yarmulke, escorted the anxious woman into his office. The tiny room was lined with bookcases packed with books bearing Hebrew titles.

"Start again," he began, pulling a pen from his pocket, "so I can write everything down on the paper. I cannot anymore hold all these details in my head." He peered at her from behind cloudy glasses. "Levine the name is, right?"

"Levin," the woman answered, looking about for an ashtray. She drew a cigarette from her purse, and lit it. "Sara Levin."

The rabbi grinned. "You see. I told you the paper is better. Already we're making progress."

Sara Levin returned his infectious smile. She was a small woman with beautifully-sculpted cheekbones and luminous eyes. Her long hair was gathered under a pink-striped kerchief. She was dressed in a full skirt that came to her mid-calf, and a blouse with delicate embroidery on its long sleeves.

"Now, how long is it that you have your civil divorce?" Czernow resumed.

"Six years."

The rabbi stroked the edge of his beard, which trailed down to his chest. "And suddenly, I am to understand, a *get*—a Jewish divorce—has become very important to you?"

"I've met someone, Rabbi." She inhaled on her cigarette, then blew out quickly. "A very fine man. We want to marry."

"Mazel tov. Forgive me for asking, Miss, Mrs.—"

"Miss. Levin's my maiden name," she said, as she crushed the cigarette in the ashtray.

"Of course. Now tell me, Miss Levin, how does it come you never thought of the Jewish divorce six years ago when you got your civil divorce?"

"It meant nothing to me," she answered, leaning back after grinding the butt to a flat disk in the ashtray. When the rabbi's thick brows drew together, she hastened to explain. "Neither Leonard, my ex-husband, nor I were religious. Passover, we went to my parents' *seder*. That was the extent of it. Six years ago, Rabbi, I don't think I even knew that the word *get* existed, or that there was a separate Jewish divorce."

Czernow gnawed his bottom lip thoughtfully. "I see. And what is different now?"

"Evan," said Sara, softening. "He gave me a book to read, *The Jewish Manifesto*. Perhaps you've heard of it?"

Czernow nodded.

"It made a big impact on me. I started going to services and taking classes. I can read Hebrew now, Rabbi. Last week I read through the *Sh'ma* in the original, all three paragraphs, and even understood some of it." She smiled at the recollection, her fingers playing with the strand of pearls at her throat. "And I'm planning to enroll Debby, my daughter, in Israel Academy, in the fall. So you see, Rabbi, I'm becoming a real Jew. Then, just recently, my rabbi was giving a sermon. He was saying that in Judaism something that starts with a religious act should finish with one. Like Shabbat starts with fire, lighting candles, and finishes with fire, the *havdala* ceremony. Marriage too, he said, starts with a religious ceremony, and if, God forbid, it ends, then it also must be done religiously. Otherwise you're still married. I sat there shocked. Evan had never mentioned this to me. He probably took it for granted that I had a Jewish divorce. I went up to the rabbi after the service, hoping I'd misunderstood him. But when I explained my situation to him, he told me that even though I had a civil divorce, according to Jewish law I was still married, and that if I married another man without first getting a *get,* I'd be committing adultery, and any child we'd have would be something called a *mamz* . . ."

"*Mamzer.*" Czernow's voice was a strangled whisper. "Mom's error?"

"*Mamzer,*" Czernow repeated. "A bastard." The eyes behind the thick glasses were full of sorrow. "Almost the worst thing that can happen to a person. The Torah tells us that a child born from the sin of adultery is forbidden to marry another Jew even after ten generations. The only person the poor child is allowed to marry is another bastard."

A tremor ran through Sara's delicate features. "I know, Rabbi," she said softly. "I just find it so hard to understand."

The rabbi turned his palms upward. "Miss Levin, if God gave to human beings a law in the Torah it means He knows human beings can keep this law. No matter how hard it may seem. It is not for us to question the reasons of the Almighty. It is unique in the Torah, the only time we see this in all the 613 commandments, that an innocent person is punished for another person's sin. The Almighty understood how difficult it would be for people to keep the seventh commandment: 'Thou shall not commit adultery.' So the Torah decreed the law of *mamzer*. You want one another so terribly, it warns the couple, that's your sin, but know that any child you conceive will be cursed till the day of its death. That knowledge, the Torah felt, should give any would-be adulterers the strength to resist."

"You don't have to frighten me, Rabbi. I want the divorce. I've come to you for help."

"So what's the problem?"

"Leonard, my ex-husband. I went to him the day after I heard the sermon and told him I needed a *get*. He only laughed at me. 'Aren't you becoming the little fanatic?' he said. Leonard said he'd give the *get* on only one condition. That I give him full custody of our daughter." Her face crumpled. "Are you telling me, Rabbi, that the only way I'll ever be allowed to remarry is by giving my child to a monster who'd blackmail me?"

The rabbi tut-tutted. "Problems human beings make, human beings can unmake. Just tell me everything from the beginning to the end."

Sara Levin clasped her fingers together. "There's nothing much else to tell. That's why I've come to you.

Everybody tells me you're the biggest expert on Jewish family law in Los Angeles. I'm praying you can find some solution. All I want is to keep my daughter, to marry Evan, to be a good Jew.'' She closed her eyes. "That's all I want."

Czernow stared at the antique desk in front of him for a long while. He cleared his throat. "I feel for you, Miss Levin. Maybe there is a way something can be done. But I must know everything about your marriage, particularly the ceremony. Where did it take place?"

"Chicago. Leonard and I are both from there."

"And do you remember the name of the rabbi who performed the ceremony?"

Sara Levin canted her face to the ceiling. "Brand . . . something or other."

Behind the thick glasses, the brown eyes became anxious. "Brandwein?"

"I think so. Yes, that's it. His first name was Naftali, right? I remember because that was my grandfather's first name."

"Naftali Brandwein," Czernow repeated in a dazed voice. "I'm shocked."

"What's the problem? He seemed like a fine old man."

"Fine old man?" Shoving his glasses up the bridge of his nose, Rabbi Czernow glared at the woman in front of him. "If you counted the great rabbis of America on the fingers of *one*, not *two* hands, Rav Naftali Brandwein would be one of them." With surprising agility, the elderly rabbi sprang up and headed for a bookcase. He pointed to a row near the top. "You may be sure that at least ten of the books here are Rav Naftali's. This is terrible."

Sara's eyes grew frightened. "You're scaring me, Rabbi. I don't understand what's going on."

Czernow shook his head. He seemed not to have heard her. "You told me you and your husband both knew nothing about Judaism. How did you come to have such a great rabbi perform your wedding?"

"It was all my grandfather's doing. He was one of the big supporters of this Rabbi Brandwein's yeshiva. He arranged everything. Could you please tell me why you're so unhappy?"

The rabbi sighed, his eyes still on the row of books. "I was hoping you'd tell me some ignoramus of an American rabbi performed your wedding. And they had oysters as an entrée, witnesses who didn't know the difference between *kiddush* and *kaddish,* and a *ketubah* —a marriage contract—with all kinds of crazy innovations. That would have been fine. The whole marriage could have been invalidated. All it would have meant was that you had lived together with this Leonard—"

"But how would that help?" interrupted Sara. "So then Debby would be a *mamz . . .* oh, whatever it is."

"Not at all. In Jewish law, if two unmarried people have a child, it's not so nice, but there's no legal problem. I know that here in America they call such a child illegitimate, a bastard. But that's not true in Judaism. Only a child of adultery or incest is a *mamzer.*"

"So I'm going to be punished now because a great rabbi performed my wedding?"

"No, no! Only, if I could find some mistake in the wedding ceremony, this would help. Even then, I'd rather convince this Leonard to give you a *get.* Just to be safe. But if he refused, no tragedy. I'd just go ahead and declare the whole marriage invalid. But if Rav Naftali Brandwein officiated, *that* is a tragedy. It means everything was done perfect. The witnesses a hundred percent kosher. And that means you cannot get remarried without a *get*."

A dull look came into the woman's eyes. "I see. It's hopeless then."

Rabbi Czernow stroked his beard. His eyes lost their sternness. "My good woman, a Jew is forbidden to ever say that a situation is hopeless. Let me tell you something. In the last thirty-five years, dozens of women have sat in the very chair you're in now. They were just as worried as you. And for every one of them we found solutions. I spoke to the husbands, sometimes many times. And in the end, men who said they'd never do things went and did the very things they said they'd never do." He lifted the pen from his desk. "I will speak to this Leonard. Tell me his whole name and phone number."

"Leonard Goode," she said, her voice listless, and then she was silent.

"Go on. Give me the number."

"It's not going to help, Rabbi. You don't know my ex-husband. Nobody convinces Leonard Goode to do anything. He's one of the most powerful lawyers in the city."

Czernow's gaunt face paled. "Oh, *that* Goode!" Slowly the elderly rabbi rolled up a shirtsleeve, and revealed a series of numbers tattooed on his bony arm. "The Jew who argues that our local Nazis here have the right to march through Fairfax."

Mutely, Sara nodded, her eyes riveted on the stark tattoo.

A new fire seemed to enter the old rabbi. "Something will be done. Tell me, has any rabbi tried to intercede yet with Goode?"

"Yes."

"Who is he?"

"Why, the rabbi whose synagogue I've been attending. Rabbi Daniel Winter."

He was cutting a thick wedge of cheesecake when he heard approaching footsteps. Automatically, the long white knife slid over a good three inches, converting the wedge into a thin sliver.

"Daniel," Brenda called as she walked into the kitchen, the *Times* crossword puzzle in one hand. "Did you hear . . ." She stopped, her narrowed green eyes shifting between Daniel and the cake. "You had such a big slice at breakfast!"

"It wasn't that big."

"It's not funny, Daniel. We've been married a little over a year, and you've put on thirteen pounds."

"Most wives would take that as a compliment to their cooking."

"I was calculating the other day," she continued, ignoring him. "At this rate, in five years you'll gain sixty-five pounds."

"Right. And if you let two fruit flies multiply, inside of five years the world will be covered with a layer of fruit flies three feet thick."

"Except for that part of the world you're occupying."

"Good line," he laughed, coming over and nuzzling her cheek. He ran his fingers through her flaming-red hair. "You smell very nice this morning, copper. New shampoo?"

"Don't change the subject, wiseguy," she said, but her face softened.

Daniel drew back and held up his right hand. "I, Rabbi Daniel Winter, being of sound mind, do hereby give my word to Mrs. Brenda Goldstein Winter that I will lose one pound within the next week. At that rate, you realize, of course, that in less than four years I'll disappear entirely. Just in time, I suppose, for the fruit flies to take my place. Anyway, what did you come in to tell me?"

"It was on the radio. The jury came in early today to ask the judge to clarify something in his instructions about the charges against Martin. From the sound of it, it looks like they're going to come in with a verdict soon."

Absently, Daniel picked up the knife and tapped its handle on the tabletop. "I really would have liked to have been around. But this conference was scheduled two months ago." He frowned at the knife in his hand.

"And there's no way you can cancel?"

"I'm one of the speakers."

"Oh, I don't think I realized that. What on?"

"A nice, light topic," he chuckled, and when he resumed, his voice was stentorian. "Will there be one Jewish people in the year 2000?"

"Aha, one of those apocalypse-now conferences, I see."

"We're going to have at least thirty rabbis there," he went on, the knife poised in midair, his blue eyes now boyishly eager. "It's the first time, Brenda, we have all the denominations represented—Reform, Conservative, Orthodox. Even two Reconstructionists, and a Hasid. Who knows, maybe we can finally make some breakthroughs?"

"It's that serious?"

"If we don't work out a uniform conversion and divorce procedure—and soon—inside of ten years, the Orthodox will be keeping family registries and not marrying anyone who can't prove their background." He gnawed his lower lip. "But I feel bad about the timing. I want to be here for Jerry and Roberta's sake.

Particularly if the news is not good. What does Joe think?'' A psychologist for the past four years with the LAPD homicide division, Brenda reported directly to Lt. Joe Cerezzi. Cerezzi had been handling the investigation into Donna Braun's murder until Ron Martin made his confession.

Brenda put on the kettle, then went over to the paneled cupboard above the sink and pulled out the coffee and two cups. "I can't remember when I've seen him follow a case so closely. Usually, once Joe testifies, he just keeps a nominal interest. Wants to find out the verdict, of course. But he doesn't go into all the nitty-gritty. This time, though, he's really keeping track. Even showing up in court when he has some free time. A big part of it, I suspect, is that he's pissed off about that priest.''

Daniel shot her a quizzical look. "Father O'Brien?''

"Precisely. You know Joe doesn't wear it on his sleeve, but deep down—not even so deep—he's a pretty serious Catholic. I know for a fact he hasn't missed a Sunday Mass in ages. But it goes much deeper than just the rituals for him, Daniel. Joe has a very strong sense of moral order. And I think he's terribly embarrassed by the way O'Brien's been carrying the torch for Martin.''

"I can relate to that.''

"Meaning?''

"Look, when you're religious, you see yourself as sort of representing your religion to the world. Then, when somebody who's the same religion as you acts badly or misguidedly, it's embarrassing, even worse, discrediting." Daniel tapped the blue knitted yarmulke on his dark hair. "If I go out without this and pick up a newspaper somewhere without paying, people get angry at me. But just let me put this yarmulke back on and do the same thing and suddenly *all* religious Jews are thieves. That's what's ticking Joe off. By showing up in court with that turned-up collar every day, and carrying on in all those TV and newspaper interviews as if the people who want Martin severely punished are somehow bigger sinners than he was for murdering Donna, Joe worries that Father O'Brien is making Catholicism look foolish, even worse, cruel.''

She poured out the coffee and handed him a cup. "Cruel? I would say O'Brien's problem is an excess of mercy."

"But to whom?" Daniel demanded, recklessly gulping down his coffee and wincing. "There's an old expression of the rabbis: 'He who is merciful to the cruel will end up being cruel to the merciful.' " Daniel's dark blue eyes grew pensive. "The funny thing is, I know O'Brien. He's probably done as much as anyone in this city to feed homeless people, and I respect him for that, but he's gotten so caught up in the drama of his born-again murderer that he'd be very happy to see Ron Martin get away with almost no jail term at all. Even though Martin killed Donna, and in doing so destroyed her parents' lives as well. Roberta and Jerry certainly got a life sentence . . . Anyway, that's neither here nor there. Cerezzi's been going to the trial, you say. What does *he* think?''

Brenda ran her fingers through her thick red hair and frowned. "When he came back to the office last week, he told me, 'Something weird's going on there.' He meant, I gather, the way Judge Feld keeps ruling for the defense.'' Suddenly she caught sight of the overhead clock. It was just after ten. "I really gotta run, honey. Just tell me your schedule.''

"I suppose I'll leave here in about twenty minutes. The conference starts at noon, so I've got plenty of time. Remember, though, I won't be back till late to-morrow afternoon."

She leaned over and put her cheek next to his. "It's going to be lonely here tonight. I don't laugh enough when you're gone. I think I'm getting pretty used to you, Rabbi."

"You know, I was thinking, Brenda . . . that Car-dozo campsite where I'm going is less than an hour's drive. Maybe Jessica could stay with a friend, and you could come over after work . . ."

Her green eyes were merry. "Not likely. Remember that last conference I surprised you at? You greeted me with such a warm kiss, and were so incredibly attentive at dinner. Then, my sweet, you disappeared till one in the morning, carrying on with five other rabbis, and loving every minute of it, I'm sure. I'm not going to come up there and spoil your fun."

"But think of it like this," Daniel said, perching on the counter and raising his thumb in the Talmudic method of argument. "What if, between one and three, I can be upstairs carrying on with this gorgeous redhead and loving it a lot more?"

She laughed, but Daniel shook his head gravely. "I'm not the mushy sort, you know that. But I want you to be the first thing I see when I wake up tomorrow morning."

"Mmm." Brenda leaned over and kissed him. "Maybe I will come, at that."

Minutes later, she drew away. "I really wish I didn't have to run now." She grabbed her blue leather purse, gave him a quick peck on the cheek, and was out the kitchen door before he could protest.

He waited till her car engine gunned, then posi-tioned the knife to make the sliver as narrow as he could—first making a lightning-quick resolution to skip lunch—mumbled a blessing, and popped half the piece of cake into his mouth. Damn it, he thought, as he swallowed, why couldn't God make carrots taste so good?

"Have you reached a verdict?" Judge Samuel Feld demanded of jury foreman Thomas Phener. The lanky Phener rose slowly to his feet, looked solemnly at the judge, and announced in a barely audible whisper, "We have, your honor."

The bailiff hurried over to take the envelope from Phener and brought it to Feld. With deliberate motions, the judge reached inside his suit jacket, withdrew a pair of dark-rimmed glasses, carefully adjusted them, and then peeled open the envelope. For a long while he stared at the paper. His face was inscrutable. Then he summoned his clerk, Donald Watson, and handed him the note.

Seconds later, the court clerk's booming voice penetrated every corner of the room. "We find the defendant Ronald Simms Martin guilty of voluntary manslaughter in the death of Donna Braun."

For a second there was absolute stillness in the crowded courtroom, then chaos. Dozens of voices erupted at once in total cacophony.

"What's it mean?" reporter Richard Brock demanded of Cerezzi.

But even as the tight-lipped lieutenant started to reply, Leonard Goode, Ron Martin, and Father Michael O'Brien were on their feet, locked in a triumvirate embrace.

"Six years max," Cerezzi spit out savagely. "Which means he murdered the girl and he's going to be eligible for parole in three years." Brock could barely hear him over the din, but there was no mistaking the police lieutenant's disgust. His eyes were on the triumphant trio at the defense table. "With time served, the son-of-a-bitch walks in about two ten."

Grim-faced, the prosecutor turned to face a barrage of reporters. Ira Nessim raised his palms in a gesture of helplessness. Seated near the rear of the courtroom, Roberta Braun was sobbing quietly, while her husband Gerald's head was slumped in his hands. A row of spectators, some of whom had attended the trial daily—activists in Women Against Violence—let loose a chorus of Bronx cheers, directed at the jury of eight women and four men. Leonard Goode had broken free of his partner's embrace and faced the judge. "Probation!" his famous voice rang out, clear above the hubbub. "We move that probation be granted."

Judge Feld acknowledged the defense lawyer's motion with a stiff nod, then banged his gavel down.

But Gerald Braun was on his feet now, his body rigid, as if it was all sculpted from one granite piece. "Outrage!" he bellowed at the jury, his furious eyes locked on the unhappy foreman's. Then again, louder now, "Outrage!" All eyes turned to the wrathful man, whose forehead bulged with swollen veins. The pandemonium in the room died. The only sound was the muted sobs of the murdered girl's mother.

Feld looked impassively at Braun. "You will sit down, sir," the judge ordered. "Immediately."

Judge Feld waited. Slowly, mechanically, Braun obeyed. Feld turned to the jury. His face was impassive. "There is a court tradition that the judge thanks the jury at the cessation of a trial. However, I would feel extremely derelict in my judicial duties if any of you left this courtroom today regarding this thank you as perfunctory. For more than three weeks I have been repeatedly impressed with your attentiveness, diligence, and obvious commitment to responsibly discharge your duties." For a few seconds his colorless eyes wandered over the hushed courtroom. "Ladies and gentlemen of the jury, I know from experience that when you leave this room, some of you will be subjected to nit-picking second-guesses from people outside. It is unfortunately extremely common for those who have never set foot in the trial to somehow become the greatest experts on the case. That's why I emphasize to you that, aside from the various attorneys and myself, you twelve are the only people who actually heard all the relevant facts of this case. You—"

"Liar!" Gerald Braun screeched. The impassive eyes fixed themselves on him. Feld turned to the court officer. "Get him out," the judge ordered crisply. But even as the burly officer started up the aisle, hand resting on his gun, Braun had swung around to face the jury. "You know less about Ron Martin than anyone!" He wheeled towards the bench, and his forefinger shot upward accusingly. "You have withheld important information from this jury about this *murderer's* history of violence against women."

The officer finally reached the enraged man, and his powerful grip locked on Braun's arm. But Braun wrenched his arm away savagely. "That gun you're carrying," he shouted at the officer, "could be put to better use keeping *him* from killing other people's daughters!" His accusing finger was pointed at Ron Martin.

There were gasps and murmurs from the crowd, some in dismay, some in horror, some sympathetic. Eyes focused straight ahead, Braun strode from the room, and the heavy oak door closed silently behind the dead girl's father. Martin turned away with a shrug. Father O'Brien put his arm around the young man's shoulders and leaned over to say something to him. Leonard Goode stood still, looking at the door that had closed behind Gerald Braun.

Reporters were jumping up to follow Braun, but Feld's gavel crashed down. "This court is still in session!" he called out sternly. Turning to the jury, he continued, "You will be doing yourselves a grave injustice if you allow the kind of hysteria just displayed here to disturb you." Juror number five, a gray-haired woman in her fifties, began weeping into a tissue. The judge's voice softened. "Bereaved people sometimes want to lash out. We all understand that, and this court has no desire to be vindictive." He turned his grave countenance to Roberta Braun, who had not moved during her husband's outburst. "Do not be concerned, Mrs. Braun. I have no intention of holding your husband in contempt." And then to the jury, for the final time: "Be proud! Your deliberations have demonstrated all that is best about America. A country where justice, not mob law, rules. So, on behalf of everyone involved in this case—"

"Not on our family's behalf," Roberta Braun called out.

But Judge Feld raced on, ignoring her. "We all want to thank you."

4

Wednesday

Afternoon

The Cardozo Institute for Jewish Learning was located thirty-five miles northwest of Los Angeles, in the Santa Susana Mountain range. During the fifties and sixties, when many TV westerns were filmed in the area, Rolf Graves, star of the long-running *Six Shooter,* had bought a ranch that adjoined Cardozo property. Later, when the show was finally canceled, he donated all nine hundred acres to Cardozo, along with about forty horses and a hundred head of cattle—the largest gift ever given by a non-Jew to a Jewish organization. Now the Institute boasted the world's only Jewish retreat center where adults could study Talmud in the morning, then put on ten-gallon hats, mount horses, and go cow-punching on the sloping green pastures in the afternoon. Since moving to Los Angeles four years before, Daniel had been invited regularly to the Institute as a scholar-in-residence. Ranch manager Johnny Sarble had even managed to teach him the rudiments of horseback riding. All had progressed well, until Sarble insisted Daniel try riding *his* horse—a giant grandson of Graves's favorite *Six Shooter* horse—whom Sarble had gleefully named Final Grave.

"I'm not ready, Johnny," Daniel had demurred.

"Rabbi Daniel," the muscular cowboy drawled, with a twinkle in his pale blue eyes, "that's always your first reaction. It took us just about forever to get you up on Annie." Annie was the most gentle filly on the ranch. "You're ready now. Trust yourself."

There was no graceful exit. They had started out all right in drizzling rain, Sarble in front, Daniel struggling valiantly to follow close behind. But it didn't take long for Final Grave to sense that his new rider was no pro. The horse trotted, then slowed, then turned, and finally broke into an irrepressible gallop.

"You're letting him take control," Daniel heard Sarble call from a rapidly growing distance.

At that second, Final Grave whipped his head up so abruptly that the reins flew out of Daniel's hands. Instinctively he grabbed at the saddle's horn, sprawled over the horse's back, and squinted at the landscape through a stinging cloud of dust. All rocks and stones. His heart seemed to burst through his chest. In the distance, he saw salvation, a large patch of grass. "If I can only hold out," he thought, knotting his fingers through Final Grave's thick mane. Even now, Daniel still remembered those tense microseconds, and the panicked question that ran through his mind, "Should I say the *Sh'ma?*" the "Hear O Israel, the Lord is our God, the Lord is one"—the final words every Jew is to have on his lips before dying. But before any words could come out, Final Grave had reached the grass and started to buck—and with a prayerful upward glance, Daniel let gravity do what it would. Seconds later he was on the wet grass, flaking the mud off his corduroys and massaging a badly sprained ankle. And ever since, despite Sarble's vigorous efforts, he had never mounted another horse.

So it was with a sense of rising panic that he now heard Rabbi Sam Kass, the program chairman, announce that at the conclusion of the afternoon session all the rabbis would ride off together—in a symbolic display of unity—to a campfire about two miles into the woods. "We brought hot dogs, hamburgers, the works," Kass said, and he looked directly at Reb Shulem Stern, the lone Hasidic representative, "and it's all *glatt* kosher, Shulem, so nobody has anything to worry about."

Except me, Daniel thought miserably.

"This places just one constraint on us," Kass continued. "We have to finish this session by two, so we can get everything done in daylight."

Daniel looked down at his notes, happy at least that he was the session's final speaker. *I guess I'm just going to have to filibuster,* he silently decided.

MARTIN GUILTY, BUT JUST. The headline dominated the front page of the *Post*, LA's afternoon tabloid. But it was not the six-point type that held Ken Levy's attention. The young insurance agent took a long puff on his Churchill cigar, then examined the picture beneath the headline once again. It showed a handsome, middle-aged man in an elegant suit coming out of the Superior Court, two uniformed policemen just a step behind. The caption read: " 'My daughter was murdered twice,' aggrieved father Gerald Braun declared this morning. 'By Martin at her apartment. And by that vile outcast in the courtroom.' "

Levy lay the cigar down carefully—he was a punctilious man—and leaned back in his leather armchair. This, he reflected uneasily, was just the sort of overwrought comment he did not like to hear. Particularly when it was directed against a lawyer to whom he had sold a two-million-dollar "key man" life insurance policy. Ken Levy's first two-million-dollar policy, no less. And in the eleven months since, to the agent's considerable consternation, this was the third time he'd heard such deep hatred directed against Leonard Goode. *And who knows how many other things I didn't hear about?*

He pushed his bulky body out of the chair, walked over to the gray file cabinet, and pulled out the lawyer's policy. He knew exactly what he'd find. All premiums paid promptly, no unusual beneficiaries, everything in perfect order.

Ken Levy wondered if he should speak to someone higher up at National Life.

Pat Hastings tucked the phone receiver under her ear. "Rabbi Daniel Winter's office," she answered. A pretty blonde in her late forties, Pat had been Daniel's secretary since his arrival at Congregation B'nai Zion four years earlier. She was so much a fixture at the synagogue that most of Daniel's callers would usually spend a minute or two in pleasantries before being passed on to the rabbi. But not this caller.

"Yes," the deep voice said gravely. "Please put me through to the rabbi."

"I'm afraid he's away, Mr. . . . ?"

"Professor," the man corrected instantly. "Professor Mortimer Allen. And where may I reach him?"

Pat scanned Daniel's diary. His number at Cardozo was listed there, but next to it was a notation, underlined in red, *Only give out in emergency.*

"I'm sorry, Professor Allen, but Rabbi Winter can't be reached right now. But I'm sure he'll be calling in to take messages. Would you like to leave one?"

The man sighed theatrically. "That won't do at all. You won't get the message right. It's too complicated."

"Try me, Professor. Some people, Rabbi Winter included, even think I'm competent."

"Pardon me, Miss. I didn't intend any insult, only—"

"Then give me your message, Professor. First, does the rabbi know you?"

"He certainly does." Unexpectedly, the man chuckled. "I'm the one who almost kept our young Daniel from graduating. He was six months late with that Gersonides paper, you see."

Pat thought quickly. "Ah, you're from Maimonides Seminary then, Professor?"

"Of course." Allen coughed as if he was about to begin a lecture. "Now please inform young Daniel that in honor of Professor Wein's seventy-fifth birthday, the academic committee has decided to present him with a *festschrift*—"

"A what?"

"A *festschrift,*" the man repeated snappishly. "What else do you expect us to give a seventy-five-year-old professor—a week in Honolulu?"

"Can you spell it for me, please?"

"Gott im himmel. I should have known this would happen. Young woman, do you not know what a *festschrift* is?"

"Frankly, no, Professor Allen. But I would like you to spell it for me."

He did.

"Thank you very much, sir. Now please go on."

Professor Mortimer Allen continued, his tone a trifle chastened. "Tell Daniel to hurry, the academic committee is planning to present it next winter. And based on a preliminary version of a paper he gave recently, the committee has assigned Daniel a topic we very much hope he'll find congenial."

"What's that?"

" '*Lex talionis:* Some Twentieth-Century Reflections.' " Professor Allen paused, then asked with the slightest hint of amusement, "Would you like me to spell that, Miss?"

She would.

It was 1:25 when Daniel rose to speak, in a tense and crowded conference room. Rabbi Bruce Barton, the leading Reform ideologue in Los Angeles, had mounted the podium earlier and opened his address with a stinging attack on the Orthodox. "Your faces are friendly," the silver-haired rabbi began, enunciating each word scrupulously so that it was impossible to overlook his challenge, "but your intentions are not. Where you have power—as you do in Israel—you deny us status as rabbis. So understand that that makes it a little hard for me to be fully comfortable with you, knowing that the *only thing* that saves my Reform colleagues and myself from being disenfranchised by you is not God, or Torah, or any Jewish values, but the *first amendment to the American Constitution.*"

The Orthodox delegates were not slow in picking up Barton's gauntlet. "You've disenfranchised yourself," Rabbi Shulem Stern accused the Reform spokesman within seconds of taking over the podium, giving his black beard a ferocious tug. "Look at all the harm you're doing. For thousands of years we Jews said, 'A Jew is one who converts to Judaism or is born to a Jewish mother.' Good enough definition for my parents and your parents, *Rabbi* Barton. But not for *you and your colleagues!* No. Suddenly everyone born to a Jewish father is also—"

Barton cut him off. "You are being imprecise, sir. Our ruling on patrilineal descent is much more complex—that a child of a Jewish father is considered Jewish *only* if he is raised with a Jewish identity."

But Rabbi Shulem Stern's thick arms had already waved off Barton's objections, as anxious murmuring spread around the room. "Second," the Orthodox delegate continued, banging the podium resoundingly with his fist, "we always taught that a Jew is required to observe the 613 laws of our holy Torah. But Reform Jews have a new standard. Pick and choose, and when the choice isn't big enough, then innovate. So kosher doesn't matter, but homosexual congregations are fine. Shabbat is observed—or rather desecrated—however anyone pleases, but God forbid a Jew should do business with South Africa."

Barton was now on his feet, shaking his prematurely white head vigorously. "Apartheid, injustice to non-Jews, you're telling me, is not a Jewish issue. Just answer. Yes or no?"

"All injustice is a Jewish issue. But how to deal with it, that's more complex. Unlike Shabbat and Kashrut, where the issue is not complex at all. They are to be observed. With no deviations!"

That pronouncement set the stage for further hostilities, and in the next thirty minutes the rancor grew. Finally Rabbi Kass came over to Daniel, in the front row. "You're on now, buddy," he whispered, "and if you don't do something quick, we're going to be barbecuing rabbis instead of hot dogs at that cookout."

Daniel stood at the podium a long time before beginning, fingering the microphone, searching out friendly faces. Individually, he got along well with almost every rabbi in the room, but now they were inspecting him—silent, suspicious, waiting to see on what side he would align himself. He was ordained an Orthodox rabbi, they all knew that, and that made the Reform and some of the Conservative mistrust him. Then again, he was serving in a Conservative pulpit, and the Orthodox were of two minds about that. Some claimed he had sold out for a big salary, others, more gracious, acknowledged that he was sincere, just that his thinking had become confused. After Rabbis Baron and Stern's speeches, now that the various issues separating the groups—the differing standards demanded of converts to Judaism, patrilineal descent, and the Reform insistence that a Jewish divorce was unnecessary—had been defined so starkly, there was little room for evasiveness and none for imprecision.

Daniel took a deep breath. "Rabbis," he began, resting his hands on the podium, "as our friend Rabbi Yitz Greenberg has said, 'I personally don't care which denomination in Judaism you belong to' "—he paused, scanning his audience—" 'as long as you're ashamed of it.' "

The crowd, surprised, burst into delighted laughter. To Daniel's relief, even Barton and Stern joined in. And from then on it was—if not easy—at least easier.

Out of 250 million Americans, he reminded his audience, a trifle over two percent were Jews. This was no revelation, of course, to the rabbis, but Daniel knew how shocking that statistic was to almost everybody else. He had once asked a non-Jewish friend to guess how many Jews there were in the United States. "America is Protestant, Catholic, and Jewish," the friend had reasoned aloud, "but then again the Jews are the smallest group. Twenty million," he finally guessed. When Daniel told him the United States had only five and a half million Jews, the man's response was immediate: "Then they all live in my city."

"But," Daniel went on to say, "by the year 2000, fully 650,000 of those five and a half million will not be accepted as full Jews by other Jews. For three reasons. First," and he ticked the points off on his fingers, "because the non-Jews being converted to Judaism by Reform and Conservative rabbis are not accepted as Jews by the Orthodox. Second, the Reform movement has declared that children of Jewish fathers and non-Jewish mothers are Jews if raised with a Jewish identity, even though Conservative and Orthodox Jews do not regard them as Jews."

He took a much needed breath, then drained the glass of water on the podium. His audience was unnervingly silent. "And then there is the third category: the 150,000 Jews whose status in the year 2000 will be *mamzerim*—labeled by the Torah itself with that horrifying term, bastards—and forbidden to marry other Jews. Through no fault of their own. Just because their parents thought it terribly important to have a Jewish marriage, and terribly unimportant to have a Jewish divorce. I need not remind any of you of the proportions of this tragedy. I know as well as everyone here the way the problem can occasionally be solved, and then only occasionally. By saying all non-Orthodox rabbis are not rabbis, and all non-Orthodox marriages are not really marriages. But does anybody here really want to say such things?" His voice abruptly lost its mildness, and his palm crashed down on the podium. "We here in this room have to start working out a solution to this problem. Because if we don't, there will, God forbid, come a time when there will be 150,000 Jews who will hate us. And we will have earned their hatred."

"*You* will have earned their hatred, Daniel, not me!"

The speaker was Rabbi John Lerner, a slight, ginger-haired Reform rabbi from Tarzana. Five years earlier, Daniel knew, Lerner had performed the wedding of Leonard Goode to his current wife, Philipa—knowing full well that Goode had never issued his first wife a *get*. "So don't lay your guilt on everybody else," Lerner continued, red patches spreading over his face. "It's not me who's earning anybody's hatred. I feel no need to carry out ancient, *sexist* Bible laws. If Judaism is about justice—and I think it is—then American divorce laws, which give men and women equal rights to initiate divorce proceedings, are a lot more Jewish."

"What the hell do American divorce laws have to do with justice?" the twice-divorced, and since remarried, Rabbi Mel Arnold called out, and everybody laughed. Except Daniel.

"John," he said, in the most neutral tone he could muster, "if you and your colleagues had told a Leonard Goode that no rabbi would marry him until he gave Sara Levin a *get*, don't you see what you could have accomplished?"

"Certainly." Lerner's mouth twisted behind the close-cropped red beard. "We would have driven Goode to a justice of the peace, and no Jewish wedding at all. Face it, Daniel. You're the one who's tormenting Sara Levin. Just send her to me. I'll perform her marriage tomorrow."

"God forbid! Any wedding you perform, *Mr.* Lerner," an Orthodox rabbi called out feelingly, "is no Jewish wedding at all."

And, of course, they were at it again.

He had come to this conference with such hopes. Only anti-Semites, Daniel thought despairingly, could ever be naïve enough to believe in a worldwide Jewish conspiracy. Any Jew knew better. Since when could you get Jews to agree on anything? Even when a split in the Jewish people was staring them in the face. All that was needed now were a few compromises. From both sides. Compromises that were fully rooted in the Jewish tradition. But, of course, no ideologue ever thought a compromise was little. Unhappy, he listened to the increasingly rancorous shouting, looking down at the sea of furious faces. Could it get any worse?

It could.

Rabbi Sam Kass was mounting the podium determinedly. "Rabbis," he called out, then waited for the crowd to quiet. "By the power vested in me as your chairman, I hereby unilaterally declare that it's time to go horseback riding. For the next three hours, all fights are off." A few weak hurrahs greeted the ceasefire. "Friends, the horses await you."

Oy vey, Daniel thought.

To his relief, a voice on the loudspeaker began paging his name. It was the Cardozo Institute secretary, calling from the front office. Weaving through the departing crowd, Daniel hurried to a phone at the back of the room and scooped up the receiver. He heard— almost drowned out by the sounds behind him—a woman's sobs.

"Brenda," he called out desperately. A dozen horrifying scenarios crowded his mind. "Brenda," he called out again, a sudden stinging pain in his throat, "is that you?"

The muffled response sounded more like *no* than anything else. Not Brenda.

"Whoever it is," Daniel persisted, "just breathe deeply. Don't rush. I'm here."

"It's me, Rabbi . . . Roberta Braun."

"Oh my God! Roberta, it's been crazy up here. Tell me, what happened?"

"It's not what happened." Roberta Braun's voice quavered. "It's what's happening, Rabbi."

"Roberta, I don't understand."

In phrases broken by sobs, the distressed woman filled him in on what had gone on after the verdict had been delivered, how Gerald had stormed out of the courtroom. "And now he's gone altogether. I have no idea where."

"Probably just driving around." Daniel heard a certitude in his voice he was very far from feeling. "Trying to get a grip on himself before he comes home."

"But that's it, Rabbi. He *did* come home."

"How do you know?"

"Because when I got back from the court a few of his drawers had been pulled open, and some clothes were gone."

"Gerald's just upset, Roberta. He's probably checked into a hotel or—"

Roberta Braun began to weep again. Precious seconds ticked by before Daniel could calm her down.

"Something else was gone, Rabbi."

"What else was missing, Roberta?"

"His gun."

5

Late

Wednesday afternoon

The long, tapered fingers made teasing, languid circles around her breast. "I want you to stay," the man said, his fingers still caressing her translucent skin.

"Mmmm," she sighed. "Don't talk. Not now."

A second later, his rough dark head was buried in her flesh. Her lanky legs twisted around his. For long moments, the only sound in the darkened room was her quickened breathing.

And then, abruptly, he stopped. He rose from the bed. "No more."

"Max!"

"Philipa!" He mimicked her petulant tone, then raised the alarm clock from his night table and waved it in front of her. "Just wanted to give you a taste.

Besides, it's barely four in the afternoon. We've got the whole night ahead.''

"Don't start on that again, sweetheart." Philipa struggled to keep her breathing even. She leaned back on her elbows, put on her little-girl face, full lips puckered, big brown eyes begging. "I want to stay here more than anything in the world. You know that?''

"More than anything?''

"More than anything.''

"Swear it!''

"Come on, Max," she whimpered.

"Swear it! I'm serious.''

She rolled her eyes. "I swear it," she said huskily.

"Say it," he ordered. "The whole thing.''

She giggled. "You lunatic! Okay. I swear if I could have whatever I wanted, I would stay in this house all night with Max Reiss." She hesitated, and then reached up to caress his face. "And forever.''

"Good. Then it's settled. You're staying.''

"Max, stop it!" She was pouting now, her smooth, slender legs over the side of the bed fumbling for her slippers. Her glance moved over the three-legged sofa, the chipped plaster, and the makeshift wood-and-brick shelves stuffed with battered paperbacks. "And if I stayed, what would we live on? Love? Darling, I grew up poor, I know better than you. Love and no money has a three-month life expectancy. Before we know it, we'd be at each other's throats. I'm not . . . I can't be poor again.''

"You really don't believe I'm ever going to make it, do you?''

She shook back her mane of blond curls. "I totally believe in your potential, darling. But two novels, however wonderful, do not guarantee a future. Or a fortune.''

"Or maybe," he spat out, "it's that you still love him?"

"Oh, Max, how can you say such cruel things?" She pulled both his arms towards her. "After what I've risked for you! Coming here whenever I can . . . Everything."

"And remaining for all of two hours. Then it's bye-bye, Max, and hello, Leonard." He pulled away. "I'm fed up with this arrangement. And fed up with the fact that you aren't." He stared moodily at the cheap wooden floor. "Now listen, darling, you're going to get your goddamned courage up and tell him the truth. *You love me.* And you want out. This is California— home of the no-fault divorce. I want you. You want me. The only thing stopping us from being together is you."

She gnawed her bottom lip. "No-fault divorce. No-money divorce also." Her voice became coaxing. "You don't want to understand, honey, do you? Leonard's got me locked into a prenuptial agreement so tight, Marvin Mitchelson couldn't break it." She sighed. "I signed it, I've got nobody else to blame. If I leave or he catches me *in flagrante,* that's it. Zilch. And my nursing skills are a little stale by now. Two months after I walk out on Leonard, I'll be hocking my jewels and furs— that is, whatever he didn't manage to repossess—and two months after that I'll be standing in line for my welfare check."

Throughout Philipa's brief monologue, Max had been pacing, stopping once to kick a wall, another time to smash the alarm clock back down on the night table. Now when he spoke, his smooth muscular back was to her. "Did you ever love him?"

"What's the—"

He turned around. *"Did you ever love him?"*

She lifted an open pack of cigarettes, shook it, and pulled one out with her lips. She lit it, and her hand trembled as she took a languorous drag. "I was twenty-two then. When I met him, what did I know? I thought he was wonderful. And he was very sweet. Not exactly sweet. That's the wrong way to put it. He was sweet on me. Unfortunately he still is. If not for that, we'd be—"

"Do you even like him?"

She studied her pink-polished nails, then glanced up at him with parted lips.

"Answer me!" he thundered.

"Like him?" she pondered. "At first. For two years —maybe a little more. Leonard's so bright, it was exciting." Her face was stripped of any expression, as she carefully pushed back a cuticle on her small finger. Sunlight, filtered through the thin curtains, gleamed on her naked body. "You know what's going to be happening in three hours? He's going to be sitting down to a perfect filet mignon. Medium rare. That's Leonard's victory meal. If I don't cook it, he gets spooked he'll lose his next case. It's like his good-luck charm. It happened just a few months ago. He got that Woodland Hills rapist off, and I forgot his stupid steak." She laughed sourly, as she casually stubbed the cigarette. "You know who his next client was? John the Gent." She laughed again. "And I'm going to be sitting there with him—my heart and soul still in this room—and getting a nonstop firsthand report about what a legal genius I'm married to. And he'll think I'm privileged, because I don't have to pay $350 an hour to hear it." She paused, and her deep voice became hushed with pain. "I'm not a person to him, Max. I'm the beautiful blonde on his arm when he walks into a room."

She went over to her lover, her slippered feet pattering over the bare floorboards. She lowered his head to her chest. "You really do love me?" she said, her slim fingers tightly gripping the back of his head. "Tell me, Max, tell me again."

Iron Will, they had nicknamed Gerald Braun in college. The man who studied thirteen hours straight for his Inorganic Chemistry final without breaking once, not even for the bathroom. Who, years later, would stop a twenty-year three-pack-a-day smoking habit cold turkey, never once even expressing a desire for a puff.

Only now, the crushed cigarette pack on the crumpled sheet beside him was nearly empty, as was the Stolichnaya bottle he was clutching by the neck.

Three hours earlier, Gerald Braun had checked into the Seville Motel. Dime-store reproductions over the bed, and whores and Johns negotiating in the rooms on both sides of him. No pretense of civility— that's what he craved now. Not like the courtroom, with its fancy robes, expensive suits, its fancy words, the façade of law and order, and underneath it all, treachery.

He emptied the vodka bottle and flicked on the TV screwed into the wall. Black and white. Even better. No pretense.

A few minutes of *General Hospital.* Nothing like that going on at Sinai Medical, he thought. But he couldn't sustain interest. Bleary-eyed, he dozed off.

It was the TV, though, that awakened him. A voice, a familiar grating voice. For a second, as he rubbed sleep from red eyes, he stumbled between reality and dreams. It seemed like he was waking from a nightmare. He was. But it was also real. There, on the screen, pin-striped suit, Leonard Goode was speaking: "I don't consider this a victory for Ron Martin. There are no victories when you're dealing with so immense a tragedy. A tragedy, which I emphasize is one for *all* the concerned parties. As much as the Braun family might not be ready to hear it, my heart is with them today as well. But the truth is, if Ron Martin spends even three more years in prison it will only constitute a pointless continuation of an already tragic situation.'' Goode hurried away, shrugging off the volley of questions from the press: "Gotta run, fellas.''

Father Confessor batted next. Braun struggled upright, knocking the vodka bottle to the floor. Now they were asking O'Brien about *him*. How dare they? "What did you think, Father, when Dr. Braun started yelling at the judge and jury this morning?''

The priest's head was slightly bowed. He spoke slowly and his face showed his pain. "The greatest, hardest teaching of Jesus is forgiveness. I can't say how I would react in such a circumstance, and fortunately God hasn't tested me.''

"Of course not,'' Braun answered the screen harshly. "You will never know what it means to lose a child.''

"But Jesus does tell us how we ought to react,'' the priest continued gently. "Ron Martin has paid a price. So now is the time to forgive and go on living. I know *I* have forgiven Ron Martin.''

"Stop already. Enough!'' Braun yelled out, covering his ears with both hands. *Donna's body is turning into ashes, and Martin gets three years in prison. Barely a thousand days for taking the rest of Donna's life. That's a price? That's a joke.* The priest's words ran through his head. "I know I have forgiven Ron Martin.'' *Easiest thing in the world for him, he didn't know Donna.* "In whose behalf do you dare forgive?'' he snapped back at the tube.

Now Ron Martin's image filled the screen. Out on bail—Judge Feld had freed him for one week to finish his photography project for Father O'Brien's church—with his current girlfriend's arm linked in his. Martin shrugged off the volley of questions from the media, "No comment. No comment." But the tanned girlfriend, Pam Lite, flashed a glowing full set of teeth at the cameras. "The worst part of the nightmare is over," she gleefully told the assembled microphones and cameras. "And I just want to make an announcement, and there's no reason it shouldn't be public. Even if Ron goes away for a few years—and I'm sure he won't, but even if he does—I'll be right here waiting for him when he gets out. And we're going to go back to my place tonight and celebrate." She then turned to Yvette Barnhard, the newswoman interviewing her. "You've been pretty fair about things, Yvette. You're invited."

Braun's fists clenched on the tangled bedsheets. The newscaster thanked Yvette Barnhard, then droned on about break-ins, fires, protests. Yet Braun could no longer hear the words. His mind had drifted back to the afternoon Donna gave a speech to her entire high school senior class. For weeks beforehand, every night when he had come home from the hospital, they had labored together over her notes. She had been so nervous. Afterwards—the applause in the high school auditorium still thundering—Donna ran to his side. She was dressed in a simple pleated skirt and a cashmere sweater, her flushed cheeks aglow, her eyes alight. "Daddy, *we* made it! You were incredible. I really mean it. Do you know how much you helped me?" Then, springing to her tip-toes, her slender arms wrapped around his neck, her beautiful face pressed close to his, she whispered, "I love you so much, Daddy."

Braun sat motionless on the bed. The memory of her trusting face—the face he could never caress again

—burned in his soul, and the sounds and images from the television set blurred. A poisonous fluid seemed to be gushing up from his stomach and spreading through his throat and tongue. He felt sick, but still his senses were keen, even heightened. *I love you so much, Daddy* kept banging up against Pam Lite's coy words, *You're invited. I really love . . . You're invited. I really . . . invited.* He trembled violently and then seemed to suddenly wake from a dream.

"What about me?" he hissed at the TV screen. "Are you inviting me to your party too, Pam?"

6

Late

Wednesday afternoon

When Evan Singer was a high school student, he had liked Rabbi Moshe Ring's approach to the Bible. "Boys," Ring instructed his class, "when Moses saw the Egyptian beating a Hebrew slave, what did he do? Did he call the Anti-Defamation League and ask them to arrange a conference on 'Oppression of the Jewish Underclass by Egyptian Overseers'? Of course not! He killed the Egyptian."

In the mid-1960s, Ring founded the Jewish Defenders, with Evan Singer, an orphaned teenager, as the group's first vice-president. Rabbi Ring was not only Singer's favorite teacher at his Brooklyn yeshiva, but a black belt in karate as well—"Take what's good from the gentiles" was a favorite motto of his. The other rabbis at the school were proud Jews, Singer thought, but meek men. When neighborhood bullies knocked their black homburgs off, they'd pay the toughs two dollars to get them back. Not Ring. The wiseguy who grabbed his hat not only handed it back, but coughed up two dollars to get his own cap returned. A week later, when a yeshiva boy was brutally mugged, with injuries that required fifty stitches, Ring led the Jewish Defenders Vengeance Squad. Singer served as his lieutenant. Four of them cornered the knife wielder. When the cops arrived what was left of him was deposited at Fillmore Emergency. Ring and Singer visited him two days later—even bringing flowers and offering a few choice words of consolation. No charges were pressed, and the attacks at the yeshiva stopped.

Two years later, Singer was serving twenty-six months in a Federal penitentiary for smashing a window at the Soviet Mission to the UN. The flying glass shards had injured the seven-month-old daughter of a Russian diplomat sleeping in the room.

When Singer was finally released, he was a more subdued man. He avoided Ring—as per his parole agreement—and took to carpet-laying for several years, till he got up enough courage to go back to college. Then he moved to California and opened a furniture store, which surprised him by being successful. Now in his late thirties, the only thing missing in his life was a wife and children. Having been a misfit and a loner so long, that took him longer to find. Until shy, slight Sara Levin came into his mid-Wilshire store to buy a love seat for her living room. Within a few months Singer was occupying that seat, and Sara told him that she wanted him to be the father of her children. The only problem was that Sara was still married to another man. At least Jewishly. And her ex-husband, Leonard, was refusing to issue a *get*.

Singer, who had remained religiously observant even in prison, did a bit of checking around and quickly realized that any pressures he might bring against Goode would likely boomerang. John Toll, a friend of Evan's and publisher of the *Valley Employment Weekly*, told him of an open-and-shut case he'd had against an employee in his paper's classified ad department. Toll had refused the man's demand for a raise, and the employee took a devastating revenge. He replaced the word "work" with another four-letter word in a giant ad for a local firm: "Secretaries wanted. Many positions available. _____ your way to the top." The firm that placed the ad received over eight hundred furious calls and was forced to disconnect its phone. The paper fired the employee. But then Goode entered the scene. Could Toll prove "beyond a reasonable doubt" that the man he'd fired was the responsible party? Of course not. And yet, Goode argued, the publisher was willing to besmirch the man's name and ruin his professional future. By the time Leonard Goode was through, John Toll was relieved at getting off with $15,000 in severance costs—one-third contingency fee to the lawyer, of course—and no suit.

"That's the kind of guy Goode is," Toll warned Singer. "You'll make concessions to him, not the other way around."

For the first time since his prison release, Singer thought back to the Vengeance Squad with nostalgia. He'd gladly visit Goode in the hospital, carry in enough flowers to fill a greenhouse—if he could only come out with the *get*. But those days, he knew, were over.

On the other hand, it was months already since

they'd decided to get married, and Sara was no closer to being free. She was an *agunah,* a chained woman, and Goode was still the one holding the key. And the rabbis she'd consulted with, Winter, and now that Czernow, reminded him of those wimps who used to pay the two-dollar ransoms, rather than of real rabbis, like Moshe Ring.

Singer was in no mood that evening to hear Sara sing the praises of her new saint, the great *tzaddik,* Rabbi Czernow. *Tzaddikim,* saints, were great in *shul* on Yom Kippur, exhorting hundreds of fasting synagogue-goers to repent. They were less effective against guys like Leonard Goode, whose Yom Kippurs—according to Sara—were spent at Vegas crap tables.

"I know what you're thinking, and you're wrong," Sara said to him quietly, as he sped over the highway to her house. "There's a power about these men, both of them, Rabbi Czernow and Rabbi Winter. They have moral authority." He glanced at her face, the gentle eyes pleading with him to stay calm, to be patient. "You'll see, this time something is going to happen."

He slammed one hand down on the dashboard. "It's hopeless!"

"A Jew," Sara responded piously, gazing ahead at the darkened lane, "is forbidden to ever say a situation is hopeless."

They drove in silence, each locked in his own private thoughts. At home, the first two messages on her answering machine were irrelevant; some pest urging Sara to apply for a Sears charge card, and her optometrist announcing that her daughter's new glasses were ready. Sara shuddered at the sound of the next voice on the tape. "It's him," she whispered, as if afraid the caller would somehow overhear.

"Your newest flame, Rabbi Czernow, called," the

harsh voice on the tape mocked. "I wish you would stop distributing my home phone number to all your rabbi friends. I have no shortage of anxious clients without nervous clergy getting into the act too. Besides, *sweetheart*"—at the sound of the cynical endearment, Evan Singer's face hardened—"this *alter kocker* sounds like a bigger *nudnick* than that Winter you sicked on me. So let me tell you once again, very clearly. You want a *get*? It's yours. The day we sign the agreement giving me custody of Debby. If you want to become a religious fanatic—and marry an ex-convict to boot, a little detail, honey bun, you must have inadvertently forgotten to tell me—that's fine. But it's certainly not the environment I intend for my daughter. Otherwise, I still might give you a *get*—after your childbearing years are over. The ball is in your court. Call me when you grow up."

Singer exploded. He leaned past the terrified Sara to yank the telephone cord out of the wall. "The ball is in our court," he yelled savagely, as Sara cried out in surprise. "Only this time, Leonard Goode's going to get slammed!"

"Why, in heaven's name, does Gerald own a gun?" Daniel asked Roberta Braun in exasperation, moments after arriving at their roomy Camden house. He was taken aback at the disarray. Papers were piled everywhere, alongside unopened mail, and ashtrays overflowing with stale butts. There was clothing strewn on almost every chair.

Roberta shook her head. Her skin was ashen; there were deep smudges of exhaustion beneath her eyes. "A few years ago, there were some break-ins south of here, in the Pico-Robertson area—one of them in the middle of the night. There were two masked robbers, and one shoved a gun in the husband's face. That's when Gerald went out and bought the handgun. And you know Gerald—Mr. Methodical, he took target classes for months.'' Roberta took a deep breath and then went on talking, as if it somehow gave her comfort to speak, somehow kept the fear which was tormenting her at bay. "He was good at it, too. He was so proud, they told him he was in the top ten percent. He tried to convince me to come. I did go a few times. But I did it more to humor him than anything else. I don't like guns.''

"Roberta,'' said Daniel, painfully conscious how worn her face had grown this past year, "come, I want you to sit down and try to relax. We'll work through this together." She nodded, then sat down on the couch beside him. Her shoulders sagged with exhaustion. "Now, you know Gerald much better than anyone. Tell me where you think he may have gone."

Roberta stood. She bunched up the red drapes, then lifted the curtains and looked out at the sunless sky. "You sound pretty worried too, Rabbi."

"I heard on the radio what Gerald said outside the courthouse today. I'm concerned he's going to try and do something to Ron Martin."

"I wish." The words came out abruptly, as if torn from her.

"What!"

"No, Rabbi. It's Gerald I'm afraid for."

"Go on."

She stroked the velvet drapes, avoiding his eyes. A ragged breath shook her frail body. "Gerald is a perfectionist, orderly, always in control. And ninety percent of the time, he really is. But I'm so worried about him. He can't live with himself when things don't go like his image." Her voice was hoarse. "And if ever a man had to undergo an assault to his sense of justice, it is him . . . us. I know what this is doing to him, Rabbi. I've seen it once before. You know, he's a wonderful doctor. He really cares about his patients. It happened early in our marriage when he was still a resident. An emergency had come up on one of his rounds, and he followed a procedure, a generally accepted one—one that almost every doctor would have used—only that time it failed. The hospital Review Committee exonerated him completely. No one sued, the family accepted it. But not Gerald. He couldn't forgive himself. He felt that if it weren't for him, that woman would still be alive. He stopped practicing. He would go off by himself for long periods. It was hard. He just cut himself off from me. I'm sure . . . I know he thought of suicide.'' Roberta looked up, as she rubbed the nape of her neck with weary strokes. "I'm afraid, Rabbi. You don't know. You can't know. Donna meant everything to him.''

"I'm afraid we have reason to worry"—Daniel chose his words with infinite care—"but maybe not for the reasons you're thinking. You see, this time Gerald has a focus for his outrage, and it's not himself. It's Martin.''

"Of course he hates Martin. But he blames himself too.'' She let the curtain fall from her hand and turned to stare at Daniel, dry-eyed, unutterably sad. "Because we didn't push Donna hard enough. He was always so gentle with her, wanting her to be happy. Martin wasn't Jewish. Me . . . it upset terribly, and Gerald too, I guess, but he thought pressure would push her the other way, make her more devoted to him.'' Her face had become so tight and pale, it resembled a mask. "Then a few weeks later, we all went out to dinner together. Martin had gone to the bathroom, when an old friend of Donna's, a boy she knew from grade school, came over to our table. He kissed her casually on the cheek, just an innocent peck. At just that moment Martin came out, rushed over to our table, grabbed the poor boy by the lapels, and threw him down. His face was so awful . . . We got out of there quick, we were so embarrassed. But even more, we were frightened. Donna swore it had never happened before, so we let it go. But, you see, Rabbi, the writing was on the wall. If we had forced her to break up with him sooner, before that vicious boy had gotten so attached to her, she might be alive, with us right now. We failed Donna. That's what's tearing Gerald apart.'' She pulled the curtain aside again, as if willing Gerald's Mercedes to appear suddenly in the driveway. ''So what do we do? What now, Rabbi?''

Several possibilities had occurred to him, but as he looked at her defeated face, none of them seemed adequate. ''This is not going to be easy for you, Roberta. Maybe the first thing we should think of doing is putting out an appeal on the radio and—''

''Oh, no!'' The woman swayed and her trembling hands gripped the windowsill. ''That'll ruin Gerald's career. It'd be like announcing to the world that he's had a nervous breakdown. I can't do that to him.''

He rose and stood behind her, then led her back to the couch.

''I wish I could do something concrete,'' he said, taking one of her cold hands in his, ''not just offer ideas, but that's all I have.''

She nodded mutely.

''I think you should hire a private investigator to locate him''—his voice was deeply compassionate— ''and, Roberta, I know you're not going to like this, but I think we have to tell the police.''

"No!" The tears she had suppressed for so long came now, trickling down her ruined face. "My daughter's dead, Rabbi. Her name ruined by that bastard Goode. And now Gerald. Not the police. No more scandals."

"Believe me, Roberta. I have a good friend on the force. I think it can be kept quiet. You even know him. Joe Cerezzi."

Her voice was a whisper. "He's been very good to us."

"He's a very decent man," Daniel said. "And he will be extremely discreet. I guarantee it. We don't have much of a choice. If your fears about Gerald are right, God forbid, then what matters most now is that the two of you avoid any more hell. I shudder at the thought of what Gerald might do, and what might happen to him as a result. Please, Roberta, you must trust me. Let me call Cerezzi."

She didn't answer. The tears slid down her cheeks. One fell, hitting Daniel's hand. He remained motionless, still cupping her cold fingers in his. Finally she nodded.

Daniel dialed Homicide. The lieutenant wasn't in. He asked to be connected to Brenda, but she wasn't there either. He hoped she'd gotten the message he'd left earlier about not going to Cardozo. Finally he left the Brauns' home number with the police switchboard operator, telling her that it was an emergency. Then he dialed his own home, used his beeper to change the outgoing message, and left the Braun number on the tape. When the phone rang ten minutes later, he grabbed it. Roberta watched him mutely.

It was Bartley Turner, station manager for KLAX, where Daniel hosted the weekly radio show *Religion and You.*

"I called your house," Turner bawled in his eighty-decibel voice. "Where the hell are you, anyway?"

"At a congregant's house—"

But Turner wasn't interested. "I've got great news—"

"Bartley, could I call you later? There's an emergency—"

"This won't take more than a minute, Danny boy. Just want to keep you informed. I'm lining up a phenomenal show for Sunday night. Only two clergy. Just that Father O'Brien and you. I spoke to the guy, and he's willing to do it. Wants to explain himself." Serenely, he cut off Daniel's exasperated protest. "I know just what you think of the padre, and that's great, because it's gonna make the show *fan*tastic. You'll have plenty of chance to give him hell. And pardon my French, Rabbi, but we're pushing this show the whole goddamned weekend. I even got half a mind to change the format this time and get that lawyer Goode on too. You know, to give the legal side. Have all of you there together, reacting on the air. Murder, crime, punishment, I mean that's what religion's concerned with too, isn't it?"

Five times already Daniel had tried to break in, but Turner had a great advantage. He could speak without taking a breath. As Turner continued in a surge of fresh enthusiasm, Daniel watched Roberta Braun at the curtains, pleating the red material anxiously with her fingers. She appeared not to hear a single word. "Don't you worry about a thing, Danny boy. It's going to be sensational," Turner concluded triumphantly. "Okay?"

"Okay," Daniel agreed. *Not okay at all, really, but anything to get him off the line.*

"I knew you'd see it that way. Bye, pal. Now you better get back to that emergency."

She had called the party for *tonight*. That means 7:30, he calculated. At the earliest.

He went downstairs to the lobby. The clerk, an acne-scarred Chicano who looked like he doubled as the bouncer, sullenly handed him the various LA phone books. Two years old. Probably the newest thing here, he thought.

He didn't open them until he was back in the room. Even then he delayed a little longer—drank a glass of tap water, and made a half-hearted effort to smooth out the sheets. He stole a look at himself in the mirror, then drew back, shocked at his expression. He filled the sink and put his head under the water. Its cold touch revived him briefly. What if she wasn't listed? But she was there, *P. Lite,* on Esther Avenue. He knew the block, all private houses. Good. No mix-ups with apartments. He prayed silently as he dialed—if only she hasn't moved! Four rings. Then an answering machine came on—yes, he recognized the voice from the TV interview. Not home yet. Better. Probably out shopping, stocking up on champagne.

He fitted his gun under his belt, put on a jacket, and went outside to retrieve his rented car. The car even had a phone. "Only ninety-five cents a minute," the girl had told him, "for business, or maybe just to tell someone you love them." For an instant he played with the idea of phoning Roberta, then decided against it. She'd wheedle it out of him in a minute, then beg, cry, maybe even threaten. No. Better she deal with it like everybody else. A *fait accompli.* In the end, she'd understand.

It was just past a quarter to six when he reached the

block. Slowly he drove past the house, a white stucco building with a carefully tended garden in front. There was no car in the driveway, and no lights on inside. He was not the sort of person who routinely petitioned the Almighty, but he couldn't deny what he was feeling. God had to be on his side—who else, Martin's? After all, it was there in the Bible, "Whoever sheds man's blood, by man shall his blood be shed."

He pulled over across the street and slouched low in his seat.

At 6:02 the streetlamp flicked on, illuminating the area in front of the house. He looked upward and smiled.

At 6:39 a white Porsche turned into the driveway, the girl at the wheel saying something, flashing her teeth. There was a man beside her. *Martin?* Sweat trickled down his forehead. He couldn't tell.

Now another car, a blue sedan, pulled in behind the white car. Two men stepped out. One black. Both big. The white guy went directly to the driver's side of the Porsche, while the black turned to scan the street. He ducked lower into his car seat.

Cops. Roberta must have noticed the missing gun, panicked. Damn it! He had been planning to wait, let the party start, then crash it. The ultimate party pooper. Now he had to be ready for anything.

He pushed himself up. It was Martin all right—standing behind the Porsche's open trunk—facing the white cop, one hand on his thigh, the other motioning arrogantly with his thumb. The black cop had joined them. After two, three minutes—or was it an hour?—the cops went back to their sedan, and sat down inside, waiting.

The girl was walking now to the front door of the house, hugging a brown grocery bag, the murderer a few steps behind her. She turned to say something to him. He was laughing now. Laughing. Donna was rotting in her grave and *he* was *laughing*.

Quietly he lowered the window. They were both facing him, the girl still in front.

He raised the gun.

The explosion nearly deafened him. Bracing, he pulled the trigger again. The acrid stink of gunpowder made his eyes tear. The girl's grocery bag went flying. For a terrible second, he panicked. Had he hit her? Thank God, no. Martin had dropped to his knees, his face writhing, his fingers clutching at his throat, desperately trying to staunch the flow of crimson which drenched the collar. But it wouldn't work, he knew. The man who had choked the life out of his daughter's throat would now choke on his own blood.

He opened his car door, stepped out, put the gun in his pocket, and walked towards the fallen figure. The girl began to scream.

The cops were already there, the white one with his gun extended, the black cop down on one knee, uselessly pressing a kerchief against the throat. The material had already turned scarlet. The girl had collapsed on the sidewalk, wailing. He stepped over the scattered groceries as he approached. He felt absurdly calm.

The black guy looked up at his partner. "He won't make it," he said.

Funny, he thought, *why don't they ask me? I'm the doctor.*

"What'd you say?" the white cop called out, swinging around. The streetlight gleamed on his outstretched gun.

Had he said something? Funny, he hadn't realized he had spoken.

Very slowly, he pointed to the gun in his pocket. He

stood still, motionless, until the cop—his face grim—had pulled out the revolver. Only then did he look down at Martin. Prone now. Quiet. No longer laughing. Would never hurt anyone's daughter again.

"An eye for an eye," Gerald Braun said clearly. "A life for a life."

Thursday

Morning

John Vieto read through the newspaper article in its entirety. When he spoke, his voice was low, but the menace in it was very deliberate.

"That bastard threw my case."

His brother Angelo grimaced. "Listen, I'm no lover of the jewboy myself. But I don't—"

"Don't give me shit!" John Vieto's thumb angrily stabbed the newspaper column. "The Martin kid wasted the girl. We're not talking slapping a broad around. Not even rape, for godsakes." Vieto raised a muscular arm in a large arc, indicating the prison's immense visitor's hall, which was nearly deserted. "That son-of-a-bitch got me twenty-five here for heroin, and this Martin'll walk in less than three."

A sly grin spread across Angelo's face. "He won't get too far."

"Whatta you mean?"

"He was blown away last night. The girl's father shot him."

John Vieto studied his brother. Then his hooded eyes filled with laughter. "Good for him." Stealing a glance behind him at two guards at the far wall, he hissed, "You got pictures?"

"I only brought one. It's enough." Angelo released the clasp on his leather attaché case and withdrew a large textbook on business administration. John Vieto saw a five-by-seven enlargement taped to an inside page. A well-endowed blonde, nude from the waist up, was on her knees, her arms locked around Leonard Goode's middle. John Vieto was ominously calm, but the fire had returned to his eyes. "Whose idea, you figure?"

"Look, your little Miss Louisiana can get any man to thinking, so who can say for sure who started it? But Varda's definitely the one pushing it now. All the way. We had a tape in their motel room last Monday, the day we shot that. She was telling Goode she had it all figured out. He'll take care of her divorce from you, then dump his bitch, and they'll live happily ever after."

"Uh-huh." Vieto nodded, but the violence with which he slammed the textbook shut was unmistakable.

"The Jew laughed. Told her he had enough enemies in life without getting into divorce work." Angelo dug back into his briefcase and pulled out a few loose sheets, a transcript of the tape. "Varda kept pushing him, but Goode wasn't buying." Too vain to wear glasses, Angelo squinted and lifted the bottom sheet till it was inches from his eyes, checked that it was the right page, then passed it to his brother.

What Vieto read was: "You are a sensational woman, Varda. And I could swear these past two months have made me ten years younger. But I feel a responsibility to level with you. We're beyond the flowers-and-candy stage. As I like to say to my clients, it's time now to do the serious talking, not about what we want but about what we can get. First of all, I'm a pretty old-fashioned sort of guy, I love my wife and I have no intention of leaving her. Second, John Vieto is even more old-fashioned than me. Try leaving him, and the only ones who'll be admiring that splendid body of yours will be the fish. Don't kid yourself, honey. I doubt there's a lawyer in this city who'd feel safe representing the woman suing John the Gent for divorce. Your husband has never exactly had a reputation for squeamishness when it came to dealing with people who crossed him. And locked away now for a minimum of ten, he probably has less. So maybe the time's come to say farewell, while the memories are—"

Vieto grabbed for the papers, his dark features taut. "Gimme the next sheet."

"That's it. End of tape," Angelo announced. "The way we figure it, your wife threw the vase at him. I guess she missed, 'cause he looked okay when he left. The bad news is, our bug was inside the vase . . . So what do you think?"

Vieto gave a harsh snort. "You know what I think? Good thing I didn't have no kids with that whore." He surveyed the ugly room, raised his head, and his somber eyes bore into his brother's. His left hand rose a few inches, drew a sharp slash across his throat, and then quickly fell. "That, little brother, is what else I'm thinking."

• • •

They were closeted together in the judge's chambers, Barney Simon for the defense, Inga Wells, from the prosecutor's office, and Judge Nicholas White.

Having requested the conference, Simon began in a deep voice: "We intend to respectfully ask, your honor, that Gerald Braun be released forthwith, ideally on his own recognizance." A successful real estate lawyer, Simon had early in his career dabbled in criminal law. But as Daniel had learned the prior evening when he quickly canvassed the more than two dozen lawyers in his congregation, Simon was the only one with any criminal experience at all. Now, all the man wanted was to fulfill his promise to Daniel. Get Braun released on bail, then run—not walk—to dump the case in someone else's lap and return to the serene, predictable world of financing, mortgages, and zoning restrictions.

"That's absurd," Inga Wells responded in outrage. From behind round, tortoise-shelled glasses, her blue eyes blazed. "The man's—"

Judge White cut the prosecutor short with an imperious wave of his hand. "Bail applications are made in the courtroom, Mr. Simon. I assume you're not so rusty on criminal procedure as to have forgotten that."

Simon accepted the rebuke. "There are some special factors here, your honor."

"Which can also be considered in court," White answered curtly, closing a manila folder.

"I want to bring a character witness."

"For a bail hearing?" The judge didn't bother to raise his bald head.

"My client's rabbi, Daniel Winter."

At that, White looked up. "Why not his first grade teacher while you're at it, counselor?"

"I'm sure you're aware, your honor, that just a few months ago Judge Feld allowed Father O'Brien to speak at Martin's bail hearing."

"Odd case, counselor, for you to be drawing precedents from." Incongruously, White flashed the briefest of smiles. "Then again, maybe in the interests of ecumenicism we should allow it here." He quirked a bushy eyebrow. "Any objections, Ms. Wells?"

The woman's tongue probed the inside of her cheek. She straightened her shoulders. "In that eventuality, I gather, the people can bring witnesses too."

"This is a bail hearing, counselors. I don't want a trial, and neither do I want a circus."

"Your honor," the assistant district attorney hurried on, pushing unruly brown curls off her forehead, "neither do the people. But we've been approached by a distinguished attorney this morning—one familiar to all of us—who specifically requested permission to address the court in the event you were contemplating releasing the defendant."

Inwardly, Barney Simon groaned. This was worse than he thought. "Who?" he demanded.

"And it seems to me, your honor," Wells raced on, her eyes never shifting from the judge's scowling face, "that this man's opinion would certainly be no less relevant than this clergyman's, in fact, I suspect more."

"And just whom are we talking about?" the judge snapped, exasperated.

Her eyes dared Simon to respond. "Leonard Goode."

White let out a belly laugh that reverberated through the book-lined room. "Mr. Goode wants to appear for the prosecution?"

"In a manner of speaking. As you can imagine, he's quite uncomfortable with the thought that the press will perceive him as working the prosecutor's side of the bench. But in the event bail is considered, I would like to reserve the right to summon him, perhaps out of sequence."

"Fine with me." Judge White pushed his chair back and stood, tugging at his tie. "I trust this conference is over, counselors."

Simon nodded and turned miserably to leave.

Wells's musical voice stopped him. "By the way, Mr. Simon, that Rabbi Winter you mentioned, isn't he the one whose wife is the psychologist in Joe Cerezzi's department?"

"Yes."

"That's what I thought." She smiled sweetly. "See you in court, counselor."

Nobody would have called Rabbi Nachum Czernow a handsome man. His nose was misshapen, his front teeth stained and crooked, and his eyes were very small. Yet to his contemporaries in the Fairfax area, Czernow was a *shayne Yid*—a beautiful Jew. As the old joke had it, a man arrived in a tiny Russian village, a *shtetl*, and asked a townsman where he could find Yankel the tailor.

"Never heard of him."

"You must know him. He's a very short man who limps."

"No, not familiar."

"He has a long scar down the right side of his face and no teeth."

The townsman shook his head.

"And he has bald spots all over his head, and his nose is always running."

"Oh, *that* Yankel. Of course I know him. Ah! A *shayne Yid!*"

Only this morning, the *shayne Yid* of Fairfax was sitting in his study, indignant. Not enough that last night this Goode had called him an *alter kocker*—the Yiddish equivalent of old fart—not enough that Goode had rebuffed his every attempt to speak about the *get,* but finally the brazen lawyer had shouted, "And you can take your Torah and shove it."

The insult to himself he could forgive, the refusal to discuss the *get* had angered him more, but Czernow had worn down many a stubborn man. But the insult to God's holy Torah was harder to bear.

He had wondered for a moment if this Goode was even a Jew. A man who defends Nazis and murderers and then curses the Torah sounds more like a descendant of Amalek than of Abraham. Imagine if Goode was not even a Jew. Czernow pondered the notion for a moment with glee. Then no Jewish marriage, no need for a Jewish divorce. Finished.

And so he checked. He called Rabbi Yechiel Veiner, a former pupil of his, and a man worldly enough to read the *Los Angeles Times* every day.

But Veiner quickly disabused him. "Oh, Goode's a Jew all right. They published a long interview with him during that Nazi business. Came out that his family name was Godzinsky, and he even grew up in a Yiddish-speaking home."

"Just trying everything," Czernow had said lamely. He hung up, knowing how foolish the whole effort had been. Of course Goode was Jewish. Would Rav Naftali Brandwein have performed a wedding without checking into the religious status of the couple? Nor, for that matter, he now thought, did many gentiles run around calling people *alter kockers*. And, after all, should he really be so shocked by Goode's contemptuous and cruel behavior? Czernow was old enough to remember

Jewish communists who rejoiced at the Hitler-Stalin pact, and who sponsored Yom Kippur dances at which they served pork.

No, Goode was a Jew. One of those, Czernow reflected with sadness, who could stir gentiles to hate Jews. With reason.

The longer he sat, the angrier he became. Rabbi Nachum Czernow had never been a man given to bad temper. But there must be a limit to *chutzpa*, to arrogance, he knew—and a man who could help Nazis, and be so cruel to a woman who had once been his wife, had far exceeded that limit.

Something had to be done.

He thought back to a ceremony he had witnessed once, more than fifty years ago, in Poland. The rabbi in charge was Yoel Roth, who later ordained him. The case had been remarkably similar. A man in Warsaw had refused for nine years to give his wife a *get*, and the woman had despaired of ever being able to remarry. Her family was one of the richest in the city, and the husband was holding out for a bribe. The family had gone high, 100,000 zloty, a huge sum by any standard. But the man demanded more.

Rabbi Roth had called in the husband. He had pleaded and cajoled, but the man refused. "I'm waiting for them to pawn their Sabbath candlesticks," he replied mockingly.

After hours of pleading, Roth made his final offer on the family's behalf: 50,000 zloty.

"You're heading in the wrong direction, Rabbi. I've already turned down 100,000."

"I'm warning you to take it."

The man laughed and left.

That night, three messengers of the rabbi forcibly escorted the man from his house to the back room of the *shul*. Ten men, a *minyan*, were present—Czernow the youngest member of the group—and they were all holding black candles, except for Rabbi Roth, who was clutching a Torah scroll to his chest. The *shofar*, the ram's horn, was blown, and Roth solemnly pronounced the ban of excommunication: "Cursed shall you be in the city and cursed shall you be in the country. The Lord will let loose against you calamity, panic, and frustration in everything you undertake, so that you shall soon be utterly wiped out because of your evildoing in forsaking Me. The Lord will strike you with madness, blindness, and dismay. You shall grope at noon as a blind man gropes in the dark, but shall be constantly abused and robbed, with none to give help." The proclamation concluded with a public warning that no one in the Jewish community was to associate with the anathematized man. Then the candles were extinguished.

Sure enough, within weeks the man's business was closed. But still he didn't give in. He refused to grant his wife her divorce.

Then word was brought to Roth that the man had purchased a boat ticket to America. The rabbi was very concerned. In America the man could disappear entirely and his wife would remain chained to him forever.

But when the man arrived at New York Harbor, a surprise awaited him. Word had reached the U.S. immigration officials that he was a wanted criminal in Poland. One report spoke of him as a thief, another as a rapist.

And back he was sent.

Two months to the day since the rabbi had first pleaded with the man, he returned to Rabbi Roth's office. This time a *get* was issued happily. No bribe was necessary.

Mentally, Czernow now set himself the same deadline. Sixty days. But what now? How do you bring pressure in a country without bans of excommunication, and without police and immigration officials one could influence?

He resolved not to get up from his chair, nor eat or drink, until he had come up with a solution to help Sara Levin. Two hours went by, but no inspiration came. Frustrated, the rabbi decided to call Judith Fein, the young wife of his favorite nephew. Judith was always trying to interest him in a religious women's group she headed, called Tzedek—Justice. Perhaps Judith would have an idea.

Daniel felt a steady but growing discomfort in the pit of his stomach as he listened to Inga Wells delineate the grave risk of allowing Gerald Braun to be released on any amount of bail. "Common sense and bitter experience," the prosecutor instructed the court, "dictate that premeditating murderers be judged in a class by themselves." Wells opened a button on her navy blue suit and leaned forward towards the judge, as if she were sharing confidential information. "If convicted, your honor, the sentence Dr. Braun faces is so great that no sum of bail money would be sufficient to dissuade him from flight. Therefore, I ask that he be remanded pending trial."

Defense lawyer Barney Simon's voice was tense and shrill, as he fought back with every rhetorical skill he could muster. Again and again he elaborated on the depth of Braun's community involvements in Los Angeles. Braun, he pointed out, was both a respected physician and a prominent member of the Jewish community. With one arm outstretched, and his voice high-pitched, Simon called out to the judge: "I submit, your honor, that there is little, if any, risk that the defendant will flee this court's jurisdiction."

Simon then summoned "Dr. Braun's clergyman and friend, Rabbi Daniel Winter" as a character witness. This was the first time Daniel had seen a courtroom in session, let alone been asked to testify. His palms were clammy. Simon's statement had only increased his anxiety. Judge White had remained stone-faced during the lawyer's address, sunk in his chair. The reporters had hardly bothered to take their pens out of their pockets. Was Gerald Braun's fate sealed? It seemed to Daniel that he alone must turn this hearing around. Now, as he took his seat on the stand, it hardly calmed him to see Braun's ravaged eyes imploring him —or was that just his imagination, he wondered—to set him free. A verse from the Torah ran through his mind like a mantra; *"Tzedek tzedek teerdoff*—Justice, justice you shall pursue."

He began his statement a moment later. *"Premeditating murderer?* Who was Prosecutor Wells speaking about, your honor? Certainly not the man whom I have come to know so well. This man is no Charles Manson." Daniel glanced down at his hands. They were trembling slightly. Yet, the hush in the courtroom was beginning to calm him. "For the last twenty-five years Gerald Braun has gotten up every morning and gone to the hospital and saved lives. Why? Because of his love for people and his desire to support his beloved family—the two people he cared for most on this earth—his wife and his daughter. Permit me to tell you, your honor, of just one episode, one illustration of Gerald's love for his daughter. Two years ago Donna fractured her leg skiing, and Gerald spent two hours a day for four months by her side, going over and over her therapy exercises with her. He didn't trust anybody else to do it exactly right. That's the sort of father he was. And what about this young woman, Donna, *ah-leha ha-shalom,* peace be upon her, who was killed? Before the trial, Leonard Goode brought tremendous attention to her diaries—"

"Rabbi," Judge White broke in, "this is an inappropriate forum for this discussion."

"Your honor, I've read those diaries. They were filled with little poems, drawings, a description of a young woman brokenhearted because she had hurt a friend's feelings—"

"Let me remind you, Rabbi, that you are here as a character witness for Gerald Braun, not for his daughter."

"Two days before Donna died, she telephoned Ron Martin's mother to apologize for any hurt she had caused him."

"Rabbi—"

"Your honor, please, unless you know these things you cannot fully understand why this terrible thing has happened. For twenty-five years this man healed the sick, carrying out the great ethical demand of the rabbis: 'He who saves one life it is as if he saved an entire world.' Then, without warning, a cruel and violent young man, in a few angry minutes, took away one of the two lives that Gerald Braun cherished most. *And* still he remained quiet and did nothing. Until yesterday, when he was forced to confront the value a court put on his only child's life: three years."

"Rabbi Winter," Judge White snapped, "although these proceedings are quite informal, and the court is willing to extend you considerable latitude in your observations, they must be relevant." A guard entered and deposited a note at the prosecutor's table. "This latitude, however, does not include lecturing this court on your personal perceptions of the propriety of judicial decisions made by a sister court and my distinguished colleague who sits on it."

Daniel felt his cheeks flush. *You're not on the pulpit,* he reminded himself, *you're here to help Gerald.* "Forgive me, your honor. I'm just trying to set Dr. Braun's act within its context. Roberta and Gerald Braun are in their fifties. They cannot bear any more children. To witness Donna's murderer given a minimal jail term—"

"Not so minimal, Rabbi," Prosecutor Wells cut in.

Daniel straightened. The words shot through him like a jolt of electricity. *My God,* he thought, as his face again flamed, *how can she believe what she is saying?* Three years for one life? What sort of topsy-turvy world had he walked into? He remembered a tale the rabbis told about Abraham's servant Eliezer, who was sent on a mission to the wicked city of Sodom. While there, a townsman threw a rock at him, causing the blood to gush from his forehead. When Eliezer summoned his assailant into court, the judge ruled that he had to pay the rock thrower for performing the medical procedure of cupping. *What sort of story would the rabbis tell about this court?* he wondered.

"Despite the impression you're trying to generate, Rabbi," Wells continued implacably, "is it not true that Ron Martin was facing years in prison?"

Daniel averted his eyes from her. *If that's the kind of question she asks,* he thought, *what good is any answer going to do?* He turned instead to the judge. "I know Gerald Braun very well, your honor. He is an asset to whatever community he has lived in. He was a danger only to Ron Martin and to no one else."

He started up from the witness stand, but Wells's firm voice arrested him: "I have a few further questions for you, Rabbi."

Daniel sat down. His heart was pounding as he turned to face the prosecutor.

"You just said, Rabbi Winter," Wells began, "that you knew Gerald Braun 'very well.' Correct?"

"Yes."

"How long have you known Dr. Braun?"

"Since I became the rabbi at Congregation B'nai Zion."

"And how long ago was that, please?"

"Almost four years."

"How many members are there in your congregation?"

"Just over seven hundred families."

"Congratulations, Rabbi." Wells smiled. "It sounds like an impressive congregation. Seven hundred families," she mused. "That must mean a total population of more than two thousand people."

"That's correct."

"I wonder, therefore, Rabbi, how well you might really know any one individual in so large a congregation."

"The Brauns have been very active members. Dr. Braun is on the synagogue's board and—"

"Furthermore—"

"*And,*" Daniel's voice overrode hers, "in the months since Donna was murdered, I've been at the Braun home frequently."

"So you believe, Rabbi, that you know Dr. Braun very well?"

"Objection, your honor!" Barney Simon jumped up, his voice weary. "Asked and answered. The witness has repeatedly emphasized his close ties to the defendant. I don't see the need for Ms. Wells to repeat the same question.''

''Ms. Wells?'' Judge White cocked a bushy white eyebrow in her direction.

''If you give me just a minute more, your honor, I believe I can tie things up, and the relevance of my last question will become apparent.''

White nodded. ''But very quickly, please!''

Wells turned to Daniel. ''So according to you, Rabbi, it would be fair to state that of the more than two thousand people in your congregation you have a better knowledge of Dr. Braun's character than of almost anyone else's?''

''I know Dr. Braun very well,'' Daniel said.

''How well, Rabbi? In your numerous visits with Dr. Braun, did it ever occur to you that he was planning to murder Ron Martin?''

''This is outrageous!'' Simon shouted, on his feet again.

''I am trying to show, your honor,'' Wells retorted, ''that Dr. Braun was merely one of thousands of people with whom the Rabbi came in contact, and that even during their visits together following the death of his daughter, the defendant was unlikely to open himself up in a manner that would justify Rabbi Winter's assertion that he knew Dr. Braun 'very well.' That is all I wish to establish, your honor. No further questions.''

Daniel returned to his seat, his mind a whirlwind of feeble retorts. He felt drained and out of place. Worst of all, he couldn't bear to look Gerald Braun in the face. He was certain he had failed him, and he felt ashamed.

Wells was addressing the court again. ''Your honor has permitted the defense the unusual privilege at a bail hearing of presenting witnesses—and though it's out of sequence, I would request the equal privilege of calling rebuttal witnesses at this time."

Judge White assented. Wells summoned Leonard Goode, "a man quite familiar to this court, though he is usually seated on Mr. Simon's side of the courtroom."

Judge White greeted Goode warmly as soon as the attorney was sworn in. The reporters were now alert, pens poised over their notebooks. *Like people sitting up straight in the theater,* Daniel thought. *The star is coming on stage.*

Small and dynamic, Goode looked out serenely at the troubled faces in the courtroom. The attorney twirled the corner of his mustache, lifted his slender arm, and pointed towards the reporters jammed into the press section. "There's something in the gut of a defense lawyer," he began. His voice caressed the words, slowly, insidiously, building. "Something that makes it hard to speak against a defendant. And though my motives might seem selfish this morning, I tell you, your honor, Gerald Braun is a most dangerous man. We live in a nation of laws. Yet when a court makes a decision which Gerald Braun disputes, what does he do? He carries out his own vindictive, vengeful definition of justice—"

The judge stirred in his chair. "Let me caution you—"

Goode tugged at his mustache. "Your honor, I feel *personally* endangered by this man." He pulled out a clipping from the previous day's *Post* and rapped hard at the caption under Braun's picture. " 'My daughter was murdered twice,' " he read.

Simon's voice rang out: "I object, your honor, most strenuously, to bringing into this courtroom the sensationalistic—"

But Judge White cut the protest short. "There is no jury here to be prejudiced or swayed by the witness's citations. And I assure you, Mr. Simon, that I am quite capable of separating substance from any hyperbole appearing in a newspaper account. Please resume, Mr. Goode."

With a gracious nod, the lawyer acknowledged White's ruling, then resumed reading. " 'My daughter was murdered twice,' " he repeated with a well-executed tremor in his voice, " 'by Martin in her house, and by that outcast in the courtroom.' " Goode scanned the courtroom, the perfectly timed silence tantalizing his listeners. "Of the two people Gerald Braun called murderers yesterday, he has already killed one." His eyes locked on the bevy of reporters, and his voice dropped to a stage whisper. "I have no desire to be number two."

A faint applause could be heard from the back of the courtroom like the pattering of feet down a hall.

"Any questions, Mr. Simon?" Judge White asked.

"No, your honor."

No questions, Daniel thought. *My God!* He had a dozen questions for Goode. *Why should Martin have had the right to be released on bail but Gerald Braun not? Why should the Nazis he defends—who want to murder every Jew in America—have the right to walk around freely, and Gerald Braun should not?* Daniel felt a pain shooting down the center of his stomach. *God Almighty,* he murmured. *It was Goode's words, Goode's lies, before and during the trial, that brought this whole situation about. The world is ruled by words,* it now occurred to him. *I try to use them to lead people, Goode to mislead them.*

Wells's voice pulled him out of his despair. "I would most respectfully request, your honor, that I be allowed to present one final witness out of sequence. I have only in the last few minutes learned that this witness would be available to the court this morning."

White's sigh was audible, but he acquiesced.

Wells signaled the guard at the back door. As the witness was escorted inside, all eyes turned to the tall, slim redhead. "I call," the prosecutor announced, "Dr. Brenda Goldstein, a psychologist with the LAPD homicide division."

While Wells swiftly qualified Brenda's psychological expertise before the judge, Brenda and Daniel stared at each other in pained dismay. The last he had known, Brenda was spending the morning at a USC conference on "Psychology, Crime, and Women." How had she come to be here—a witness for the prosecution? Had she deliberately omitted telling him? Was she afraid that, if he knew, he'd try and argue her out of it? He felt a stinging sense of betrayal.

"During the time you spent with Gerald Braun, Dr. Goldstein," the prosecutor began firmly, "did you form any impression as to his current frame of mind, most particularly as to whether or not he would constitute a danger to the community if released?"

"I feel a conflict here, your honor," Brenda started, turning towards the bench. "Dr. Braun, you see, is a member of my husband's congregation."

Judge White's brows drew together. *"Your husband's congregation?* Do I understand then, Dr. Goldstein, that it is not your congregation as well?"

"I mean the congregation where my husband serves as spiritual leader."

"Your husband is a clergyman?"

"Of course. He's here in the courtroom."

"He is?"

"Rabbi Winter. He's sitting over there, behind Dr. Braun."

A smile lightened the judge's face, while Leonard Goode's rich chuckle echoed through the courtroom. "I see," the judge said, "that we have a very ingenious representative from the prosecutor's office this morning. Highly unusual, but nothing improper. Please go on, Dr. Goldstein."

Brenda's glance took in Daniel's sickened look. "I want to further emphasize," she said, "that though I do not know Dr. Braun well, I have had very warm feelings towards him, and I feel uncomfortable saying anything that might be injurious to him."

"I understand your reservations, Dr. Goldstein. And your comments will be one of many—in this case, *very* many—factors that the court will consider. So please address Ms. Wells's question. Based on your observations, have you formed any impressions as to whether or not Dr. Braun might pose a danger if released from custody?"

"I would only say this, your honor. Dr. Braun's anger towards Leonard Goode is tangible, even fierce. He is convinced that Goode slandered his daughter's memory during the trial."

"I repeat. In your opinion, is Dr. Braun a danger if released?"

She inhaled slowly. "I . . . I really have nothing more to say, your honor."

White smiled politely. "The witness may stand down."

The skirmish between Simon and Wells continued for twenty minutes more. It was the weary White who decreed a halt with the banging of his gavel.

"Bail is set at $250,000," he announced peremptorily. Then he glared at the defendant. "And will be revoked upon the slightest provocation." Again the gavel descended. "Next case."

• • •

"You're gracing me with your presence early today."

Max Reiss opened the door wearing a rumpled white undershirt and Levi's. It was not yet noon.

"That's a real friendly greeting," Philipa Goode answered sweetly. She leaned up and kissed him, rubbing her pink-lacquered fingers lightly against the stubble on his cheek. "Leonard's in court."

"But he just finished a case yesterday?"

Deftly, she slid under his arm into the room. "You heard what happened?"

"Of course." He let out an exaggerated groan. "If only good ol' Lenny boy had showed up with Martin last night at the party."

Philipa visibly shivered, her silk dress shimmering. "It's not a joke, darling. Leonard's really scared."

Reiss stared at her. "Of the *doctor?*"

"That's why he's in court this morning. Trying to convince the judge not to let Braun out on bail."

"He's really afraid this guy will shoot him too?"

"Leonard thinks he might have gone too far this time. That stuff about the sex diary, her kicking Martin in the balls. This Braun seems like he's on a vendetta."

"Mmm." Max scratched his chin. "What would happen to that pre-nuptial agreement you signed if, *God forbid*, anything happened to Leonard?"

"It wouldn't apply. Why?"

"You mean you'd inherit?"

She shrugged. "Whatever he left me."

The corner of Reiss's mouth lifted slightly. "And knowing you, my suntanned little ascetic, I'm sure you've never given a moment's thought to how much that would come to?"

She smiled and reached for a cigarette. "I have a pretty good idea."

"How much?"

"Well, first, I get the house."

"Big deal. How much of it's actually paid for?"

"There's a $300,000 mortgage, but just a few doors down from ours, this other house, no Jacuzzi even, went for eight-fifty."

He picked up a notebook from his desk and wrote 550 in large numerals.

"Max, what are you *doing*?"

"Just writing. What else you got?"

"Max, you're being ridiculous."

"Just curious, darling, and imaginative. I'm a novelist. I'm entitled. What else you got?"

She shrugged, and sat down sideways on Reiss's desk chair, first picking up and depositing on an already messy couch his sweater and shirt. "Leonard's got assets—the usual, some real estate, stocks."

"How much?"

"I don't know."

"Sure you don't. How much?"

She frowned thoughtfully. "He's been doing well. I'd guess two, two and a half million, something in that area."

"And how much of that area goes to you?"

"Darling, you're starting to make me nervous."

He watched the long, curving eyelashes play against her cheek. "I'm just thinking of this as a case for Nurock." Max's first two murder mysteries starred Professor Jason Nurock, a mathematician who had left a tenured Ivy League position to go to Vegas to become a professional gambler. Nurock's trademark line was "I am not a gambler, just a businessman," and his pure mathematical logic was always indispensable to his solution of the murders in his cases. "My plots always work better the closer they are to real life. So, you were saying, assets, two, two and a half million. How much to you?"

She rolled her beautiful brown eyes. "A lot goes to his daughter."

"Of course. That's not what I asked."

She stood up abruptly and went to the refrigerator. He waited by the kitchen door. "You were saying?" She pulled out a Diet Coke and cast around for a clean cup. In the corner of the cupboard, she thought she found one, but a quick look at its insides and she started sipping from the can.

"Nu?" he said.

She put the can down. "I don't know. A third. Maybe a half."

Under the 550, he scribbled 650. "Just being conservative. What else—insurance?"

"Yes. He has a big policy."

"How big is big?"

"Two million."

Max Reiss whistled. "And the division?"

"A million to the firm, half of the remainder to his daughter, the other half to me."

He added 500 to the list, drew a line under that, and wrote $1,700,000. A few inches away from it he drew a zero and quickly sketched a heart around it. "In other words, if you leave Leonard, and file for divorce, you end up with this"—his pen traced a big zero in the air—"give or take a few irrelevant thousands. But if he were to die, you'd be sitting on a mill seven. Am I correct?"

"Max, you're frightening me."

"No I'm not. You wouldn't be so familiar with the breakdown of his will and insurance if the same thought hadn't gone through your pretty little head a time or two. As for me, that's simply the way you think when you write murder mysteries. All I'm doing, sweetheart, is thinking the way Nurock does. With extreme precision. Leonard dies and you get a million seven. Correct?"

"Yes, but—"

"And there's a guy out there who Leonard is scared shitless wants to kill him?"

She nodded.

"And at this very moment Leonard is complaining to a courtroom that this old guy wants to bump him off. Which means that if anything happens to Lenny, the cops will also be inclined to think this Braun guy is responsible. Am I right?"

Her eyes widened. "Don't even—"

"I'm just asking questions. Nobody ever died from a question. Anyway, seems to me this Braun would be in a bad spot if anything happened to Lenny. It's bad enough to be suspected after a murder happens, but imagine being suspected *before.*"

"Max, stop—"

"There's nothing to stop, honey. My mind's just playing. Besides, for all we know, this Braun might really do it. Sounds mad enough. And he did have the balls to ice the kid. Interesting to speculate how easy our lives would then become, isn't it?"

"There's no reason to think—"

"Oh, that's where you're wrong, darling. There are a lot of reasons to think about it. One million seven hundred thousand and one, to be precise."

"What's the one?"

He sliced an arrow through the heart he had drawn and studied the deadly valentine impassively. Without looking up, he said, "That one, my darling, is the biggest reason of all. That's you, honey."

•   •   •

"How in heaven's name," Daniel struggled to control his voice, "did you get yourself involved in this?"

Brenda panted from the effort to catch up with him. From the moment the judge had dismissed them, Daniel had swiftly headed for the parking lot, without bothering to slow his long steps to match hers. "Don't start with me, Daniel. I was at the conference when they paged me. Wells had gotten hold of my secretary, who tracked me down. Wells insisted I come to court immediately. So I rushed down here, and what's the first thing I see? You! Do you realize the ridiculous position you put me in?"

Daniel stopped and swung around to face her. "How did Wells know to call you at all? She seemed awfully sure of what you were going to say."

"Because last night she came down to headquarters and spoke very informally to Joe and me. I simply told her my impressions of Braun—his ferocious hostility towards Goode—and mentioned that I knew him slightly through you. It was all so casual I didn't think to mention it to you when I got home last night. Daniel—"

A couple neared them, laughing. Impatiently, Daniel moved aside to let them pass. "Could you imagine if, God forbid, they had denied Jerry bail today? He'd be locked up for months until his trial. Wasting away. Maybe because of you and Goode. Then they could try what would be left of him."

A tinge of red appeared on her cheeks. "One way of looking at it."

"You have another?"

"Jerry Braun killed someone, and I think you keep trying to forget that. I know the provocation, but killing is murder; there's no way around it. It's barbaric, worse, where will it lead? I'm not as sure as you are,

Daniel, that it would be the most evil thing in the world if Jerry Braun is locked up till his trial. Besides, what if he murders Goode?"

"He won't. Jerry's not a violent man. He's broken."

Brenda looked around self-consciously, but they were alone again. The parking lot was empty. She took a step close to Daniel and rested her hand on his arm. "Daniel, let me ask you something. If somebody from the congregation asked you a question about Jewish law and I contradicted your answer, would you be a little annoyed with me?"

"Probably."

"Probably? You'd be furious. You'd want to know how an ignoramus like me, who barely knew what Shabbat was before we met, was suddenly giving rulings about Jewish law."

Daniel gave a small smile. "I would hopefully phrase it a bit more tactfully."

Her cheeks flamed the color of her hair. "Well, did it ever occur to you that I'm the one who works in homicide? That I've spent as much time studying psychology as you've spent studying the Talmud, and that I also have a lot—"

"Jerry Braun will be destroyed if he's kept in prison."

"And if he murders Leonard Goode, then Goode and Braun will both be destroyed. Remember that proverb you told me yesterday—'He who is merciful when he should be cruel will be cruel when he should be merciful'? I'm telling you, Daniel Winter, your mercy to Gerald Braun this morning might be no favor to him at all."

A horn blared from the corner of the lot, and someone yelled a curse. Daniel wound his keychain round and round his finger. He searched for an answer but all that came to him were retorts. "And your cruelty was no mercy."

But Brenda wasn't listening. One hand above her eyes to shade them from the midday sun, she stared up at him.

"Deep down, Daniel, did you ever stop to think that maybe you wouldn't mind if Goode gets murdered?"

8

Thursday

Evening

Russell Kahn, president of Daniel's congregation, opened the board meeting abruptly, with a sharp slap of his palm across the top of the gleaming mahogany table. "I appreciate your all coming to this emergency session on such short notice," he began, as the buzzing around the table quickly halted. The idea for the meeting had only come to Kahn during last night's TV news, so he was pleased to see more than forty of his fifty-member board present. "And as I'm sure no one here wants to waste time on formalities, we'll dispense with reading the minutes of last month's meeting. Any objections?" In the half second he paused, there were none. "Good. Then let's go right into the only item on tonight's agenda—the appropriate policy for us to take concerning Jerry Braun's membership on this board. I want you to know that I spoke with Jerry late this afternoon"—around the table faces strained forward expectantly—"and stressed, of course, our deep concern for him and Roberta. But the bottom line is, he's not intending to resign his seat. I told him my thinking. He's making a dreadful mistake, both for him and for us. Speaking as your president—not as Jerry's friend, because all of us here are his friends—I believe it incumbent on us to insist that Jerry vacate his board seat *immediately.*"

A few approving murmurs greeted the announcement. Over at the side of the room, away from the table, Daniel's hand shot up.

Kahn craned his neck sideways, a tight smile on his lean face. "With all due respect, Rabbi, given the urgency of tonight's agenda, and the fact that you are not a board member—"

But Daniel was already on his feet. "I have something to say, Russell, as rabbi of this congregation."

"This is a *board* issue," Kahn's basso voice boomed, as he stretched himself to his full six-feet-three-inches. "It does not fall within your purview."

"This is a *Jewish* issue," Daniel shot back, "as much as if the board was voting on a motion to shift the Sabbath from Saturday to Wednesday."

"That's the most ridiculous—"

"What's this Jewish angle you're getting at?" Sam Bornstein, Kahn's predecessor as the synagogue's president, broke in.

"Oh, for heaven's sake, Sam," Kahn snapped. "I'm in charge here now, not you."

"Why don't you let the rabbi answer the question?" Sonya Wrighter, a new board appointee, called out.

Kahn bit back a curse; a vein started to throb on his

neck. He remembered how vigorously his wife Joyce
had lobbied him six months earlier, when Bornstein
first approached him about the presidency. "You're
too damn honest, honey. You've never learned how to
hold back your real feelings. When someone speaks
like a fool, you let them know exactly what you're
thinking. You'll resign inside of two months. They
need a politician there, a diplomat." His mother had
even telephoned from Florida to support Joyce. "Before you know it, you'll be fighting with everyone. And
for what?" she went on, reaching back to her Yiddish
roots. *"A bissel kovod"*—a little honor.

But Kahn had ignored both of them, encouraging
Bornstein to present his candidacy, and two months
ago—in the absence of any opposition—he had been
unanimously elected. And to his wife's and mother's
amazement, he had so far succeeded in defying their
dire predictions. But ever since hearing about the
shooting the previous night, a terrible unease had
been building in him. In just four days the congregation was initiating a four-million-dollar campaign for
capital improvement of the synagogue facilities and for
construction of the Myron Kahn Community Center—
in memory of his father—alongside it. And now this!
Bad enough to have it come out that there was a killer
in the congregation—but on the *board*? What had happened was sad, tragic. He could even understand what
Braun had done, however pointless and foolish it was.
But sad was one thing; *takhliss*—the bottom line—was
another. You can't start a four-million-dollar campaign,
try and generate p.r., newspaper publicity, and large
contributions, with a man about to be tried for murder
as one of your leaders. And since this afternoon—with
the hourly radio reports avidly detailing the stunt Winter had pulled in the courtroom—Kahn's unease had

turned to fury. How dare the rabbi go into open court and give his imprimatur to vigilantism and killing? And without even consulting him, without requesting his permission. He could already see the headlines a few days down the road: VENGEANCE KILLER'S CONGREGATION OPENS FUND DRIVE. Who the hell did this rabbi think was paying his salary—those loony Women Against Violence, or those Justice for Donna pickets?

Kahn turned now to Sonya Wrighter and lifted a dark blue volume off the table. "Tonight's discussion will be conducted in full accordance with Robert's Rules of Order. In this room," his lips parted slightly, though the smile did not reach his eyes, "this book is our Bible. If my own Joyce was here tonight, I wouldn't even let her speak up. Can you imagine that?" Scattered laughter greeted this pronouncement. Kahn turned grim. "This is a *board* meeting, about a *board* problem, for *board* members." His eyes bore down on Daniel, and the accumulated rage he'd been trying to contain finally started seeping out. "Besides, Rabbi, don't you think you've spoken up more than enough today?"

Daniel's blue eyes narrowed. "What is that supposed to mean?"

"That your wife, Rabbi, has shown a lot more sense than you have. I know enough Bible to recognize the wisdom of King Solomon. 'There is a time to speak, and a time to be silent.' And in court today, it was time for Jerry's lawyer to speak, and for his rabbi, *the rabbi of this congregation*, to be silent. Let me share some wisdom with you, Rabbi. Not out of the Talmud, but from the real world. Before coming to Los Angeles, my family lived in Atlanta for three generations." He looked around the table. "I suppose most of you here know that. And I remember my grandfather telling me about the terror the Jewish community there felt when Leo Frank was charged back in 1913 with murdering that young girl, Mary Phagan. *Terror*. My grandfather felt it, all the Jews there did. So you think they went out into the streets and the courts and tried to turn it into a Jewish issue? Of course not. They worked behind the scenes, enlisting prominent non-Jews, getting the cream of the gentile community involved, denouncing the false accusation. *That's responsibility*. And Leo Frank, for God's sake, was an innocent man. He hadn't killed someone with two police officers as eyewitnesses. In light of all that's going on, the last thing in the world that's going to help Jerry, or this congregation's health and future expansion, is if people out there—and the media—start seeing this as some sort of Jewish/Catholic fight, you on one side, that priest on the other, or some Jewish revenge thing—you know that business about the vengeful God of the Old Testament."

An uncomfortable silence settled over the boardroom. Daniel remained in his seat, but there was a dull red patch over his cheekbones, and when he spoke his voice was very low and precise. "Am I permitted to say something now?"

"Damn right you are," Sam Bornstein called out.

Kahn regarded Bornstein with a frozen smile. "Thank you, Sam. It's good for the board to know you're ready to step back in as president if I resign." He turned to Daniel. "Now that I've spoken about you directly, Rabbi, of course you can answer."

"Thank you," Daniel said, his voice clipped. "First, Russell, I want to make one historical observation."

Kahn's eyes rolled upwards. "You're not on the pulpit here, Rabbi. Could you please confine yourself to the issues I raised?"

"It's about what you raised, Russell—the Frank case, and a major detail you left out. For all that Atlanta Jewry let responsible non-Jews speak up, and for all that some did, it was all worthless. In the end, Leo Frank was lynched. So I hardly think we should use that example as a model for how we should act. Second, and more importantly, since Donna was murdered, Jerry and Roberta have desperately needed our help and support. They still do. Can you see us in good conscience denying it to them? These two people are not strangers to us. Most of you in this room were here less than three years ago when Donna came before us to request a grant to send three of our college youth to that mammoth Soviet Jewry demonstration in Washington. She had earned the money for her own ticket, but that's the sort of person she was, worrying about others, and not just herself." His voice became forceful. "Don't you remember her organizing the Meals-on-Wheels for elderly invalids who couldn't leave their houses? That's the twenty-four-year-old girl whose murderer has now been killed. As a rabbi, as *your* rabbi, I would consider it Jewishly despicable to throw Jerry off the board just to make a good impression on non-Jews." His eyes shifted around the conference table. Some met his gaze, others dropped theirs. "If you think that Jerry Braun deserves to be thrown off the board at this time, then throw him off. Not to make an impression on anybody. And not to make our fund-raising easier. But only because you're *convinced* that killing the man who strangled his daughter was *immoral*, not just *illegal.*" He turned back to Kahn. "As a guest of the board, Mr. President, I will intrude on this meeting no longer."

He stood, nodded to the board members, and walked out of the hushed room.

9

Friday
Morning

David Hanks, newly appointed to the *Herald Examiner* city desk, scanned the maze of picket signs in front of the office building at 9696 Wilshire. The sun beat down so fiercely that perspiration gleamed on the faces of many picketers, and bystanders shielded their eyes with cupped hands. At the opposite end of the street a police officer was talking into a hand-held radio. Must be forty people here, Hanks quickly estimated, mainly women—and each one seemed to be carrying her own message. One grandmotherly type was holding up a cardboard sign with huge black lettering: LEONARD GOODE = NO GOOD. In front of the parked squad car, a pert brunette was holding a cardboard sign that read: GOODE DEFENDS THE FIRST AMENDMENT AND VIOLATES THE THIR-

TEENTH. Next to her a thin young man in a patched T-shirt and knitted skullcap—one of the few men there —was waving a banner which read: GET GOODE. The crowd had picked up the chant, and as the minutes crept by the ominous words grew louder and more sullen.

Hanks's eyes narrowed. Thirteenth Amendment? Prohibition? Women's right to vote? His brow furrowed. Later than the thirteenth, weren't they? For a second he regretted spending most of his eleventh-grade civics class drooling over Loni Parsons's legs. Finally he gave up, approached the brunette, and introduced himself.

"Judith Fein," she said when he finished, though she did not lower her sign to extend a hand. "I'm president of Tzedek. That's Hebrew for justice. We're the group that organized this demonstration."

Hanks flashed a boyish smile. "You want to refresh me, Ms. Fein, on the Thirteenth Amendment?"

"That's the one forbidding involuntary servitude."

"Come again!"

"Slavery. The Thirteenth was Lincoln's amendment forbidding slavery."

She looks normal enough, Hanks thought. Then again . . . "You're telling me," he said, vainly trying to suppress a smile, "that Leonard Goode is violating the law against slavery?"

Judith Fein gave a very deliberate nod. She was really, Hanks decided, very pretty. "In spirit, most definitely."

He could play along. After all, there might be an angle for a good story in it. "How?"

"Twelve years ago Mr. Goode married Sara Levin in a Jewish ceremony. Yet now, though they have a civil divorce and he has remarried, he refuses to give her a

Jewish divorce. According to Jewish law, Sara is still married to him and forbidden to anyone else. In Hebrew a woman who is victimized by such a man is called an *agunah*, a chained woman." Her voice was chilling in its contempt. "Tell me, Mr. Hanks, if some woman was arbitrarily vetoing your right to marry the woman you loved, what would you call her?"

"My mother."

Fein glared at him, then reluctantly laughed. "Seriously. If a woman forced you to stay married to her against your will, wouldn't you consider that pure unadulterated slavery?"

Hanks gulped. A joyfully secular Southern Californian pagan, he got quickly lost in the thicket of religious disputes. "Seeing as an American court has already declared the lady divorced, why don't your rabbis just do the same?"

"They are forbidden to do so."

"By whom?"

"According to our Torah, the Five Books of Moses, it is the man who initiates the marriage ceremony. He proposes, and the woman either accepts or rejects his offer. And since, legally speaking, the man is the initiator of the marriage, only he can dissolve it."

Hanks studied Judith Fein's intelligent face, fashionable flowered skirt and top, even the pale blue kerchief covering her hair. Together, it didn't add up to this primitive theology she was spouting. Hanks was the scion of a Unitarian home, of the sort encompassed in Whitehead's definition, "A Unitarian is a person who believes there is, at most, one God." He remembered a riddle he had brought home from Sunday school once. It had irked the hell out of his mother, though his father had roared with laughter. "When is the only time you hear Jesus Christ's name mentioned in a Unitarian Church?" Answer: "When the janitor trips on the ladder." And so he regarded Fein's matter-of-fact acceptance of a sexist, supposedly God-given legal code as more than a little puzzling, disorienting, in fact. As if they had been walking along together and suddenly had come to a door through which only she could pass, while he was left outside, bewildered. He squinted down at her. "You really believe all that?"

"I do."

The monotonous chant of her fellow demonstrators—"Get Goode, Get Goode"—was starting to make Hanks's head throb.

"We all do," she went on. "The rabbis, of course, didn't want men to abuse this law. They often ordered men to grant their wives a Jewish divorce, a *get*. In fact, one of the leading rabbis in this city, Nachum Czernow, ordered Leonard Goode to do so."

"And what did Goode say?"

"He refused. That's why we're all here. And we intend to keep coming back, *religiously*, Monday, Tuesday, Wednesday, Thursday, till Leonard Goode sets Sara Levin free. People tell me Mr. Goode likes publicity. In that case, we'll give him plenty. More than even *he* wants."

Russell Kahn jerked his thumb in the direction of Daniel's office. "Is he in?"

Pat Hastings looked up from her typewriter. "The rabbi?"

No, the plumber, Kahn felt like answering. He would have liked nothing more than to give some scathing retort to Daniel's secretary. But he controlled himself. Besides, his wife Joyce—whose instincts about relationships, he had to admit, were a hundred times better than his—had sent him out of the house this morning with only two words of advice: "Be nice."

Be nice, he reminded himself now. "Yes, of course, the rabbi," he told Pat, amazed at how benevolent he sounded.

"I'll let Rabbi Winter know you're here." Pat lifted the receiver, but Kahn's hand was already pushing open the door to the inner office. He walked straight over to Daniel and gave the surprised rabbi a crushing handshake.

"Shalom aleichem," Daniel said, putting aside the large black Talmud he had been poring over.

"Ah . . . yes. Good day, Rabbi." Kahn took a seat opposite him, crossed his long legs, and managed a strained smile. "I suppose we both got a little hot under the collar last night."

"I suppose we did," Daniel said. "You see, I—"

"No need to apologize, Rabbi. I understand what you were going through. And the bottom line is, it was a good thing for us hardheaded businessmen—the guys who have to make the practical decisions—to hear a rabbi's compassionate voice."

"Thank you, Russell. I'm touched, I really am. Do I take it then that the motion concerning Jerry has been dropped?"

Are you nuts? Kahn almost jumped up, shouting. But again he restrained himself. He had let the rabbi get under his skin last night, but now *he* was holding all the aces. "The board voted thirty-six to four to vacate Jerry's seat immediately."

There was a pause. "I see."

"You know very well how much I urged Jerry to resign and not to force our hand. But he left us no choice. In three days we have our first fund-raising meeting, and I don't want anybody there thinking about anything else."

"I see."

"Stop saying that," Kahn snapped. "I want to know what you're thinking."

"As I see it, what you were doing was wrong last night, and I think it's wrong now."

"The man committed a *murder.*"

"The man killed his daughter's murderer," Daniel responded. "I should think that makes it a little different."

Kahn smiled thinly. "Don't make me out to be the bad guy, Rabbi. This is a civilized country—the U.S. of A."

"Oh, really? Why don't you tell me, Russell, what's so civilized about a country in which a man snuffs out a woman's life and the court sentences him to prison for only three years?"

"Six years."

"He would have been paroled in three. Parole is a right murderers now have too."

"Listen, Rabbi, I'm not interested in scoring debating points. I'm just telling you, until this business is cleared up, the whole leadership of this synagogue must distance themselves from Jerry."

"I see."

"*And will you stop saying that?*" Kahn shouted. The vein in his neck began to throb painfully. *Be nice,* he thought. "You're putting me in an extremely awkward position, Rabbi. I don't like having to give you a direct order, but you're leaving me no choice. As the president of this synagogue, I'm telling you. Stop talking about this case, and stop associating with Jerry Braun. As of right now."

Daniel was quiet, but his piercing gaze did not leave

Kahn's face. "As an employee of this synagogue," he said, "you can instruct me on matters of synagogue business. On religious matters, Russell, I listen to a higher authority. And in Judaism, how you treat other human beings is a *religious* matter."

10

Friday
Evening

"It was beautiful, Rabbi," Sara Levin said. "Thirty-four women and five men, I counted them, marched in front of Leonard's office for over two hours. And Judith Fein promised me they'll be back on Monday."

"That's a wonderful beginning." Daniel smiled, as he filled her glass with white wine. He was seated around the gleaming Friday night Shabbat table with Brenda and their first-time guests, Sara Levin and Evan Singer. Sara wore a red and white dress, which contrasted richly with her olive skin, while Evan was clad in a dark suit and white shirt, the top buttons undone. It was a rare weekend for both couples, alone, their children away. Conversation was merry as the four devoured Brenda's gefilte fish and arugula salad, and steaming Hawaiian chicken.

"The truth is," Singer said, shrugging his broad shoulders, "all that happened was that thirty-four women got two hours of exercise."

"Evan, stop!" Sara snapped. Her delicate features tensed. "Anything that puts pressure on Leonard is good. Isn't that true, Rabbi?"

"Of course."

"The pressure will work," she insisted. "It'll make him give me the *get*, won't it?"

"I hope so."

Singer rubbed his finger along the edge of his wineglass. "But you can't say for sure, can you?" he asked softly.

Daniel's eye caught Brenda's. "How can anyone say for sure?"

"And if he doesn't give it, Rabbi, Evan and I won't be able to marry, will we?" The light of the candlesticks revealed the fear in Sara's eyes.

The only sound that could be heard was the ticking of the grandfather clock on the mantel behind Daniel. "No, Sara," he said.

"You don't think I should give him my daughter, do you?"

"How could anyone ask a mother to give up her child? Particularly to the moral influence of a Leonard Goode. Our best bet—and I think it's a very good bet —is to keep up the pressure."

"Pressure?" Singer sneered. "What do you think Leonard's afraid of? That everyone on Wilshire Boulevard will find out he's a naughty boy? You think that's going to make him even flinch?"

"Do you have a better idea, Evan?" Daniel asked.

Evan bent forward in his chair, his elbow on the

table. His eyes were dark with anger. "In my teenage days back in the Jewish Defenders, Rabbi Ring was once approached in a case like this. He sent four of us to speak to the guy. And we told him: 'Next week, your wife will be permitted to marry. Either as a divorcée or as a widow. It's up to you, buddy.' "

"And what happened?" Brenda asked. Her green eyes looked over at Singer with a mixture of curiosity and disbelief.

"The first week, nothing. So we went back and dragged the guy over to my friend's basement. I started showing off my karate skills. Chopped right through a brick. Then I started measuring his neck." Singer threw back his head and laughed. "The guy got so scared he wet his pants." He saw Sara's face redden, and turned to Brenda, "Excuse me, Rebbetzin. Anyway, we knew we had him then. So we took him straight over to the rabbi's house. The rabbi called in a scribe and witnesses. And within the hour the guy's wife was free."

"And you weren't concerned he'd go to the police?" Daniel asked.

"Police shme-lice. We knew from the wife that he was doing a big business in diamonds, and reporting zilch on his returns. He didn't want the police involved any more than we did." Singer took a gulp of the clear Yarden wine, then plunged ahead. "Besides, when we had the guy in the basement we took about a dozen pictures of him naked. Told him if he ever so much as called his ex-wife to wish her a Happy Passover, we'd plaster them all over the neighborhood."

Brenda grimaced. "I can't believe you did that. That's a horrible thing to do."

"Six years his wife had been trying to get a divorce. Nice refined rabbis speaking to him three, four times a week. And he wouldn't give it. *That's* what was horrible."

"What about your threat?" Daniel pressed. "Would you really have killed him?"

Singer was silent a long moment, prodding the tablecloth with his fork. Then he shrugged. "I've wondered about that sometimes. I don't know. After that encounter in the basement, he didn't know either." He looked at Brenda. "I suppose if we *had* killed him, we could have called in your husband."

Daniel's face reddened. "What's that supposed to mean?" he asked.

"To come testify at our bail hearing." Evan was smiling.

"Enough, Evan!" Sara said nervously. "I'm sorry, Rabbi. He just likes to be provocative."

"Don't patronize me, Sara. The rabbi and his wife seem to think what I did was horrible. Even though he figures it was great for Braun to blow away that Martin kid."

"I don't think it was great. But I do understand it."

"So why don't you under—"

"Rabbi," Sara broke in, more firmly this time, "speaking of the Brauns, how are they doing? You know I always sit near them in services."

"I was making a *point, darling.*"

Sara stared up at Singer. Her lips trembled. He scowled and then his mouth tightened. He turned to Daniel. "Sorry if I offended you, Rabbi."

"You know the greeting we give today," Daniel responded, " 'Shabbat shalom—A peaceful Sabbath.' " He smiled at them. "Maybe we really should speak of less controversial things."

"I wasn't just being polite before, Rabbi," Sara said.

"I really am concerned about the Brauns. How are they?"

"About what you'd expect for a couple who've lost their only child. Now Jerry's facing a murder charge and Roberta's chain-smoking like a fiend."

"I hate being around smoke," Evan said. "Thank God we can't smoke on Shabbat. At least one day a week, Sara can't smell up the house."

"Evan has my word of honor," Sara said. "The day I marry, the moment before I step under the *chuppah,* that's my last cigarette. Besides," she went on, as she patted his hand, "this character won't kiss me if he smells cigarette smoke on my breath."

"It's not just her breath," Evan said, leaning his elbows on the table. "It gets in her hair, and even her fingertips reek from the way she grinds those filthy butts down. Makes me nauseous."

"Excuse me," Daniel said, "I think it's time to get the *benchers.*" He saw Sara's puzzled look. "You know, the prayer books for the *birkat ha-mazon,* the grace after meals. It's time we did a little Shabbat singing."

Evan took advantage of the break and excused himself.

Sara waited till the men had stepped out of the room, then leaned towards Brenda. "How long, if I may ask, Rebbetzin Winter, did you and the rabbi know each other before you got married?"

"A little less than a year."

"And were you religious before you met him?"

Brenda smiled at the recollection. "Not really."

"Like Evan and me." Sara smiled and her voice grew dreamy. "I know Evan can be hotheaded at times, but if not for him, who knows if I would ever have been exposed to the beauty of Torah, the peace and tranquility of Shabbat, the glory of worshiping Hashem?

Do you know Evan was the first man I ever dated who wore a yarmulke? Seeing him walk around like that, such a strong man but so pious, makes me feel safe."

They finished the evening over a babka, served with tea. The *birkat ha-mazon*, which they sang straight through in high spirits, lasted a good ten minutes.

They exchanged their parting Shabbat shaloms, then Daniel escorted the couple to the front door. Evan skipped down the front steps to the street, breathing deeply of the cool fresh air. After the heat of that morning, the evening breeze was welcome. Sara turned to Daniel. "I hope you realize how much I want to marry Evan, Rabbi."

"I do."

"More than anything I've ever wanted in my life."

"I plan to dance at your wedding, Sara."

"Thank you, Rabbi. Thank you."

The door was closed gently, and Daniel stood for a few seconds staring through the window at their retreating backs.

"She worries me," Brenda said when he returned to the dining room. She had stretched out luxuriously on the couch, weary after the extensive Shabbat preparations.

"*She?* You mean he, don't you?"

She shook her head. "I suspect Evan's bark is worse than his bite. When I was in private practice, I must have seen two patients a day like him. Big dramatic stories, in which they were always the heroes."

"You think Evan made up that whole incident?"

"I'll put it to you this way. If the three guys who were with him, and the guy they were leaning on, were also here, I bet we'd be hearing some very different versions of what happened."

Daniel laughed. "Okay, Dr. Rashomon, fair

enough. So what is it about Sara that's got your psychological antennae up?"

"Her immense capacity for self-destructiveness."

Daniel shook his head. "I don't see it. It seems to me, in fact, that that's exactly what she's now freeing herself from. Her becoming religious is a perfect example—it's a move towards stability."

Brenda propped herself up more comfortably, a cushion behind her head. Daniel sat beside her on the sofa, and Brenda rested her legs across his lap. "It's a move towards getting married, that's what I think. She struck me as a little desperate. When you left the room, she told me that she became religious because of Evan."

"Which proves very little. Didn't you become religious in large measure because of me? But now it's part of your life."

"That's because I adopted what made sense to me. And fortunately you made so much of it seem sensible. But a few months after I met you, I wasn't going around telling people 'Daniel exposed me to the beauty of Torah, to the glory of worshiping Hashem.' That's how she was speaking when you went out. By the way, my friend, if you wouldn't show up in every courtroom in the country, maybe I could express my ideas a little more freely too. I definitely did not want Jerry Braun released on bail."

"Oh, we're back to that again. By the way, just to keep things accurate, I showed up in *one* courtroom."

"You can joke your way out of anything, Daniel, but you have to realize what you did in that courtroom yesterday. You didn't just speak out on behalf of Jerry. You spoke out on behalf of murder."

"Do you see killing Ron Martin as murder?"

She pushed herself up. "Do I understand why he did it? Yes. Was it wrong? Yes. Was it murder? Yes."

"Murder is when you kill an innocent person. I hope, at least, you don't consider Ron Martin an innocent person."

"Ron Martin was vile, Daniel. But he was judged and sentenced in a court of law. And with all the failings of the courts, they're all that stand between us and anarchy. Can you imagine if everyone who's angry about a court's ruling took it into their heads to exact their private revenge?"

"A lot of injustice would occur," Daniel conceded. "But this was not one of them. And I'm not going to watch Jerry Braun crucified because of what may hypothetically happen." He stopped abruptly and moved over, inching himself closer to her. His hands gently kneaded the back of her neck. "I'm starting to feel like a fool for giving Sara and Evan that little sermon about a peaceful Shabbat. Look at how the two of us are observing the Shabbat."

She lifted her hand and stroked his cheek. For a long moment the room was silent. Slowly Brenda reached up and caressed Daniel's arm. Her face puckered mischievously. "For such an observant man, Rabbi, there's still one Shabbat law we haven't observed tonight."

Daniel frowned. "What are you talking about, copper?"

" 'Rabbinic scholars,' " Brenda quoted from the Talmud with a suspiciously pious expression, " 'are to have relations with their wives on Friday night.' "

"Why is it," he said, in mock exasperation, "that of all the Talmudic laws I ever taught you, that's the only one you can quote?"

"I told you, buster. I adopted what made sense to

STOP! *DANGER... INTRIGUE...and SUSPENSE AHEAD!*

1. Detach the Free Gift seal at the right.

2. Follow the trail of footprints to the next page.

3. And affix your Gift Seal in the space provided inside to receive:

FREE GIFT

A free 362-page Agatha Christie Bedside Companion.

A free preview of the mystery classic...
And Then There Were None!

Follow the trail
into Agatha Chris

FREE PREVIEW! The Bedside Companion is your **FREE GIFT** just for viewing Agatha Christie's renowned mystery classic. **And Then There We None,** for 15 days risk free. It's one of the most captivating murder myster ever written! Will you discover whodunit before the author reveals the solution?

And Then There Were None demonstrates the exciting mystery entert ment that awaits you in **The Agatha Christie Mystery Collection.** The Co lection brings you Agatha Christie's novels in hardbound collector's edition that are not available in any bookstore. Each book is bound in simulated leather — rich, Sussex blue in color, and decorated with distinctive gold em bossing. The covers are padded and soft to the touch. The bindings are sew (not glued), and the pages are of acid-free paper that will last for generation All in all, each volume is a masterpiece of the bookbinder's art and will disp elegantly in your home.

You might expect to pay $20 more in bookstores for luxurious volumes like these. Yet they are yours for only $12.95 each (plus shipping and handl

NO OBLIGATION — EVER! Send for **And Then There Were None** and enjoy it for 15 days risk free. If you like, return it, owe nothing, and that wil that. If you keep it, you'll receive additional volumes in **The Agatha Christi Mystery Collection** about once a month — and always with 15-day previe privileges. Keep only those volumes you want. Cancel any time. And whate you decide at the outset, **The Bedside Companion** is yours to keep **FREE.**

footprints below World of Mystery!

Take advantage of this generous offer today!

FREE ...Fascinating 362-page Agatha Christie
Bedside Companion!

FREE ...Preview of **And Then There Were None!**

me. And that one always made the most sense of all.'' She sat up, reached over, loosened his dark red tie, and slipped it slowly off his shirt. ''Don't you agree?''

"Maybe you should get a move on upstairs," he murmured. "Wouldn't want us to start neglecting any Shabbat laws."

11

Saturday

It was a quiet Shabbat morning service, no bar or bat mitzvahs, or would-be grooms to be called to the Torah, and therefore no large *kiddush* celebration at the end. Synagogue attendance, as a result, was lower than usual, two hundred people at most. At the start of services, Russell Kahn, his back ramrod straight, walked up to the *bimah* to take his place as president at the front of the congregation, next to Daniel. He extended neither hand nor Shabbat greeting. "What's the sermon this morning?" was all he asked.

"I was thinking of speaking on *Lex talionis.*"

Kahn nodded approvingly. "Fine, nothing controversial. Has a scholarly ring to it." He cleared his throat. "By the way, what does that mean exactly?"

"*Lex talionis?*"

"Yes."

"It's Latin, Russell. Means an eye for an eye."

Kahn's eyes blazed. "Rabbi, I'm shocked that you would choose such a topic now, of all times. Only you—"

Daniel grinned. "Don't worry. I was pulling your leg, trying to lighten the mood between us."

The president's eyes still flashed, but he gave a perfunctory laugh. "Oh, excuse me, Rabbi. Very funny." Fortunately, at that moment, Cantor Bloch's "*Barukh ata . . .*" inaugurated the service.

The next hour proceeded uneventfully. The worshipers recited and sang their prayers beneath the synagogue's twelve stained-glass windows, depicting the tribes of Israel. Then, while the *gabbai* was summoning the third *aliyah* to the Torah, Daniel saw Roberta and Gerald Braun entering at the back of the synagogue. He waved a greeting at them. Russell Kahn stared at him angrily.

"What the hell are they doing here?" he hissed.

"You only threw him off the *board*, Russell, not out of the synagogue."

"But he was so furious he swore up and down he'd never set foot in here again."

"I know."

"How? I didn't tell you that."

"I called Jerry as soon as you left my office. When he told me what he was feeling, I insisted he come."

"What did you do that for, Rabbi? Haven't you done enough meddling?"

"I didn't want Jerry and Roberta to feel totally excommunicated from Jewish life. Sometimes, Russell, the purpose of religion is to comfort the afflicted."

The melodic chant of the Torah resumed. But Russell Kahn hadn't noticed. "Really!" he said. "Sometimes, Rabbi, I believe you think its purpose is to afflict *me.*"

Max Reiss sat at his desk, arranging the scattered pages of a manuscript. Philipa came up behind him, but he went on working. She started rubbing his shoulders. "Don't be upset, sweetheart. I'll only be at the health farm five days."

He picked up a page and tore it into smaller and smaller pieces. "What do you need a health farm for? It's for two-ton slobs."

"Which is what I'll be if I don't go soon. After my workout last week, I stepped on the scale. 124. I was shocked. I've never been over 118 in my life." Her hands went back to his neck, and she placed her soft curls against his cheek. "I'll really miss you, darling. What are you going to be working on?"

"New book idea," he said, handing her the title page. *Goode Mourning,* she read, and the sheet dropped right out of her hands. With a satisfied smile, Max lifted it.

"Are you crazy?"

Max laughed, and rested the sheet on his cluttered desk. It lay there amid piles of edited pages, crumpled notes, and unpaid bills.

Philipa reached for a cigarette. "What's the matter with you, Max?"

He handed her a thick sheaf of pages. "Don't get hysterical. It's just another Nurock mystery I'm starting. *The Stabbing.*"

"And that?" she said, pointing to the title sheet on his desk.

"That," he answered softly, "is just wishful thinking."

"I knew we shouldn't go," Gerald Braun said to his wife. She had set out a simple Shabbat lunch, tuna salad and a fruit plate. But Gerald hadn't touched a thing. He simply rested his elbows on the smooth pine table and held his head in his hands. His face was gray with fatigue and pain.

"Enough, darling. It's good we went. You saw how happy the rabbi was to see us. And the Weins, and that young woman, Sara something, and the Horowitzes—"

"And who else?" Jerry pushed back his chair and got up from the table. "Staring at me like at a freak show." He stalked over to a small round mirror on the wall and fingered his cheeks: "Does it show on me—that I killed someone?"

Her hands began to tremble. They had begun to shake a lot in these past months since Donna died. Compulsively, she picked through the ashtray in search of a long butt. She had vowed yesterday not to buy a pack of cigarettes—it was forbidden to smoke on the Sabbath. But she could no longer restrain herself. "You're talking like a fool."

"Am I? Do they realize, any of them, what it feels like to have your child murdered?"

"Did we? Before Donna . . . before this happened to us, did you and I know what it meant to lose someone so senselessly? It's like that with everything. When a woman gives birth to a Down's syndrome child, suddenly she and her husband can't understand why other people don't know what they're going through. Beforehand, maybe they would have given a pitying glance and thrown a dollar in a box."

"Bravo! So that's the *profound* wisdom you've been picking up at Compassionate Friends?"

"One of many things, darling, I've learned there. I wish you'd come with me just once."

"So they're ignoring us in synagogue because their child didn't have the life snuffed out of her?"

She watched him. It hurt. The lines of grief and rage deeply carved his gaunt cheeks. He was turning into an embittered old man before her eyes. "Come back to the table, Jerry."

"It's because they think I'm a killer. To them, I'm just another Ron Martin, no better or worse than he is."

She rose and stood behind him. "God forbid. Who would draw such a ridiculous comparison?"

"What do you think they threw me off their precious board for—parking in front of a fire hydrant?"

"They're like any establishment group, afraid of any hint of a scandal. That's all Kahn cares about. It's no moral judgment on you."

"It's that son-of-a-bitch Goode's fault."

His savage voice frightened her. "What does Leonard Goode have to do with it?"

"The general opinion is that Donna got what was coming—"

"Stop it!" she shouted, and every muscle in her face was taut. "Stop it!"

"When Goode started that bluff about the sex diaries, every damn paper in town gobbled it up. And when it came out that it was all phony, who the hell even saw it mentioned? They think Donna's a tramp."

She bent her head so he would not see the tears stinging her eyes. "They all know that's Goode's method. He even has a name for it. 'Desanctifying' the victim. Everybody knows it's a sham."

"You're wrong. People always like to believe the worst. Who knows what nonsense they'll come up with next? That I killed Martin to stop him from revealing more filth about Donna. And if they run short of ideas, I'm sure Leonard Goode will happily provide some new ones." His face sagged. With heavy steps he went over to the hard chair in the corner. He sat there, staring past the hanging copper pans, the woolen potholders that Donna had knitted, his eyes focused on some unknown object that seemed to hover in the air.

"Eat something," Roberta urged.

"Eat something," he repeated, then started to laugh. When he caught his breath, he surprised her with a riddle. "You know the difference between Leonard Goode and a vulture?"

"What?"

"A vulture waits till you're dead to eat your heart out."

12

Sunday

All weekend long KLAX had been pushing Daniel's
Sunday night talk show, *Religion and You*, like a
prizefight: "Listen in as Daniel Winter takes on Father
Michael O'Brien and Leonard Goode in a far-ranging
debate on all aspects of the Donna Braun passion slaying and revenge killing. *Love your enemy* or *A life for a
life*, punishment or forgiveness—which way is right?
The debate that Winter started with Goode in the
courtroom this Friday morning continues now *only on
KLAX.*"

Normally, *Religion and You*'s format was simple:
three clergy, a minister, a priest, and a rabbi, with Daniel moderating. Thanks to Bartley Turner, however, tonight's show had been totally transformed. Daniel

would still moderate the call-in show, but this time he was also an advocate. And he was nervous. Leonard Goode had that effect on him. Repelled him, too. Whenever he saw the attorney, he also saw Donna's face. Shy, innocent, and dead. He knew he was being melodramatic, but he felt that tonight he was representing every victim whose rapist or killer Leonard Goode had set free. And that made him even more anxious. What reason did he have to assume he would come off any better against Goode on the air than they had in the courtroom?

Goode and Father O'Brien arrived at the station together, followed seconds later by Bartley Turner. O'Brien gave Daniel a hearty handshake. Daniel was struck—not for the first time—by the Father's genuine warmth, and by the lack of lines in his face. The man seemed to exude tranquility.

Goode's manner was gruffer. "No opening statements, Rabbi. I don't want you controlling the show's direction. So let's go straight to calls." Daniel bristled, but Turner, who was standing behind the diminutive lawyer, swiftly pulled Daniel aside. "Don't make a fuss, Danny," the worried station manager whispered. "You'll do great under any conditions. And we can't risk him suddenly deciding to walk."

At 8:06, right after the news, they went on the air. The first call came in on capital punishment, and Goode cut the woman caller short in seconds. "Don't use that term, cap-i-tal pun-ish-ment," he told her, dragging out each syllable. "The only people who like to speak about cap-i-tal pun-ish-ment are the people who support it, who want to sanitize what they're doing. Let's call it what it really is: legalized murder."

"Which you always oppose, Mr. Goode?" the caller asked.

"Always."

Daniel leaned forward. "I'm surprised. Your entire career, Mr. Goode, is based on justifying capital punishment. The punishment *your* clients inflict on their victims. Isn't that what you did in this case, in arguing that Donna Braun provoked Ron Martin to murder her?"

"You're being demagogic, Rabbi. I never ever, in any way, argued that Ron should have killed that unfortunate girl. I simply pointed out that we were dealing with an immense tragedy for all concerned, and that it made no sense to put all the blame on one person."

"Even if that person was the murderer?"

Goode blew out audibly, so that all the listeners could share in his weariness. "Did it ever occur to you, my all-knowing friend, that the twelve-member jury, which heard the *whole* story, might have been in a somewhat better position to decide the case than Rabbi Daniel Winter?" As Goode built towards his climax, Father O'Brien's long, narrow face grew creased, pained by the sharp tone of the other two participants.

"If they'd heard the whole story," Daniel answered, "you would be right. But they didn't, and you're the one who made sure of that. You stopped Mona Lance, Martin's former girlfriend, from testifying that he had severely beaten her seven times, and once even tried to strangle her."

Goode's voice was icily professional. "No criminal prosecution was involved. Lance's allegations were never scrutinized by a police officer, let alone by a jury. Her testimony would have unfairly prejudiced the jury against the defendant."

"It would have prejudiced them, I'm sure. The way I'm prejudiced against Eichmann."

"That is an ugly comparison," Father O'Brien interrupted in his melodious voice, "to draw about a young man who is now dead."

"If there is some religious or moral wrong, Father, in speaking ill of a dead person who murdered someone, I'd appreciate it if you would explain to me what it is."

"We come out of different traditions, Rabbi. The Old Testament speaks of an eye for an eye, which in its own time was quite probably a tremendous advance. But the New Testament goes beyond that. It demands from us a total forgiveness of sin. That's what Jesus taught: 'If you forgive men their trespasses, your heavenly Father will also forgive you; but if you do not forgive men their trespasses, neither will your Father forgive your trespasses.' You see, Rabbi, we think differently—"

"Not at all, Father. It seems to me that verse is just Jesus's restatement of an eye for an eye."

"What . . . what are you saying?"

"According to Jesus, if you forgive others, God will forgive you. If you don't forgive others, He won't forgive you. In other words, God treats you exactly as you treat others. Which is what the Hebrew Bible demands."

"That's a preposterous way of interpreting Jesus's words!"

"Furthermore, Father, forgive my tactlessness, but did it ever occur to you that if you spent your life speaking as vigorously against hurting people as you now speak about forgiving sinners, maybe a Ron Martin would never have killed Donna Braun."

O'Brien's light blue eyes hardened. "And if you had spoken as vigorously about forgiving sinners as you now speak about avenging evil, maybe Gerald Braun wouldn't have killed Ron Martin."

"Are you seriously equating the two acts?" Daniel asked.

"I should hope not," Leonard Goode intervened. "What Ron did was tragic, but it was impetuous, in the heat of passion, and under terrible provocation. Gerald Braun's act of murder was a premeditated, deliberate act of revenge."

"In other words," Daniel said to Goode, fighting off a rising feeling of nausea, "you believe that Gerald Braun's killing of his daughter's murderer was worse than Ron Martin's killing of Donna Braun?"

Goode gave a measured nod. "Insofar as premeditated murder is worse than a killing committed in a moment of passion, most definitely."

"Mr. Goode," Daniel's voice became steely, "until this moment I assumed you defended Nazis only because you thought every one was entitled to a defense. I now realize it's probably because you've worked out some ingenious rationale as to why they have more right on their side than the Jews."

"Ha, ha, ha!" Goode chortled sarcastically. "I'm not falling for your provocations and tearjerkers, Rabbi. But for the sake of our listeners, let me explain something. I defended the Nazis because I realized that when we start regulating First Amendment rights according to our personal likes and dislikes, you can kiss the First Amendment good-bye. As regards the Holocaust, I consider every one of the six million Jews who perished in it as my brother and sister."

"I don't believe you for a moment."

"Why not?"

"If you really felt the six million were your brothers and sisters, really felt it, you would not have defended the people who identify with their murderers any more than you would defend someone who would, God forbid, murder your real brothers and sisters. It's only because these victims, whether they be Jews in the Holocaust, or a Donna Braun murdered by a vicious and vile ex-boyfriend, are strangers to you that their suffering and fate bothers you so little."

"Do you really believe I'm happy Donna Braun was killed?"

"All I know is that you celebrated in court when the jury announced its verdict. I happen to know, Mr. Goode, that you have a young daughter. If a few years from now, after Mr. Martin would have been released from prison, your daughter had brought him home as a fiancé, would that have made you uncomfortable?"

"Ron Martin is dead, Rabbi. Because of the premeditated act of a man you went into court to publicly support. A man who has directed public threats towards me. A man who would not be walking the streets had you not come to his rescue in some sort of misguided belief that you know when it's proper to take another human being's life. I'm not going to dignify your ridiculous speculations with a response."

"Of course not. If you answered truthfully you know how damning your response would be. You wouldn't have wanted a Ron Martin to date your daughter because you love your daughter, and you wouldn't want her to be savagely beaten and perhaps killed. But other Americans love their daughters as much as Leonard Goode loves his. Can't you spare a little compassion for them? Don't you give a damn when you send a murderer back into society?"

Goode's face was white with anger. "Rabbi, you're the first Jewish Inquisitor I've ever met. And like most Inquisitors you talk more than you listen. So why don't you pay attention while I give you an elementary lesson about what a criminal defense lawyer is. Someday, you or someone very dear to you is going to be charged with breaking some law. And when that day comes, who do you want as their defense attorney? Someone who feels paralyzed at the thought that if he gets them off, they might commit a crime again? Or somebody who feels terribly and totally responsible for the fate of that person who is so dear to you?"

"That's one way of looking at it," Daniel said. "On the other hand, it doesn't increase my good will for you to know that if I'm mugged and murdered when I leave here tonight you'll be standing first in line trying to make sure my murderer gets away with it. I understand, Mr. Goode, why anyone contemplating murder or rape should have kind feelings towards you. But what is it about you exactly that the rest of us—victims and potential victims—are supposed to be enamored of?"

Goode twiddled his fingers, and surveyed Daniel as if he was some large unpleasant insect that persisted in buzzing around. "Do you believe, Rabbi, that every accused criminal is entitled to a defense?"

"A *truthful* defense, yes. But that's not what you offer. In American courts, it's only *the witnesses*—certainly not the defense lawyers—who swear to 'tell the truth, the whole truth, and nothing but the truth.' *The whole truth,*" Daniel repeated, "without impugning Donna's character, and implying she's a tramp, without blaming her for provoking her own murder, *without* excluding a Mona Lance from testifying how Ron Martin had a history of savagely beating the women he dated."

"Your problem, Rabbi, is with the Constitution, not me. It was Judge Feld who ruled that Lance's testimony was remote to the case and prejudicial."

"And we both know that if the jury had heard her testimony they'd have sent Martin away for life."

"Which only proves how prejudicial it was."

"Which only proves how revealing it was about Martin's character. To people like you, the adversary system is a game. The stronger the prosecution's case, the greater lawyer you are for beating them in the courtroom. To religious people, for whom every human being is created in the image of God, murder is the most evil thing a person can do. If, God forbid, Father O'Brien, it was a relative of yours who had been murdered, would you be satisfied with the verdict?"

"If I had seen repentance such as I saw in Ron Martin, most definitely."

"What repentance? You speak as if Martin were killed distributing food at a Salvation Army kitchen. He was going to a party, Father, a party, to celebrate getting off so lightly."

O'Brien's forehead tightened, and his eyes hardened. "Stop slandering this young man's name. It's not worthy of you. Two fine young people are dead, and this name-calling must stop. I know far better than you what agony and shame Ron went through. You're putting cynical interpretations on everything. Ron wasn't celebrating that he had killed Donna. He was happy that he would finally be able to start putting this very sad episode behind him."

"You have a rare capacity for faith in human nature, Father."

"Since you twisted the last biblical verse I cited, I'll offer one now that's too clear to be misinterpreted." Father O'Brien opened a small black Bible and removed his bookmark at a page in Matthew: " 'For if you love those who love you, what reward shall you have? Even the tax collectors do that.' "

"And I believe," Daniel said, "that a man is only as good as what he loves."

"What is that supposed to mean?" Goode rapped out.

"That if you love a Mother Teresa, that tells me something about you. And if you love a Ron Martin that tells me something about you. And if you love them both equally, then you have made the word love meaningless."

"In God's eyes all of us, even a Mother Teresa, are sinners," O'Brien answered.

"Tell me, Father, in God's eyes are all sins equal?"

"The worst sin is to lose faith, to despair of God's love and forgiveness."

"I should think," Daniel said, "that the worst sin is cruelty, to hurt someone. How much more so to murder an innocent person."

"According to your Old Testament God of vengeance," Goode asked, "do you believe that Ron Martin deserved to die?"

"Forget dying," Daniel answered. "You were trying to get him paroled with no jail at all!"

"True, I was. I still think he should have been. And now *you* answer my question. Do you believe that Ron Martin deserved to die?"

Daniel sat forward in his chair, and his fingers tapped the desk in front of him lightly. Three hundred thousand people out there were listening, ready to pounce on any imprecision. The president of his synagogue, Russell Kahn, he could be sure was one of those listeners. "Mr. Inquisitor," Leonard Goode persisted, "the Father and I are entitled to an answer. Do you believe Ron Martin deserved to die?"

Daniel's mouth felt dry, and he waited. He did not want his voice to sound hesitant. "Yes. I would say his

death was more just than three years in prison would
have been."

"*Holy shit,*" he could faintly hear Bartley Turner
shouting just outside the studio. "*What a show!*"

At 9:45, Jerry Braun came into the bedroom. Roberta
was in her nightgown, listening to Daniel's show.

"I'm going—"

"Sh . . ." she said. "I'll speak with you soon, darling. It's only another fifteen minutes."

He came over to her night table and twisted the
volume down to a murmur. "I've been listening to that
crap too. Enough. I'm going to sleep."

"Can't you just wait till the end of the show? Anyway, it's not even ten o'clock."

"I have to be up early." She watched as he picked
up the alarm clock and adjusted it. 6:15.

The radio show was forgotten. "Why are you getting up at six in the morning?"

"Six-fifteen," he corrected. He moved over to his
side of the bed, slipped off his shoes, and started peel-
ing off his socks.

She hugged her chest. "Why? You're not working
tomorrow."

"I have things to do."

"What things?"

"I like to be out early in the morning. It's the only
time it's quiet in the streets. I can go walking without
being honked at."

"You've never gone walking in your life. I want to
know, Jerry, why you're getting up so early?"

"I told you."

"No, you haven't."

He leaned over her and turned the volume up.
Goode was arguing with some caller. But neither Ger-

ald nor Roberta was listening. He lifted his pajamas in one hand, then grabbed the alarm clock in the other. "Enjoy the show," he said in an angry tone. "I'm sleeping downstairs."

Roberta stared after him as his shadow trailed down the dark hallway.

13

Monday
Morning

When Lyn Means was hired by Leonard Goode, the lawyer had given her no illusions about her responsibilities. "You're here," he told the woman, who was plump, forty-five years old, and unmarried, "to do the donkey work. And if sometimes it's interesting, consider that your bonus." Means had accepted the job without hesitation. Donkey work or not, she would be working with Leonard Goode, a definite step up from maintaining files for the Los Angeles office of the Social Security Administration. For over two years now, working long into the evening, Means had meticulously organized all the research on pending cases, filing the separate bits of information into their own folders. Occasionally Goode allowed her to test a client's alibi—"He tells me he made it to his house in under twenty-five minutes," Goode would tell her, "see how long it takes you." And, happily, the bonuses turned out to be not so rare. It was Means who discovered that Ron Martin's old girlfriend, Mona Lance, had been arrested years earlier on a drug charge, information which her boss had used to devastating effect in the courtroom. Of course, Means had also discovered that Lance's accusations about Martin's beatings of her were one hundred percent true, but that only made the discrediting testimony all the more critical. For a crime buff who read three or four true crime books a week, working with Leonard Goode was pure heaven.

"Donkey work" was, in fact, what brought her to the Goode house this morning at a few minutes before eight. She had already assembled more than five hundred notecards on a pending rape and torture case, and with the trial only ten days away, Goode wanted them in order, now. With Philipa off to Ferguson's Health Clinic, Goode insisted they work at his house, away from the telephone and distractions of his office. And, Means suspected—though Goode had not said so, of course—away from Judith Fein and the Tzedek pickets.

Means parked her car and approached the sprawling ranch house, whistling softly. The birds seemed to be calling back to her as they flitted between the great oaks that framed Goode's lush front lawn. She lifted the brass knocker and tapped loudly. No answer. She tried the button, setting off a series of lyrical chimes. Nothing. Finally she rapped her own little tune on the front door, waited, and then rattled the doorknob. The door was unlocked. *Must have left it open for me,* she thought as she stepped inside.

"It's Lyn, boss."

No answer.

"Hello! It's me," she called out, louder now.

She stood on the white marble floor and glanced around her. The foyer was immaculate, and perfectly still. Dominating one side was a huge purple vase filled with blue silk flowers and twigs. The song of the birds filtered faintly through the open door. Frowning slightly, she headed towards the kitchen. *Maybe he's forgotten and gone straight to the office.*

But Leonard Goode had not forgotten.

He was sprawled on the kitchen floor, arms clutched over his chest. His white shirt was more red than white, and blood pooled around him. Without stopping to think about what she was doing, Lyn pulled up his right arm, then gasped in horror as it fell limply to his side.

"Mrs. Braun?"

"Yes?"

"Lieutenant Cerezzi of—"

"You don't have to identify yourself, Lieutenant. We've spoken often enough."

"Yes. Thank you, Mrs. Braun. Could I have a word with your husband, please?"

"Oh, Jerry's not in."

"I have his work number at the hospital. Would I find him there?"

"Oh, no. Jerry hasn't been at work since the trial began. He's on an extended leave."

"Of course. I think I knew that. When do you expect him home?"

"I'm really not sure. Should I have him—"

"Perhaps you could tell me what time he left the house this morning, Mrs. Braun?"

She paused. "Quite early."

"Could you be a bit more specific?"

"I'd feel more comfortable, Lieutenant, if you told me the reason for your questions."

"Well, for one thing, Dr. Braun is required to check in with his probation officer—"

"Of course."

"—and he was supposed to do so today by ten a.m. Officer Mejia just informed me that he has not seen or heard from him."

"I'm very sorry to hear that, but I'm sure there's a reason. It's not like Jerry. I'm sure he'll be there soon. It is only ten forty-five."

"I know. But your husband is out on a homicide charge, Mrs. Braun. Do you have any idea where he is?"

"I know he got up very early, Lieutenant."

"What time?"

"I can't be sure, because I was still sleeping. But he set the alarm last night for six-fifteen."

"Is that unusual for him?"

"I really don't know anymore what's unusual or not. You know how depressed Jerry's been. He told me he wanted to go out walking early."

"Has he been doing that often recently?"

"Not really."

"And you got up when?"

"About seven."

"Was he still home?"

"He was gone."

"So it would seem he left the house before seven, perhaps considerably before, and you haven't seen or heard from him since?"

"You make it sound very ominous, Lieutenant.

Should I have him call you or Officer Mejia as soon as I hear from him?''

"It's *urgent* that he do so.''

"Lieutenant?''

"Yes?''

"You said 'for one thing' before?''

"What?''

"When I asked the reason for your questions, you said 'for one thing.' ''

"Yes, I did.''

"Well, is there another reason for your questions?''

"I'm afraid there is.''

"What is it?''

"Mrs. Braun, at sometime between six-thirty and seven-thirty this morning, Leonard Goode was murdered.''

Max was poised over a yellow legal-size pad, pen in hand, when he heard the click catching in the door. Only one other person had that key, he knew, and she was too far away to be making surprise visits. He reached for the pistol in the top drawer of his desk.

The woman in the doorway stared at the outstretched gun in mute horror.

"Philipa! What the hell are you doing here?''

She stayed by the door. *"What have you done?"*

Carefully, he rested the gun on his desk. Her eyes flicked over it, and she shivered.

"You maniac,'' she spat out furiously. "I thought Leonard had a heart of stone but—''

"You want to tell me what you're talking about?''

"Don't give me that crap, Max! I never wanted this.''

"What?''

"I'm sick to my stomach.'' Her petite body sagged.

Curls fell over her pallid face. She would not look at him.

He held up his hand. "Philipa," he said, "something very strange is going on here. I haven't the faintest idea what you're talking about. Please close the door and come inside." She did not move. "Let me tell you what I do know," he continued. "My name is Max Reiss, I write murder mysteries, and I love you very much. But that's it. I have no idea why you're here. The last I knew, you were fifty miles away, at some health farm. And unless it's the food they've been serving you there, I certainly don't know why you are sick to your stomach."

"Leonard's dead, Max!"

Max's eyebrows came together and his forehead tensed and wrinkled. "Are you serious?"

The Stabbing, you bastard," she screamed. She rushed towards his desk and violently swept the pages of his manuscript off it. As the papers flew in the air and then scattered on the floor, Max watched without moving.

"What happened?" he asked.

"*Stop it! Just stop it!* Is it your normal habit to greet visitors with a gun?"

"How did Leonard die?" he demanded.

"Check your lousy pages of *Goode Mourning.* Maybe it's in there."

"That was a joke, Philipa."

"Was *The Stabbing* also a joke?"

"No, of course not."

"Well, Leonard was knifed. Does that surprise you, Max?"

Max was silent. He stared at the pages strewn on the floor.

"Say something." But Max sat motionless. She

started kicking wildly at the pages on the floor. "Say something, damn you!"

"When was he killed, Philipa?"

"As if you didn't know."

"When was he killed?"

"Early this morning."

"I didn't get up till almost eleven. I worked last night till after three."

She glared at him.

Finally he raised his hawklike eyes and watched her inscrutably for several minutes. He lifted a pen from his desk and began chewing on its tip. "You're the only one I told about *The Stabbing.*"

The crimson lipstick Philipa wore was smudged on one cheek, like blood. She stared at him in mute horror.

" 'Methinks,' " Max murmured softly, " 'the lady doth protest too much.' " He shook his head. "I don't buy any of this, Philipa. You say Leonard was murdered early this morning. Maybe you left your fat farm during the night. Would anyone have noticed?" He tapped the pen on his desk pensively. "And now you're getting ready to appoint me as your fall guy. What for? To save your pretty little ass if the police can't pin the murder on that poor doctor?" He stood up.

"Don't come near me."

But he came closer. Philipa watched him, stiff with rage, but she did not move. He stopped and threw his hands up in the air. "My God, let's take a breath for a minute and try and calm ourselves. Are we two sorts of nuts? Of course, you didn't do it, and of course I didn't either. It's terrible what happened, and we're both just very shaken." He fingered one of her blond curls, then pulled her roughly forward and covered her whimpers with his mouth.

14

Monday
Afternoon

The blue Mercedes was just passing Leucadia, south on Freeway 5, when the flashing lights of the CHP patrol car signaled it to the right. A balding officer with a pronounced potbelly came forward to the passenger side, while his petite partner hung back, hand resting on her gun.

"Your registration, sir?" the cop said impassively, as the window rolled down.

"This is ridiculous," the driver protested. "I've been on cruise control the whole time. I haven't gone an inch over fifty-five."

"Registration, please," the officer repeated dully.

With a muttered curse, the man flicked open his glove compartment and drew out the papers. "With all the crime out there," he grumbled as he handed them over, "you people beat your brains out deciding whether somebody was going fifty-five or fifty-six."

"Gerald Braun," the officer read aloud.

"Yes. Now please tell—"

The cop signaled his partner to come over, and he passed her the registration. "Call it in," he said in a low voice. "I think he's our boy."

The woman walked swiftly back to the patrol car, and the big cop's hand shifted almost imperceptibly to his gun.

"What is—" Braun began.

"Where are you heading, Mr. Braun?"

"*Dr.* Braun."

"Dr. Braun."

"To San Diego."

The policewoman returned from the patrol car, signaling a thumbs-up.

"Keep your hands at all times where we can see them," the big cop said. Braun's eyes moved from one to the other.

"I realize I forgot to be in touch with Mejia," he said, his tone slightly more civil.

"Mejia?"

"Officer Mejia."

The officer shook his head. "Don't know him."

"Then what is—"

"The Los Angeles Police Department has requested, Dr. Braun, that you be brought in."

"*For not being in touch with Mejia?*"

"They want to speak with you right away."

"So I'll go to LA, okay?" Braun was resigned now. "You can go now. Don't worry. I'll head right back."

"We're taking you to our local airstrip," the cop

said, as his partner moved to the other side of Braun's car. "They're sending out a helicopter."

"That's ridiculous! What about my car?"

The officer had one hand on the door. "Officer Keaton and I will arrange to have it towed to a garage here in Leucadia. They'll be in touch with you about picking it up."

Gerald Braun remained in his seat. A variety of emotions played on his face. "Let me tell you something, Officer. My life has been ruined by you people. Not one of you is interested in justice. It's all a sham. You're a bunch of clowns. People out there are being murdered and mugged, and the best you can manage is to pull in a few drivers off the highway for moving violations. I'm sick to death of your hollow laws. This country has no law. It has no order."

"I'd prefer, Doctor," the big cop said, "that you come with us peacefully. But peacefully or not, you're coming with us."

Braun accepted their offer of a ride to the airport. Peacefully.

JETSET TOURS OF ENCINO—WE MAKE LIFE FUN, the sign read, and if the color photos in the window were anything to go by, Jetset kept its word. Whether they were water-skiing in Waikiki, careening down steep hills in Vale, or mountain-climbing in the Alps, the vacationers all had perfect bodies, perfect teeth, and blissful smiles. Somehow, the compulsive nail-biting of the harried blonde now coming through Jetset's entrance served almost as a rebuke to the happy faces in the window.

The woman walked swiftly over to the one available agent, her red stiletto heels clicking. The panel on the desk read Simon Hutch.

"I want to go to Alexandria," the woman said.

Simon Hutch had worked for Jetset for nearly ten years. His smile was as glorious as those in the pictures. "Planning on going down to the pyramids?"

The blonde looked at him blankly.

"Alexandria, Egypt, Miss?"

"No, no," the woman said. "Alex—"

"I'm sorry," he interrupted, graciously motioning her to the plaid armchair by his desk. "Why don't you have a seat first?"

The blonde's very short skirt rose even higher as she sat down, revealing legs more than worthy of Jetset's window. Hutch nodded approvingly. "I just finished scheduling a whole itinerary for a college group traveling to the Middle East," he explained. He picked up the domestic airline guide. "Alexandria, Virginia, right?"

"Louisiana," the blonde corrected. "Alexandria, Louisiana. And I want the next flight."

Hutch flipped through the guide quickly. "Let's see what we have. Mmm." He flashed her another smile. "Nothing direct, ma'am."

"I know that," the woman said impatiently.

"You have to go through Dallas or Houston."

"What's the next flight?"

"Continental 894 to Houston." Hutch glanced at the clock which was mounted over a large poster of a couple tanning on a Tahiti beach. "Leaves in just over an hour. At two-forty."

"Book it," the woman commanded.

"Round-trip?"

The blonde nibbled at her lip. "One way," she finally said.

Hutch keyed up the flight information on his computer. "No problem. Still plenty of room. Economy or—"

The woman was already inspecting the interior of her red purse. "First class."

"Name?"

"Vard—" The woman's eyes narrowed. "None of your business."

"It's not personal, Miss. I need your name for the ticket."

"Oh, of course. Lisa Lemon," she finally said.

"Thank you, Miss Lemon." He punched it into the computer. "That will be $657, including tax. Will you be paying with check or credit card?"

The woman withdrew seven one-hundred-dollar bills.

"Now don't take any chances," Hutch called out cheerfully as he handed her the ticket. "You'd better—"

Her shoulders stiffened. "What d'ya mean by that?"

"By what?"

"About taking chances."

"You have only a little over an hour till the flight, Miss Lemon. Don't take any chances. You're cutting it awfully close. You better start out for the airport right away."

The chic blonde wheeled around, stepped out onto Ventura Boulevard, and turned right. A woman with two children stopped her to ask directions, but she pushed them aside and raced on. She was practically running by the time she reached her cream-colored Seville.

After hanging up with Cerezzi, Roberta Braun had quickly disconnected her listed phone, before the reporters and other busybodies started calling. The last year of tragedy had cruelly taught her how little respect for privacy the media had when they scented a story. Every few minutes, though, she found herself compulsively checking their private line. Just to make sure the dial tone was working. She'd hang up, then immediately worry that Jerry had tried to call during the five seconds the receiver had been lifted. When she wasn't checking the phone, she paced up and down the kitchen, smoking, unable to concentrate, her ear cocked to KNOX, Los Angeles's all-news station. A little before noon, she jumped when she heard a ring. But even as she scooped up the receiver, she realized with a sinking heart that it was the doorbell. Six of LA's finest trooped into the house. Sergeant Robert Mitchell was leading the delegation, and he showed her a search warrant. Speechless with terror, she again retreated to the kitchen. Officer Janet Bow followed.

"Where is my husband?" Roberta managed to gasp.

"I don't know," Bow said kindly. "That's what we all want to know."

The news summary was coming on, and the slaying was now the lead-off item: "Los Angeles's own real-life Perry Mason, Leonard Goode, was found stabbed to death this morning at his Beverly Hills mansion. While no further information is available at this time, you will recall that just three days ago, fearing for his own safety, Goode appealed to Judge Nicholas White not to release Ron Martin's revenge-killer Dr. Gerald Braun on bail. Judge White rejected Goode's arguments, listening to the pleas, rather, of Braun's character witness, Rabbi Daniel Winter, spiritual leader of Congregation B'nai Zion. A source has informed KNOX that Gerald Braun's whereabouts are currently unknown, and that the LAPD has issued an all-points bulletin for Dr. Braun, who made headlines when he murdered the man convicted of his daughter's death.''

"What do you think you're going to find here?" Roberta Braun asked the policewoman as the broadcaster moved on to the next item. She stood by the wall, her back flattened against it.

"I think, ma'am, you really should speak to Sergeant Mitchell.''

Roberta Braun felt as if her home was being stampeded. These men were trudging over her carpets, moving furniture, stripping down her wall hangings, and all she could do was stand there. In a helpless tone, she answered her appointed guard, "I will. I will speak to him.''

But she didn't. She stayed in the kitchen, pressing her fingers against the wall, her back to Officer Bow. Over an hour had passed before Sergeant Mitchell came in. "Sorry for the inconvenience," was all he said, and they all left. Roberta sat alone in her ransacked house like a wounded soldier looking at a deserted battlefield. Suddenly, a few minutes after three, the jangling ring hit her like lightning.

"Barney Simon, Roberta.''

"My God! Barney, are you with Jerry?''

"Yes, I am, but you cannot speak to him right now." The lawyer's voice was hesitant. "I can only stay on a minute. We're at homicide headquarters.''

"Is Jerry all right?''

"Not really, Roberta.''

"What's the matter with him?'' she cried. But she knew the answer.

"It's nothing physical, if that's what you mean. But we've got ourselves a problem, a big problem. We must find Jerry a criminal lawyer quick.''

"You're our lawyer, Barney. I don't know these

things. Just call up whoever you think is best.'' She hung up abruptly. She didn't have the strength to continue.

Barney Simon sat staring at the receiver in his hand. ''Too bad,'' he said to no one in particular, ''the guy who's best is no longer available.''

In his thirty-eight years, Daniel Winter had questioned many things about himself. In his adolescence, he wondered if he would ever be attractive to girls. In his yeshiva days, particularly during the hours spent studying *musar*—ethical texts—he wondered if he was generous enough, unselfish enough, idealistic enough, to be a religious leader. The one thing he had never questioned, however, his intelligence, was exactly what he was questioning now.

Was Brenda right all along? he wondered. *Am I suddenly such a fool?* He was wandering around what was charitably known as the Venice Boardwalk, a stretch of asphalt with benches overlooking the ocean, and a motley collection of restaurants, and stores selling novelty items. The chilly ocean air sliced through his shirt, but Daniel was oblivious to the cold. He bought a bag of potato chips at a corner market, and munched on them while watching a streetfront missionary haranguing a mixed bag of afternoon strollers and drunks. Then he kicked off his cordovan loafers, pulled off his socks, and wandered out onto the soft sand. About twenty feet from the ocean, he sat down on a large mound of sand and stared out at the frothy waves, hypnotized by their power and unending force. Now and then he watched a white sail bobbing in the distance. He was overcome with a longing to remain there, to lean back on a beach chair, and just watch.

Brenda's call to him had been a terse, staccato recitation of facts. Goode was dead, Braun had been picked up a hundred miles away, and police had found blood in Braun's car, which was being rushed from a garage in Leucadia to the forensic lab in LA. She had said little more. Certainly no "I told you so." But he knew exactly what she was thinking, because he was thinking exactly the same. *Did I cause Goode's death—no, don't sanitize it—Goode's murder?* He had despised the man. Goode's ethics were the mirror-opposite of almost every value he held dear. But the sanctity of life was one of Daniel's highest values. And Goode was dead now, apparently at the hands of a man Daniel had helped release. After he hung up with Brenda, he slipped out the back door of his office—without even telling Pat he was leaving—and headed, as if impelled by a power greater than himself, straight for the ocean.

The rolling waters pacified him, but they were a brief distraction from his thoughts. When the guilt got overwhelming, he'd recall what he knew of Goode's life—his defense of the Nazis, his refusal to grant Sara the *get*, his cynical hatchet job on Donna's reputation, his celebration in the courtroom—and for a minute the guilt would ease. But only for a minute. Goode, after all, was no Ron Martin. He had never ruthlessly laced his fingers around a young woman's throat and squeezed until she choked to death. And even if the world was a less evil place without him, it was certainly worse because of the evil Gerald Braun had now done. *Pseek raisha ve-lo yamut,* the Talmud said. You can't cut off the head of a chicken and then say you're not responsible for its death. He had helped Braun gain his freedom. Now he couldn't disavow responsibility for what Braun had done with it.

The waves lolled him, but the miserable thoughts kept gnawing. He kept remembering Brenda's words in front of the courthouse. *Killing is murder. It's barbaric. Worse, where will it lead?*

"Four o'clock," he heard the missionary's voice bellowing from the boardwalk, "and which of you are one hour closer to damnation?"

Damnation? He was overcome with fatigue. He thought of the words of Rabbi Eleazar in the Talmud. Suddenly thrust into awesome responsibilities at the age of eighteen, Rabbi Eleazar complained to his colleagues, "I am now like a man of seventy." Daniel felt very weary.

As the day slipped by, the waves grew more and more turbulent. He thought of Pat at the office. He knew he should hurry back, but he could not stir from his spot. A bedraggled young man, unshaven, with a guitar strapped to his chest like a wandering minstrel, walked barefoot over the sand, singing a familiar folk tune, *In the Early Morn'n Rain.*

The young man sat down a few feet away and, gazing into Daniel's face, serenaded him. There was an eerie kindness in the washed-out face. The man's bloodshot eyes were defeated, Daniel thought, but they were not bitter. He found himself wondering what dark stroke of fate had broken this lost soul's spirit. He shivered. It was getting dark, and the cold air was creeping into his bones. Yet he remained motionless. Only when the singer had wandered off, did Daniel come to himself.

My God, it's past five. He rushed back onto the asphalt and pushed a quarter in the phone.

"Where have you been, Daniel?" Pat cried out. "Do you know—"

"I'm okay. Don't worry."

"Don't worry? I've been going insane here! Russell Kahn called up with the news, and when I buzz your

office, you've vanished into thin air. I've been checking everywhere. I wasn't going to leave till I heard from you."

"I'm sorry, Pat. You're an angel. I was just in shock. I had to get away."

"I needed to find you, Daniel. It's important."

This is the only thing I'm missing, he thought. *An important message.*

"Lieutenant Cerezzi called," Pat said. "You have to get over to his office immediately. They're holding Gerald Braun there, and he insists he's innocent. But he won't say anything more. He told Cerezzi he's a lost soul without you. He will not say a word unless his rabbi is with him."

Now Gerald Braun was lost, he thought. He was torn between fury at the man and understanding for his anguish. He shook the sand from his hands and feet. "Tell Cerezzi I'm coming."

"When?"

He thought back to another lyric of his wandering minstrel and said, "I'll be on my way."

Evan Singer came into Sara Levin's house, both arms upraised, singing an off-tune version of Handel's *Messiah.* "Hallelujah, Hallelujah, Hallelujah." He stopped, grabbed her to him, and swung her around. "We're free. Sara, we're going out to celebrate."

"Evan! We can't do that. I don't think it's right. Stay here, I'll make something for you."

"No way. Not tonight, Sara. Tonight I want to dance in the streets." He climbed up on the coffee table and started stamping his feet, like a flamenco dancer. "Aaai, aaai, aaai." He snapped his fingers over his head. His dark face, set off by a new short haircut, was exuberant. Sara stared.

"C'mon, baby," he said, jumping down off the table. "You're sitting there looking like death warmed over. I want to go, go, go. I don't think you fully realize what all this means."

Her face revealed a mixture of worry, fatigue, and amusement. "I think I do, Evan."

"So?"

She turned away. "I keep thinking of Debby. It's a nightmare for her. Remember, Leonard was her daddy."

"Wait till she finds out what a lousy bastard her father was! The only good thing is that now he's a dead bastard."

"I know what Leonard was, Evan. I'm not being suddenly sentimental. But we can't dance around and throw parties in front of Debby. She's twelve years old. At that age little girls love their fathers, no matter who they are."

"Did you call her?" Debby had been visiting with Sara's parents in Chicago for the past week.

"We spoke for over an hour. It was very painful. Philipa also called her, which I think was very sweet. Thank God, Debby was told before it hit the news. She's coming back tonight. I have to be quiet for a while and get ready for her. Her flight's due in at ten-ten."

"So we'll start acting sad at ten-oh-nine. But not one minute sooner. This time is for us. I haven't felt like this, Sara, since my first night out of prison. No bars and locked doors. No one stopping me from doing what I want when I want. Don't you feel totally relieved?"

She walked over to Evan and drew his head to her chest. Stroking his short dark hair, she murmured, "Of course I'm relieved. But the way it happened, the violence," she shuddered, "I hate that."

He pulled away from her abruptly. "Goddamnit, Sara, don't look a gift horse in the mouth. Would it have been better if he had been run over by a car?"

"It would have been better if he had given me the *get*."

"And he never would have. Do you doubt that?"

Her delicate features tightened. "No, I know that very well."

"Good." He grabbed Sara's coat and held it open like a bullfighter teasing a bull. "Then get your coat on, sweetheart. C'mon. We've got our whole lives ahead. Let's not waste a minute."

"Thank you for coming, Rabbi."

Braun's voice was brittle with relief. The doctor moved towards the door, but Daniel gently backed off to the side. He extended a hand, and reluctantly Daniel accepted it.

Standing behind Braun, a glum Barney Simon pulled his client back to his chair.

"Okay, Dr. Braun," Cerezzi broke in, his fingers tapping the only bare spot on his cluttered desk. "We've met your—"

"I know, Lieutenant," Braun said. "I'll talk now."

"Good." Cerezzi pressed a buzzer. "Send Marty in," he barked. A moment later a lanky man with thinning gray hair walked in. There was a small video camera poised on his shoulder. He pointed it at the lieutenant's burly figure.

"You're ready?" Cerezzi asked the technician.

"Take it away, Lou."

"This is Lieutenant Joseph Cerezzi," he began, clearing a space on his desk. "It is Monday, March 27, six-oh-five p.m., and I am speaking to Dr. Gerald Braun, pursuant to the LAPD investigation into the homicide this morning of Leonard Goode. Present with me are Dr. Braun's attorney, Mr. Barney Simon"—and the camera panned to the silver-haired attorney—"and Rabbi Daniel Winter." Cerezzi looked across at Braun. "Why don't you identify yourself, Doctor, and we'll begin?"

"I didn't do it," Braun said.

"Could you please identify yourself first, Doctor?"

Braun did so.

"Now," Cerezzi resumed. "The first thing I want to do is get some answers to the questions I posed to you earlier this afternoon."

"Lieutenant," Barney Simon said, "I want to reserve my client's right to refuse—"

Braun waved his hands angrily. "Barney, stop! If you go on like this, I'll fire you."

Simon slumped back in his chair. "I wish you would, Jerry."

"Look, Barney, I appreciate everything you've done. But I explained to you before. I don't need any legal advice now." He undid the collar buttons on his shirt, as if he found the room confining. "I've got nothing to hide. Ask anything you want, Lieutenant."

"Good. Let's start from the beginning, Doctor. At what time did you get up this morning?"

"Six-fifteen. That is, I set my alarm for then. But the truth is, I was up even earlier, from about five."

"Are you usually such an early riser?"

"Not since I've stopped working. But I had something to do."

Cerezzi waited, but Braun didn't continue.

"And what was that, Doctor?" the lieutenant prompted.

Braun looked at him defiantly. "To see Goode."

"You had made an appointment with Leonard Goode?"

"No."

"So you were planning a surprise visit to his house?"

"I needed to speak to him."

"Why?"

The dark eyes that looked at Cerezzi were reproachful. "My name is mud in this town, Lieutenant, in case you hadn't noticed. And then"—his thumb indicated Daniel—"on the rabbi's radio show last night I heard Goode saying again how I've been threatening him. I had to speak with him . . . I wasn't going to tell him any lies, sweet-talk him, I didn't care if he knew how much I despised him. But I just needed to tell him I wasn't going to do anything to him and to ask him to stop telling people I was. The press can do what they want with me. But this publicity, these accusations are destroying my wife."

"That was the message," Cerezzi said somberly, "you intended to convey to Mr. Goode."

"Yes."

"If you wanted to reassure him of your peaceful intentions, wouldn't it have made a little more sense to go to his office?"

"I knew if he didn't have to see me, he'd shun me. I'd end up sitting out there the whole day with his secretary, while he'd slip out through some side door."

"And you thought he'd let you into his *house*?"

Barney Simon, who had been shifting uncomfortably in his chair, sprang up. "Lieutenant, I insist this must stop. I must meet with my client alone."

Cerezzi's eyes moved impassively from Simon to Braun. "Is that what you want, Dr. Braun?"

"No. Barney, please, I told you. I'm no longer your client. Keep out of this."

When Braun resumed, his words were spoken with enormous effort. "I got to Goode's house early, even before seven, and just stood in front there, figuring I'd wait until he came out. You see, I had it all planned, Lieutenant. I'd keep both my hands up in the air, like in those Westerns, assuring him there was no danger. And I was just going to give him my message and leave."

"And what happened?"

"I stood in front, waiting. Then I went back to my car for a while—I didn't want any of the neighbors noticing and calling the cops. And you know what it's like after you wait for a while. I started looking into his yard, and I saw the front door was almost wide open. So I walked up to it, rang the bell, called out his name. And then I stuck my head in. You know it didn't seem right, the house being open, so I walked in. There was a smell of coffee or something. I walked through the front hall into the kitchen, where the light was on. And he was lying there." Braun raised one arm to the side, the other towards his chest, mimicking Goode's body. "I'm a doctor, I didn't even think for a moment who he was, I just bent down. I could see right away he was dead."

"Really, so that's how it happened?" Cerezzi picked up a tab from a long-discarded can of soda and rolled it between his thumb and forefinger. "And what did you do then?"

"Lieutenant, I panicked. I didn't know what to do. Of course, I should have called nine-one-one. But I knew he was dead. I knew what they would think, me sitting there with the body of the man I hated most in the world. Who would believe me? So I ran to my car. I just started driving."

"Where?"

"Anywhere. Nowhere."

"You want to be a little more specific?"

"South. Towards San Diego. Mexico. I tell you I wasn't thinking."

"During a police search this afternoon, blood matching that of the decedent was found in your car."

"Barney told me. It makes sense, Lieutenant. There was a lot of blood around the body. You must have seen that. Obviously, inadvertently, I stepped into some."

Cerezzi's face was grave. "You wouldn't be the first murderer, Doctor, trying out an alibi like that."

Gerald Braun turned towards Daniel. His fingers bit into Daniel's wrists. His eyes were colorless in his ruined face. "I swear to you, Rabbi. On my Donna's grave, I swear to you. I did not kill Leonard Goode."

The room was quiet. Cerezzi's hooded eyes went back and forth between Daniel and Braun. Barney Simon fidgeted with his silver tie clip, but he did not look up. Daniel stared at Braun. There was sympathy and doubt on his face.

"Everything you've told us, Jerry, it's all true?" he asked him.

Braun shuddered, but his voice was firm. "Everything, Rabbi."

"The early meeting, the inadvertent stepping in the blood, all of it?"

"You know better than anybody how much Donna meant to me, Rabbi. That child was my life. You know that, Rabbi, don't you?"

"Of course."

"On her grave, Rabbi. I swear it *on her grave*. I killed Martin and, if I have to, I'm willing to pay the price for it. And I hated Goode. But I didn't kill him. I wouldn't bring you down here to make a fool of you."

Daniel's eyes searched Braun's ravaged face. The only sound that could be heard was the clattering of a loud typewriter from an adjoining room. Nobody uttered a word.

15

Monday

Evening

Shang-Chai West, Los Angeles's premier kosher Chinese restaurant, opened for dinner at 6:00 p.m. When Evan Singer and Sara Levin arrived at 6:50, however, it was still quite empty.

He ordered Shang-Chai's specialty, "Peking Duck for Two." To Evan's surprise, Sara ate heartily.

A short Chinese waiter, a yarmulke perched on his head, brought in their fried banana. It erupted in flames, making them both laugh. Evan raised her hand to his mouth, then kissed each fingertip one by one. "You were making me a little nervous before," he said.

"Oh, my darling, it had nothing to do with you. I feel much better now, just sitting here together. I'm just so worried about Debby. Ever since I've heard the news, I've been thinking about something Rabbi Winter taught. When God dried up the Red Sea, the Jews crossed it, then when the Egyptians chased in after them, the water came back and drowned them."

"That's not your great Rabbi Winter who said that. It's in the Torah."

"I know, I know," she hurried on. "Anyway, the rabbi told a *midrash,* that when the angels in heaven saw the Egyptians drowning, they started singing a song to God. And God said, 'My creatures are drowning, and you're celebrating?' That's why when we count off the Ten Plagues during the Passover *seder* we dip a drop of wine with our pinky onto the plate after we say each one. To show a little sorrow."

"A little sorrow?"

She nodded. "Yes. I thought we should show a little sorrow too."

"I can live with that." Evan sighed happily, stretching himself luxuriantly. "A little sorrow and a lot of joy." He lifted his wine glass high in the air. "To us! May the past never haunt us, Sara, and may our future years together be filled with a little sorrow—and a lot of joy."

Sara clinked his glass with hers and watched as he greedily gulped the fizzling red wine.

"Drink," he commanded.

She did. And a little drop of the wine rolled over her finger and dropped onto the colorful oriental plate.

District Attorney Ryan Sanders convened the press conference for 8:30. "At least that'll keep us off the early news," he told his top aide, Rosalyn Kheel, as they sat in his plush office.

"But that's exactly the sort of forum you sparkle

in," the young woman responded, not bothering to hide her irritation. "Excuse me, Chief, but that was a dumb move. Look! A big murder was committed, and the arrest was made inside of a day. We've got just seven months to the election, and you're downplaying, throwing away a golden opportunity."

"You think so, Rosie?"

"No, I don't think so. I'm just saying it because I get a kick out of calling you dumb."

"Well, you're thinking very short-term, lady. You're excited about a little extra TV coverage, and I'm talking damage control. This is one case where no one, and I mean *no one,* comes out smelling like a . . . rosie"—Sanders's craggy face creased into a smile as the woman winced. "What glory's in it for me? A confessed murderer blows away a guy, gets released on bail, and kills another. You think that'll make the public want to run out and push the lever under my name?"

"How the blazes can anyone blame you? Judge White made the bail decision. Our office argued like hell against it."

"And lost. Which is the only thing the public will remember. Nope"—and he shook his gray head emphatically—"it won't end up helping me. The glory and headlines in this one'll come when we try Braun. Until then, our job is to get the public's attention focused elsewhere."

"Like on Judge White?"

Sanders looked at the fair-haired woman's face. Somebody, he thought, should tell Rosie not to wear so much makeup. "I'm going to teach you a valuable lesson, Rosie, and don't ever forget it. It never does one damn bit of good to alienate the judges. If I go out now and denounce Judge White, John Q. Public will get pissed off for as long as it takes some new scandal to drive this crime off the front page. And then he'll forget. He won't remember if the judge's name was White, Black, or Green. But Judge Nicholas White will remember. For as long as he's on the bench. And it'll be hell for our people who have to come up against him."

"So who can you finger?"

Sanders swiveled in his leather armchair, smiling pensively. "My mother didn't raise an idiot. I can think of a couple of nosybodies who can take a few lumps on this case without doing us much harm in return." He eyed the little gold clock on his desk. "Come along, Rosie. I think you'll enjoy this."

The local stations and papers were all there. So were the *New York Times*, *Newsweek*, and *Time* reporters too. Even stringers from a few European and Japanese papers were clustered in the crowded room. Sanders waited graciously as the technicians adjusted the lights and checked out their mikes. At 8:35, he opened the press conference with a statement announcing Gerald Braun's arrest, and elaborated for a few minutes. "While the evidence implicating Dr. Braun is very—"

"Has he confessed?" the *Los Angeles Times* reporter called out.

"No. That is, at least not yet. The state intends, in any case, to have Dr. Braun examined by several psychiatrists. If he is found competent to stand trial, I intend to go into court as soon as possible."

"Goode was murdered in his home," the *Herald-Examiner* newswoman stated. "Right?"

"That is correct."

"Where was his wife?"

"From what I understand, and Lieutenant Cerezzi is, of course, the one handling the investigation, Mrs.

Goode was away on a previously scheduled trip. The deceased was by himself."

"Did he have any children living at home?" KRAR asked.

"No. His daughter lives with her mother, Mr. Goode's first wife."

"What's the girl's name? How old is she?"

Sanders placidly ignored the barrage of questions. "I see no advantage to be gained by exposing a young child to such publicity. She is suffering enough. Any other questions?"

"The knife wound was near Goode's heart, right?"

"Yes. A coroner's report with precise details will be released in the next few days."

"What makes you so sure it wasn't suicide?"

"If you don't find your answer to that question in the report, you'll find it out in court."

Sanders scanned the crammed room back and forth, then his eyes rested on the plump figure of Shirley Anty—universally known as Aunt Shirley—from the *Evening Opinion*.

"Your turn, Shirley."

"What do you think of Judge White's decision to release Dr. Braun on bail just one day after he murdered Ron Martin?"

The question he had been waiting for. The one he knew had to come. Sanders steeled himself. "That's an excellent and important point, Shirley. There is no question that after a day like today it would be easy to point the finger at one judge or another and blame him for the terrible crime that has ensued. But that would be both the easy and the wrong thing to do. The judiciary is not the right place to be assigning our blame. Judges, after all, are only human. And like all of us, their decisions are made on the basis of advice they receive from sources they assume to be reliable." Sanders relished the sensation of hundreds of interested eyes fixed on him. "Yet twice during this past year, men in our communities whose appropriate roles are in churches and synagogues have chosen to intrude themselves into the judicial process. I'm referring, of course, to Father Michael O'Brien's repeated intercessions on behalf of the late Ron Martin, and the recent appearance of Rabbi Daniel Winter at the bail hearing of Gerald Braun. Naturally, I know that both these men had nothing but the best intentions. But rabbis and priests, whose job should be to lead people to heaven, ought to know better than anyone else that the road to hell is paved with good intentions. I would be pleased if the lesson learned from the tragic and senseless slaying of Leonard Goode is that criminal work is best left to the professionals qualified to handle it. Clergymen can play a crucial role in helping to raise a generation of young Americans who never end up in front of a judge. But once a person has already been arrested, and even acknowledged his guilt—as happened in *both* these cases —it is time for some of our activist clergymen to— quite frankly—butt out. If Rabbi Winter had done so in this case, Leonard Goode might still be alive."

Hands started frantically waving. The noise was deafening.

"Does that mean—" the *New York Times* was asking.

"Daniel who?" the *Neue Freie Presse* asked his neighbor.

Ryan Sanders regarded them all with a benevolent smile. "Thank you, ladies and gentlemen, and good night."

While driving over at a very leisurely pace, Daniel forced himself to think of places he'd dislike being at

more than Russell Kahn's fund-raiser. Like the Gulag
Archipelago. Or on a plane hijacked by the PLO. But
the list was very short. The gathering at Kahn's Beverly
Hills mansion had been set up as a coffee and dessert
meeting for the board and a few select contributors.
Daniel had postponed his arrival for as long as he
could, and by the time he got there it was well after
9:30. Brenda spotted him immediately—her eyes had
been on the front door from the moment she had arrived—and came right over, the fixed smile on her face
turning into a real one.

"Am I an idiot for showing up here?" he asked,
greeting her.

"Depends on whether you're in a masochistic
mood or not."

"That bad?"

She nodded glumly.

"I can tell," he said, quickly scanning the room.
The expansive living room was alive with chatter,
glasses clinking, and an occasional burst of laughter.
"When I enter a synagogue meeting, people normally
notice. This time not a soul's come over."

"They've noticed, Daniel, don't worry."

"Has anybody said anything?"

"About you?"

"Uh-huh."

"They've been studiously speaking to me about everything except you. On the other hand, every time I
pass by a group, you and Gerald seem to be the topic of
conversation."

He saw the tall figure of Russell Kahn, with two vice
presidents flanking him, coming over. In the room,
chattering went on, but eyes subtly turned in their direction. "I think I know what Isaac felt when Abraham
started preparing to slaughter him."

"Hello, Rabbi," Kahn said, not smiling.

"Hello, Russell." Daniel turned to the other two men and extended a hand. "Mike, Don."

Their handshakes were perfunctory.

"Did you hear Sanders's press conference?" Kahn asked.

"I did," Daniel said.

"Pretty powerful, wasn't it?"

He chose to treat the question as rhetorical and said nothing.

"You know, Rabbi, I was going to announce a million-dollar contribution tonight."

"I'd heard."

"You think I'd get any splash for my bucks in this environment?" Kahn waited, but Daniel could easily imagine the splash he'd provoke if he said anything. "Donald here tells me that we'd be damn fools trying to raise two cents now. They're starting in with the jokes already." He pointed to a bald man across the room who was laughing raucously at some joke. "That pain-in-the-ass Abe Walker is telling everybody we're going to be building specialty rooms at the new Community Center. A Gerald Braun firing and slashing range. A Leonard Goode meditation room where people can reflect on what happens to them if they get into a fight with a member of our board. And a Daniel Winter common-sense room, where it's forbidden to act logically. I was thinking of telling—"

"This is very unfair, Russell," Brenda interrupted. Her green eyes sparked fire.

Kahn looked down at her from his great height. "I've got no beef with you, Rebbetzin. I told the rabbi, I just wish he acted with your intelligence and caution."

"Daniel has as much intelligence in his pinky as this whole—"

The chattering in the room seemed to have suddenly stopped. Someone's laughter was abruptly stifled.

Daniel's face was stiff. "Please—"

"You know what I think your problem is, Rabbi?" Don Sohn broke in. "You're a very bright guy, and right, ninety percent of the time. But you think you're right a hundred percent of the time. And the ten percent of the time you're wrong, Rabbi, you're a hundred percent wrong."

Kahn shifted his feet. The veins pulsed visibly on his neck. "Do you know what—excuse my French, Rebbetzin—*crap* we're going to be taking on this, Rabbi?"

Necks started craning in their direction.

"I think," Daniel said softly, "that Gerald Braun is innocent."

"And I think," Kahn answered savagely, "that the cow jumped over the moon in 1492."

Mike Bernstein, second vice president of the board, had remained silent. Now he stroked his thin goatee, a pale spark of interest in his eyes. "Why do you think Jerry's innocent?"

Kahn's fist crashed into his palm. "This is an absurd discussion!"

"I want to hear," Bernstein said calmly, "what the rabbi has to say."

"A few reasons," Daniel answered. "First of all, he denies it."

"Oh, come off it," Sohn said, rolling his eyes.

"Think about it," Daniel answered. "When Jerry killed Martin he didn't deny it. Why deny it this time?"

"Because," answered Kahn, "he figured he could

get away with Martin's killing. Everybody would be sympathetic."

"Second, Goode was murdered with a knife from the kitchen rack in his house."

"So?"

"It means that in all likelihood the murder was unplanned. Somebody came to Goode's house and picked up a weapon there. But if your theory's correct, that Jerry went there intending to murder Goode, he would have brought a weapon with him, right?"

"Maybe he did," Sohn said. "Then when he saw the knife there, he just figured that would be more convenient to use, you know, less suspicious."

"Maybe," Daniel answered. "Though everything about Goode's murder suggests that it was spontaneous, unplanned. And then there's one more thing, as far as I'm concerned probably the most important . . ." He stopped, and his blue eyes focused on Kahn. "Jerry swore to me on Donna's grave that he didn't do it." He felt Brenda's grip on his arm.

"Really," Kahn said, his voice ominously mild. "And that's why you take him seriously." The red flush on his neck was turning purple. "Well, I'll swear to you, Rabbi, on your contract's grave, that if your meddling screws up our fund-raising and our synagogue's name, I will personally run you out of here. And if you believe Jerry Braun's oath, Rabbi, you'd better believe mine."

Daniel looked up at the president. "I'll tell you what I believe, Russell. You've gotten so caught up with your big edifice complex that you've lost sight of the purpose of what we're doing here. The only justification for raising money and putting up buildings is because we're doing God's work. Creating a place where people are influenced to be better, where we can fight against the injustices that everybody else takes for granted. And, most important, a place where we help those who are hurt, not turn our backs on them. A synagogue's not meant to be a place where people pray on Saturday and then prey on each other the rest of the week. And that's exactly what I'm afraid you're going to turn our synagogue into. A place that turns its back on someone, because helping him might cost us a few big contributions. If that's what we're becoming, Russell, you don't have to tear up my contract. I'll do it myself. Gladly.'' He turned to Brenda. ''I think it's time we went home.''

"And I think it's time you stayed there,'' Kahn shouted at his departing back. ''At least that's one place I can be sure you'll stay out of trouble!''

16

Tuesday

Morning

"Good morning, Lieutenant." A short, dark man, the top of his head a barren desert down the middle, with growths of black hair on both sides, extended a card. JASON D. PERKINS—PRIVATE INVESTIGATOR, Cerezzi read, and under that: *The "D" stands for discretion.*

"I'm particularly busy this morning," Cerezzi said, handing back the card. He looked pointedly at his watch. "And I don't like it when people make big mysteries of why they want to see me. You've got precisely ninety seconds to convince me this isn't a waste of time, Mr. Perkins."

Jason D. Perkins was unfazed. He plunked his thick body onto the chair. "I have not the slightest doubt,

Lieutenant, I will be staying here much longer. And at your request.''

"Shoot."

"You saw the D on my card?"

Cerezzi's fingers were restlessly tapping his desk. "I'm not illiterate."

"To me, Lieutenant, discretion is a sacred word. I always tell my clients that my obligation is to learn as much as possible while disclosing as little as possible."

"An ability," Cerezzi responded, "which you seem to possess to an extraordinary degree. You're down now to one minute."

"Sometimes, though, it is wrong to be discreet. In this instance, for example. If you continue pushing your case against Gerald Braun, you might—I stress *might*—be making a catastrophic error. Five weeks ago I was hired by Leonard Goode to check on his wife Philipa's movements. He wanted to know if she had a lover." Perkins looked down at his digital watch and sighed. "How unfortunate, Lieutenant. My ninety seconds are almost up."

Cerezzi half-grinned. "Wasn't really checking my watch. I just wanted you to get to the point. Go on."

Perkins lowered his bald head and crossed his legs. "Normally, of course, I would never violate a client's confidence. Particularly one with whom I have had such a long-standing relationship. You see, I have done investigative work for Mr. Goode, on and off, for seven years. But now, with Mr. Goode's demise, he is no longer my—"

"The point, Mr. Perkins!"

The detective pulled out a breast-pocket memo book and consulted it. "On February 15, I met with Leonard . . . ah, Mr. Goode at his office. He was highly agitated. He told me that he had inadvertently caught his wife, Philipa, in a series of small lies. She told him she'd be lunching at a certain restaurant at a certain time, and when he needed to reach her, she wasn't there. That night he asked her casually about the lunch, and she pretended she had been there. A few days later, she told him she was rushing out to Hammacher Schlemmer, and when he said he wanted to accompany her, she insisted she had to go alone, because she wished to surprise him with a gift.'' Perkins paused dramatically. "Mr. Goode then went to the store himself. Philipa wasn't there, and hadn't been there."

"I get the picture."

"Are you familiar, Lieutenant, with the pre-nuptial agreement Philipa Goode signed prior to the marriage?"

"Don't know a thing about it." Cerezzi's phone buzzed. He picked it up and listened for a moment. "I know about that appointment," he said. "Call and say I'll be late." He paused. "And hold all calls." Out of the corner of his eye he caught Perkins's satisfied smile. "Go on."

"If Mrs. Goode either sued for divorce or committed adultery, she'd end up with almost nothing."

"And in the event of Goode's death?"

"Mr. Goode disclosed nothing to me about a will."

Goode's will, Cerezzi scrawled on his pad. "Okay. Now what did you discover about the lady?"

"As I always tell my clients, there is seldom smoke without fire. Philipa Goode was indeed, shall we say . . . *involved.*"

"And you reported this to Goode?"

"That was my job."

Cerezzi felt like he was pulling teeth. "How did Goode react? Did he intend to divorce her?"

"My clients pay me to provide them with information. They seldom tell me what they're going to do with it. But based on his tremendous agitation and persistent questions, I would say that he was deeply in love with her."

Cerezzi's fingers tapped on the desk again. It was over a year since he had given up smoking, but sometimes his fingers still ached for a cigarette. "So that even after learning of his wife's affair, your impression is that Goode intended to stay married to her?"

"I believe so. He told me once that it was just a spite affair."

"A spite affair?"

"When I brought him my findings, he was real upset. He was probably embarrassed that I knew his wife was having an affair, and he wanted me to know that he was still a vital man. That's not unusual, Lieutenant. A lot of my clients act like that."

"You're losing me, Perkins."

"Excuse me, I've been running ahead of myself. Goode told me that Philipa had found out about an affair he was having."

"With whom?"

Perkins shook his head. His plump jowls quivered. "That, Lieutenant, he did not confide."

"So for all you know, it could have been a story Goode made up to you to save his pride."

"Perhaps. I have no way of knowing."

"Let's move on then to what you do know, Mr. Perkins. What exactly did you find out about Philipa Goode?"

Perkins flipped the pages of his memo book. "Three or four times a week, and almost always during the afternoon, she would go to 320 North Horn. It's a two-story rental building, with garden apartments."

"Horn. That's West Hollywood, right?"

"Yes. She would go to the apartment of a Mr. Max Reiss, number 427, and remain there between one and three hours."

"And what did you find out about Reiss?"

Perkins flipped to the back of his memo book and read, "Thirty-four years old. Native Angelino. Never married, though he has an illegitimate nine-year-old daughter from a woman he lived with. Taught English at Los Angeles Community College for seven years. Left three years ago, and now writes murder mysteries." Perkins's right hand rose to pat a tuft of unruly hair over his ear. "Lieutenant, if I were to acknowledge to you a minor infraction of the law that might have been committed during the investigation, can I rely upon your understanding?"

"How minor?"

"Perhaps entering an apartment without the permission of the resident?"

"Was anything taken?"

Perkins's face was a picture of horror. "What do you take me for, Lieutenant? I was just fulfilling a request of my client."

"To break into Reiss's apartment?"

"Mr. Goode wanted definitive evidence, which was very hard in this case, since Philipa and Reiss never left the apartment, and the window shades were always drawn. Look, they weren't in there playing Scrabble, but I suppose Goode was secretly hoping Reiss might turn out to be a masseur or acupuncturist or something that could give the whole matter an innocent explanation. So I— Wait. Lieutenant, before I continue, am I safe in assuming my license will not be endangered by anything I confide to you?"

"If the story is as you say, it won't be."

"I rely on your word. Three days ago, on March 25, I waited outside Reiss's apartment. He went off in a car at about two-thirty, and I was able to get in."

"How?"

"That, Lieutenant, shall remain a professional secret. The first thing I checked was the clothing closets. I found several female outfits."

"How do you know to whom they belonged?"

"I have no reason, Lieutenant, to believe Reiss is a transvestite."

"But how can you be sure these garments are Mrs. Goode's?"

"I took pictures."

Perkins shook out the contents of a small manila envelope and passed several photos to Cerezzi. One of a sleeveless red gown. A polka-dot bathing suit. A French maid's uniform, the photograph of which was marked on the bottom in pen, "from Frederickson's." And several pairs of jeans. "I also," Perkins said, "made a note of the exact size of all the garments. Either they were hers, Lieutenant, or they belonged to someone with a very similar size and frame."

"You showed these pictures to Goode, I gather?"

"I had no opportunity."

"When did you last see—"

Perkins sat up abruptly. "Just let me finish first. You see, after going through the clothes closets, I took additional pictures. Mr. Goode wanted to have a sense of who his rival was."

Cerezzi broke the seal on a package of Lifesavers and popped a cherry one in his mouth.

"On Reiss's desk," Perkins continued, "I saw a manuscript, and two title pages. I gather it's a book on which he is currently working."

"We're talking homicide here, Perkins, not literary criticism. Just tell me what's relevant."

Perkins handed another photograph to Cerezzi. "Here's the first title page," he said. Cerezzi examined the photo, much of it dominated by the words *The Stabbing*.

The lieutenant let out a low whistle.

"And here's the other title page." He handed over a picture highlighting the words *Goode Mourning*.

"Do you see," Perkins asked, his chubby face eager, "the book lying alongside the manuscript?"

Cerezzi brought it within inches of his face. "Can't make it out."

"Reeson's *Sharp Edges: A History of Knife Murders in America.*"

Cerezzi bit down on the candy. "So Reiss seems to be working on a mystery dealing with a knifing. And another title that implies he was considering the possibility of Mr. Goode's death. You didn't photograph any pages from the manuscript itself, did you?"

"Of course not. I was just there to find out what was relevant, Lieutenant, not, as you say, to do literary criticism. One more thing. Philipa Goode was supposed to be at Ferguson's Health Clinic from Saturday to Tuesday."

"We know all about that."

"Friday morning Mr. Goode told me about the trip and asked that I keep tabs on her. He was afraid Reiss might join her at Ferguson's for a tryst. I couldn't afford to spend three days there on the chance that might happen, but a woman I used to know in Los Angeles, Bonnie Melton, works there, and she agreed to serve as Santa's little helper."

"Did Reiss show?"

"No. At least not at any time Bonnie was there.

Early Monday morning, though, at about four-thirty a.m., Bonnie was working the night shift at the front desk and heard a car pulling out. Since nobody had dropped a key off with her, she was worried a guest might be skipping town without paying the bill. So she rushed outside. Fortunately Philipa drives a red Ferrari sports car, and Bonnie recognized it. So she called me."

"At four-thirty in the morning?"

"Actually closer to five. She was under instructions to call me immediately if she saw anything unusual. I told her to ring Mrs. Goode's room first, you know, make sure the car wasn't stolen. When she got no response, she rushed away from the desk for a few minutes and let herself in the room with a key. Mrs. Goode was gone."

"Was the room cleared out?"

"Not at all. Her clothes and toiletries were all there. When Bonnie called me back, I told her I would take over from my end. I knew it would take Mrs. Goode a good hour to get back into LA, so I caught a little shut-eye, then hurried over to stake out Reiss's house. I stayed there till a little after eight, then left. Mrs. Goode never showed."

"And did you see Reiss?"

"No."

"Do you know if he was home?"

"As I told you, Lieutenant, the window shades were always down."

"What about his car?"

"The apartments there don't have parking spaces. His car could have been anywhere within a few blocks."

"Any lights on?"

"No. Though by six a.m. it was getting light already."

Cerezzi swallowed the remains of the Lifesaver and popped an orange one in his mouth. It didn't stop the nicotine craving, though. "Do you have any idea if Goode ever spoke or met with Reiss?"

Perkins shook his head. "No way of knowing. He did ask me, though, for Reiss's address and phone number."

"Our department," Cerezzi said, "contacted Philipa Goode at Ferguson's at about nine-thirty a.m., the morning of the murder. She acted as if she was awakened from a deep sleep."

"I'm not surprised."

"Does your operative know what time she returned?"

"No. You see, Bonnie—and if you speak to her, just make sure she doesn't catch any hell from the hotel about this—was only there that night because she was covering for a friend whose fiancé's army leave was ending that night. The girl showed up a little after five, and Bonnie went home."

"Didn't she tell the girlfriend to watch out for Philipa?"

"Of course not. This was nobody else's business." Perkins leaned back in his chair and rubbed his eyes. "That's it. I don't have anything more to tell."

Cerezzi pushed back his chair and regarded the bald man cynically. "Something's curious to me," Cerezzi said. "In the thirty years I've been in this office very few p.i.'s have ever come in on their own. We usually have to hunt you guys down, make all sorts of threats. So why you?"

"Leonard Goode always played fair with me. Paid his bills on time and in full, which is no small thing in this business. Usually, once people get the information they're after, they don't want to see or know from you. And Mr. Goode defended me free of charge two times when I got into a little trouble. Saved my license. And like I said before, confidentiality doesn't apply now. With Mr. Goode's demise he is no longer my client, and I hardly expect the widow to pay the bill, particularly when she finds out why her husband hired me. That's it, Lieutenant. No tricks. I'm on your side on this one. I want justice. And now I think I'm entitled to know what you're going to do with all this information."

"Check your story out minute by minute, detail by detail."

"Even though Braun's already been charged?"

"We're not railroading anybody, Perkins. If there's a chance of an error, I want to find it out."

"So where are you going to start?"

"By getting your business card back from you, Mr. Perkins. We will be in touch."

Perkins handed the card over. "You're not exactly generous with information, Lieutenant. This is the third time I'm asking. Then what?"

"Then I'll give you my card." Cerezzi pulled out a small business card from the top drawer of his desk, unscrewed a black felt-tip pen and quickly marked something on the card. He passed it over to Perkins. Between Cerezzi's first and last name, a large D had been inserted.

Cerezzi's lips curved into a small smile. "Do you want to take a guess what the D stands for?" he asked.

"She's *going to what?*" Evan Singer shouted into the phone.

"Evan, please," Sara pleaded. "I'm not happy about it either. But Leonard was her father."

"And who gave you this brilliant ruling?"

"It all came about . . . I called up Rabbi Czernow to thank him—"

"For what?"

"Evan, don't be like that!"

"I'm serious. What good did he do for us?"

"He was so nice to me when I met with him, so warm. And more than that. He's the one who got Judith Fein from Tzedek involved."

"Yeah, yeah. And with all that, the reason we're getting married has nothing to do with your saintly Rabbi Czernow or your Rabbi Winter. You want to thank someone? Call up Gerald Braun. He's the one who put an end to that son-of-a—"

"Evan, I asked you not to talk that way. There's nothing to be angry about anymore. Just think of Debby's feelings."

"Okay, okay. Without the lectures. I'm sorry. End of issue. So what did Rabbi Czernow tell you?"

"That despite all the ugliness between Leonard and me, as far as Debby is concerned, the laws of mourning apply. She has to keep *shiva* all seven days."

"But why in your . . . in what is going to be our house?"

"Where else? That is where she lives."

"No. That is where she lives with you. When she spent time with her father, it was at his house. She should mourn him there."

"Be reasonable. Debby needs me to be with her. I can't leave a young girl alone there. She's not close to Philipa."

"You told me how sweetly Philipa acted towards her."

"That was one phone call. Debby is heartbroken. She loved her father."

"Look, Sara, you've told me that a million times, and I will do my very best to respect that fact. But we all have our limits. I will not—understand me—*will not* allow Debby to sit on a low stool all day long mourning that scumbag Leonard Goode in the house where I will soon be living with the woman I love. If Jewish law says he has to be mourned by his daughter, he has to be mourned. But not in our house."

"Do you realize what a position you're putting me in?"

"You can spend time with Debby at his house."

"Evan, how do you think I feel about going into Leonard's house? The very thought horrifies me."

"Listen, Sara. Everything about this disgusts me. Starting with having to put on an act in front of Debby as if a real human being had died. But I love you, and I understand Debby's feelings. So I'm going to do what you want. But now I'm asking you to do this for me. Do I have your word?"

"Maybe we—"

"Don't start with alternatives. This is not open for discussion."

"Okay, Evan, okay."

"Good, you're a doll. I'll speak with you later."

"You believe what they're saying about me, don't you?"

Roberta Braun turned from the haggard face of her husband. "I don't know what to believe anymore."

The meeting room at the detention center was newly painted, clean and very cold. Gerald sat at his assigned table looking across at her helplessly. "I'm not a what, Roberta, I'm a who."

A tear streaked down her face. "Gerald! Gerald! What's become of you?"

"I didn't do it!"

"Did a little demon come and put bloody footprints into your car?"

"My God! You too? What are you all thinking?"

She lowered her head. The harsh fluorescent lights highlighted the weary lines in her face. For a while she sat quietly, crushing an empty pack of cigarettes in her hands. At other metal tables, inmates sat with wives, girlfriends, mothers. One Mexican man was surrounded by seven children. The three smallest noisily competed to sit on his lap and called him "Poppi." Roberta watched and winced. *Gerald does not belong here,* she thought. *He needs help.*

"The shock has been too much for you, darling," she finally managed to say. "You're not yourself. Maybe the best thing would be to try and just not think about anything for a while."

"Great advice! Particularly when Cerezzi and the others ask me questions."

"Don't talk to them. They can't force you—"

"Stop treating me like an imbecile, Roberta. Do you think I made up the story about going to Goode's house? Of course there were footprints—I stepped in the blood."

"My poor darling," she whimpered. "It's too much, Gerald. Just too much. You need rest. That's what we have to get for you."

His face contorted. "Go rest yourself! You and the others. You, Roberta, of all people, were the one person I was sure would trust me."

"Did you trust me when you came up with this brilliant scheme to surprise Goode at his house?"

"I couldn't trust your reactions."

The room was cool, yet beads of sweat moistened his forehead. The Mexican children were now playing tag, and the atmosphere had grown boisterous. Gerald and Roberta looked at each other across the table, yet it seemed to her that a great distance separated them.

"Can't you at least believe me?" he finally mumbled.

She met his gaze. "It's a very hard story, Gerald— for anyone to believe. Just don't talk about it anymore. I love you very much, I really do, Jerry. *That* you must believe."

"You're the one who's crazy, Roberta. All of you. Get out of here. Just go away and don't come back until you can believe me."

Braun slumped over the small table. He didn't look up when she touched the back of his neck and whispered good-bye. As she walked out, the playful cries of the children echoed through her heart.

For the first time in ten days—it seemed more like ten years—Daniel had managed to block out the morning for study. Funny, he thought, how much congregations wanted their rabbis to be scholars—the very word "rabbi" meant "teacher"—then loaded them down with so many hospital visits, counseling sessions, committee meetings, and administrative and fund-raising duties that ultimately time was allotted for everything except study. And then members would complain if a rabbi's sermons started sounding repetitive.

He eagerly pulled out a few volumes from an overstuffed bookcase and retrieved some notes from his file cabinet. It had been over a year since he had delivered a paper at a rabbinical convention comparing aspects of Torah law, the even more ancient legal code of Hammurabi, and Christianity. But inexorably drawn by

the terrible events of these past days, that was precisely
the material to which he now gravitated. He loosened
his tie, flung his suit jacket over the arm of his swivel
chair, and sat down at his oak desk like a hungry man
sitting down to a large feast.

It was so preeminently obvious to Father O'Brien,
he thought, that forgiveness was always a great virtue.
And on this issue O'Brien, he knew, was not idiosyn-
cratic, but representative of Church teaching. When
the Turkish fanatic Ali Agca had shot and almost killed
Pope John Paul II, the Pope forgave him from his hospital bed, even though the would-be assassin had not
requested forgiveness. Every Catholic whom Daniel
knew thought the Pope's action was noble, that anything less would have been unworthy of the Vicar of
Christ on earth. Every Jew he knew thought it was
crazy. An unrepentant killer tries to kill you—and is
not trying again only because he is in jail—so what are
you forgiving him for? After Eichmann directed the
murder of six million Jews, Israel staked out agents all
over the world till they kidnapped the Nazi from his
hiding-place in Argentina, tried him in Jerusalem, and
hanged him. *How did it come about,* he wondered, *that
good people of different religions could see the world so differently?* It went back, he thought, to a theme that had
recently occurred to him. For Judaism, the greatest sin
was cruelty, for Christianity, historically, it was non-be-
lief in Christ. And the issue went even deeper.

Christianity had always been obsessed with afterlife.
But as soon as stress is put on the next world, the sins
of this world inevitably start seeming less consequen-
tial. Even in the worst-case scenario, a person is murdered, so what—the next world is the one that really
counts. He remembered a Christian funeral he had
attended recently where the minister had urged peo-

ple not to cry but to be happy, because the dead person was now in a better world. Though Judaism believes in an afterlife, its emphasis was on this world. Which is why almost the greatest evil that could befall a man was to be cut off from his life. Murder in Judaism was not just another crime. *Because it was irrevocable, it was the unforgivable crime.* The victim, the only one empowered to grant forgiveness, was incapable of doing so. Judaism was never obsessed with forgiveness, but with justice—"Justice, justice you shall pursue," the Torah commanded—and forgiving murderers is unjust to their victims. The point was not to demoralize would-be penitents, but to underscore how cautious people must be before committing acts that have irrevocable consequences.

Then again, once you declare some things unforgivable, where does it end? What he called justice, he knew Father O'Brien would label revenge.

He picked up a batch of notecards and leaned back on his chair. His expression changed as the internal dialogue flowed on. He barely noticed that a canister of pens tipped over and spilled to the edge of the desk. The scribbled notecards were filled with citations from one of the oldest legal codes extant, the almost-four-thousand-year-old laws of King Hammurabi of Babylonia. To Hammurabi, an eye for an eye was exacted with terrifying literalness. If a man killed another man's daughter, then the killer's daughter was executed. If a man built a house for another man, and the house collapsed, killing the son of the owner, then the builder's son was killed. Children were not regarded as human beings, but as the parents' property. You hurt another man's property, then your property—your child—is destroyed. Daniel's face tensed, and his eyes hardened.

As much as Jewish law rejected a Father O'Brien's "All is forgiven" attitude, so too did it repudiate the cruel vengefulness of Hammurabi's code. Of course, children should not be put to death for their parents' crimes. People should only be punished for their own sins. Furthermore, the very basis for capital punishment in the Bible, the belief in a "life for a life," was rooted in a principle unknown to Hammurabi. It meant that all lives were equal. In Hammurabi's code, if you murdered someone of an inferior social class, all death sentences were suspended. Kill an inferior, and Hammurabi only assessed a fine. The Torah abhorred that thinking. "And you shall not take reparations for the soul of a murderer who deserves to die," it ruled. All people are created in the "image of God"; therefore, the spilled blood of a murdered servant diminishes God's image as much as the blood of the richest man in the land. That's why the Torah outlawed fines for murderers. Human life was too precious to be paid for with money. All human life was holy. Except for the lives of people who murdered. *By denying innocent people the right to live, murderers forfeit their right to live.* He wrote this last thought down on a piece of paper, then reread it. It seemed as obvious to him as if he was saying two plus two equals four. And yet he knew that if he uttered this thought publicly, many people would dismiss him as a vengeful fanatic.

Was he? Was Gerald Braun? He looked longingly at the books on his desk, wishing that he had not just hours, but days and weeks to study. He wanted answers now, not for sermons, and not to defeat a Russell Kahn or a Father O'Brien in an argument, but because he realized that the hardest thing sometimes was not to do what was right, but to know what was right. He shook some sugar into the cold coffee on his desk and then

left the coffee untouched. He picked up a Torah
Shelemah, a twentieth-century compilation of commentaries on the Torah. Maybe he'd find some answers
there.

17

Tuesday

Afternoon

Cerezzi, wearing his one black suit, was about to press the doorbell when he noticed that the door was ajar. He pushed against it gently and stepped onto a white marble floor. In the background, he could hear a murmur of voices. A moment later a trim, dark-haired woman dressed in an expensive black knit suit approached him.

"Myra Zoltes," she said, her matching ebony bracelets jingling as she extended a hand.

"Joseph Cerezzi."

"Ce-re-zzi," the woman repeated. "Doesn't sound familiar. I'm Philipa's sister. Are you a friend of theirs?"

"Not exactly. I'm actually—"

A knowing smile crossed her carefully reddened lips. "You probably worked with Leonard?"

"If anything, on the opposite side."

The smile vanished. "Just who are you?"

"I'm with the police department, Ms. Zoltes. I came here—"

"Why didn't you say so when you walked in?"

"Ms. Zoltes, I'm here to speak with your sister. I didn't want to make a scene by coming in and announcing myself as a police officer."

The woman's slanted eyes narrowed. "My sister buried her husband this morning. Do you think it's decent—"

"Ma'am," he said, restraining himself, "I'm directing the investigation into the murder of Mrs. Goode's husband. I think it's highly decent to do whatever is possible to catch the killer. Do you agree?"

Her face grew solemn. She nodded.

"Now there are a number of questions I need to ask your sister which could help us in this investigation. I thought that rather than insist that she come down to headquarters and speak with me there, I'd just come here and take care of matters. You want to know why? Because I knew the funeral had been this morning. That's why. Does that sound decent enough?"

"I'm sorry, Lieutenant."

"Thank you. Now, why don't you do the decent thing and bring your sister out to me?"

A chastened Myra Zoltes headed back towards the living room. A few minutes later Philipa emerged alone, her flowing black dress contrasting dramatically with her long golden curls. She seemed unnaturally well-groomed and serene for a woman who had just buried her slain husband, Cerezzi thought.

"Myra told me you had some questions, Lieuten-

ant," she said, coming forward with her hand outstretched. "As you can imagine, I'm more than
anxious to cooperate with you. I want to see that man
punished. But I'm just so drained today. Couldn't this
wait a few days?"

"If it could, Mrs. Goode, I promise you I would not
be here. But I do need to speak to you for a few moments."

"Of course, Lieutenant. Please go right ahead."

Cerezzi glanced towards the crowded living room.
"I really think it would be better if we continued this
conversation in a more private place."

"Very well."

She led the way up a wide staircase, covered with
thick maroon carpeting. They walked down a long hallway and entered a book-lined study. Philipa went to the
levered chair in front of the desk. She sat down at the
chair's edge and crossed her slender stockinged legs.
Cerezzi eased his large frame into a more modest chair
opposite her.

"The day your husband was murdered you were at
Ferguson's Health Clinic. Correct?"

"Lieutenant, I went over this a hundred times with
that sergeant—"

"Collins. Yes, that's how I know about Ferguson's.
Now, according to Ferguson's records, you arrived—"

Philipa straightened. "Have you been checking up
on me?" Shrillness lurked in her voice.

"It's a matter of routine, Mrs. Goode. We check all
the movements of people close to the victim. I'm sure
you know that from your husband, don't you?" She
gave a grudging nod. "Okay. So let's just review this.
You checked into Ferguson's Saturday afternoon?"

"That's correct."

"And you intended to stay there for how long?"

"Until Thursday. Ideally, it's best to stay at least a week. But Leonard and I had a banquet honoring a friend this Thursday evening. I had to get back."

"Between your arrival and the time you learned of your husband's death, did you have any occasion to leave the clinic's grounds?"

She stared at the books along the wall behind Cerezzi. Then she reached down to smooth out the stocking around her ankle and answered casually, "I went jogging Sunday morning. I don't know, I probably crossed out of the boundaries—"

"Any other times?"

"No."

"Are you absolutely sure?"

"Lieutenant," she said coolly, "I answered your question."

He looked meditatively at her. "Would you characterize your marriage as a good one?"

"Is this really part of your standard list of questions?"

"Usually."

"Yes, Lieutenant, our marriage was excellent."

"There's something I'm curious about."

"What's that?"

"You and Mr. Goode had signed a pre-nuptial agreement which—"

"Lieutenant, you've obviously been doing quite a bit of homework on me."

Someone knocked impatiently. "Aunt Philie," a child's voice called out peevishly, "I can't find that pen set you bought me!"

Philipa rose and called out, "Jeremy, honey, look in Uncle Lenny's room. On top of the television. Okay, sweetie? I'll be out very soon."

Cerezzi stayed seated. He watched as the widow returned to her chair, taking small careful steps in her heels.

"In homicide investigations," he said, "we check out all leads."

"I thought Braun had been charged."

"We're tying up some loose ends."

"Then let me apologize if I sounded snappish before. You can imagine what a hard day this has been for me. I just realized something, Lieutenant. I did, in fact, leave Ferguson's one other time."

"When was that?"

"It was in the middle of the night, Monday morning—I was half dead—that's why it slipped my mind. Ferguson's is great, but they really starve you there. You know what it's like, you pay three hundred dollars a day for two sticks of carrots and all the lettuce you can eat. I woke up in the middle of the night, I was so hungry. Of all things, I desperately wanted a milkshake, something nice and fattening. And I remembered seeing a Denny's Restaurant when I was driving up. Well, you know, they're open all night. So I jumped into my car—"

"Did you go out the front lobby?"

"What for? My car was next to my room. Have you been to Ferguson's?"

"No."

"It's set up like a motel. You can just go right out."

"You left at about what time?"

"Well after four. I don't really remember."

"And arrived at Denny's—"

"When I got to the restaurant, there was a sign, 'Closed for repairs' till some date in April."

"So no one at Denny's saw you?"

"Of course not. The restaurant was closed, and it must have been nearly five in the morning."

"And you immediately returned to Ferguson's?"

"No. I was starving. I drove around trying to find another twenty-four-hour restaurant. No luck. They roll up the sidewalks there at ten. There were one or two gasoline stations open. But they were the old kinds, without the little supermarkets. I finally gave up and went back to Ferguson's." She swept up her long hair and began twisting it behind her head into a bun. Her liquid brown eyes were empty of expression.

"At what time?"

"I can't tell you exactly. Maybe five-thirty, even closer to six, who knows, maybe even later?" She was twisting the thick ends of her hair. Her voice sounded distracted. "I suppose my exhaustion was finally more intense than my hunger. I fell asleep right away."

"You said Ferguson's was costing you three hundred dollars a day, correct?"

"Yes."

"Just to lose weight?"

"Nobody goes there for their tennis courts and golf."

"Isn't it a little odd that you'd throw away that kind of money and then sneak out at night for a milkshake?"

"Have you ever dieted, Lieutenant?" She was now looking sideways at the mirror on the opposite wall, patting her sleek hairdo.

"I have." Cerezzi thought back to the hideous time when he had just stopped smoking. He'd put on a very unneeded fifteen pounds and earned a stiff reprimand from his superior, Captain Robert Grier, who gave him just sixty days to take it off. It had been a miserable two months. He repressed a sigh.

"So you know how tough it can be?"

"It's tough."

"Didn't you ever break your diet?"

"Not if I was spending three hundred dollars a day on it."

"I don't want to sound snide, Lieutenant, but perhaps three hundred dollars means a lot more to you than to me."

"Let's move on to something else."

The knocking on the door started again. "It's not there," the boy wailed.

She stood up, calling, "Jeremy, baby, one minute," and started towards the door. "Lieutenant, you've obviously asked the most pressing questions, and I trust I've answered them quite adequately. Can't this wait a few days?"

"Do you know a Mr. Max Reiss?"

If the question threw her, Cerezzi thought later, she didn't show it. Her short, careful steps didn't waver. She held the door by its brass knob. Outside, the boy gave a series of hard, aggressive knocks. "Uncle Lenny's room is all messed up!" She opened the door just a little and glanced back towards Cerezzi as she eased her generous curves through the narrow opening. "Forgive me, Lieutenant, I'm just too busy now. I'll answer anything you want to know in a few days. I'm sure you can find your own way out."

Doris Touhey, Brenda's secretary, greeted him, her mouth struggling with a large wad of chewing gum. "Longtimenosee, Rabbi." Or at least that's how it came out; Doris's words always ran together.

"How have you been?" Daniel asked.

The bleached-blond young woman flipped her palm. "Could be better."

"What's the matter?"

"Jim and I broke up last night."

He had known Doris almost from the time he had met Brenda. In those two years Doris and Jim had broken up an average of once every two months. "I'm sorry. Does it seem serious this time?"

"I gave him an ultimatum. We've been engaged a year already, you know."

"I understand. And you want to get married?"

"That I'm not a hundred percent sure of. Our relationship sometimes seems a bit unstable."

He suppressed a smile. "Unstable" was putting it mildly. "What do you want then?"

"An engagement ring."

Daniel laughed.

"I'm serious, Rabbi," she said. "Just because we're not totally sure about marriage doesn't mean he can't give me a ring. I mean, that's a token of what he's feeling, isn't it?"

"I suppose so."

Doris cracked her gum as she picked at her glossy purple nail polish. "I told him if he's serious, now is the time to prove it. Otherwise, maybe I'll find someone who is."

"You certainly didn't pull any punches. How did Jim react?"

"He stormed out."

"I'm sorry to hear that, Doris." He looked towards the closed office door. "Is Brenda free?"

Doris checked the phone. One line was lit. "She's been on awhile. I'll bet she'll be off in a minute." Her elfin face puckered into a smile. "Talking of betting, does Judaism permit it, Rabbi?"

"It's not crazy about it, but it doesn't normally forbid it."

"Then I'll make you a bet."

"That Brenda's going to be off in a minute?"

"I'll bet you, Rabbi, that by next Tuesday"—and she extended her left hand—"I'll have a ring on my fourth finger."

Daniel looked at her thoughtfully. "A bet like that, Doris," he finally said, "I am definitely not going to make."

"Why not?"

"Because I would be rooting too hard for you to win." The phone light switched off. With a smile, he left Doris and walked in.

Brenda looked up from behind her desk. "Oh, it's you."

He gestured to the outer office. "Why do I think I'm more popular out there?"

"Do you know who I just got off the phone with?" Brenda didn't bother waiting for a response. "Judge Nicholas White. He blasted me, Daniel. Told me he's been getting hell from everyone—even the mayor called him—for releasing Jerry Braun on bail."

"And he blamed you?"

"As a matter of fact, he did. Said he discounted Leonard Goode's protests, because Goode always exaggerated everything. But I should have been more definitive. He said because I hedged so much, he didn't feel he had the right to deny bail."

"That's totally unfair."

Brenda raised her red eyebrows. "No, Daniel, it was fair. I froze when I saw you in the courtroom, so I fudged. Of course I was afraid Jerry would be dangerous if he was released. You never wanted to acknowledge how dangerous he was, because you didn't think his revenge killing of Martin was wrong. But I do. Except when it's self-defense, killing is murder." Brenda stood up now, gripping her desk tensely. "But I downplayed what I believed about Jerry's dangerousness. I knew how unhappy you would be if I said exactly what I was thinking. I compromised myself professionally, Daniel, because of you. Now somebody's dead as a result."

It would have been a scant consolation, he thought miserably, to tell her that Leonard Goode had routinely gotten violent criminals released, without feeling so much as a twinge of guilt when they raped or murdered again. "Do doctors feel guilty," Daniel had once heard him challenge a TV interviewer, "when they surgically repair someone's trigger finger, and the person then uses it to shoot someone?"

He walked behind her and his fingers massaged the back of her neck. "I'm sorry you feel that way, Brenda."

She didn't turn. Her voice rose sharply as if from a distance. "What do you mean you're sorry I feel that way? How do *you* feel?"

"You know exactly what I think, Brenda. That Jerry's innocent."

She swung around, pulling away from him abruptly. "Oh, Daniel, cut it out! You're feeling as guilty as I am. That's why you're denying Jerry's guilt. You can't bear to own up to what you did. But Jerry did it. Which means you are partially responsible, and I am too."

"Only if he's guilty."

Brenda shook her head violently. When she spoke each word came out hard, like a bullet. "You are impossible."

They stared at each other like two old friends who suddenly found themselves with nothing to say. Brenda walked over to the window, her back turned to him in silence, her slender figure silhouetted against the diffused light coming into the room.

"You are impossible," she repeated, her face away from him.

With that cheerless adieu, he too walked away. He went out past Doris and found himself heading for Cerezzi's office down the hall.

"Tell me something, Joe," he said, before even sitting down. "Am I the only lunatic in this city who thinks Jerry Braun is innocent?"

"I know one more," Cerezzi said.

"This," Russell Kahn bellowed, "is the straw that broke this camel's back."

He pointed to the LA *Times* on his immaculate mahogany desk. "We're not just being ridiculed in the Jewish community anymore, it's the whole city now." He cleared his throat and raised the paper. " 'Towards the end of District Attorney Ryan Sanders's press conference,' " he read, " 'in an unprecedented attack, he singled out a local clergyman, Rabbi Daniel Winter of West Los Angeles's Congregation B'nai Zion—' "

"We knew all about that last night," the congregation's first vice president Donald Sohn interrupted. He smiled bleakly. "At least you can't deny one thing. The rabbi's finally getting us some newspaper coverage." Beside Sohn, treasurer Sidney Cass gave a nervous laugh.

"You'd be cracking jokes at your grandmother's funeral," Kahn snapped. "Anyway, I didn't summon you guys to my office for fun and games. Now listen up. It gets worse."

"We know all about it, Russell," Cass said. "We read the newspapers too."

"But you don't understand what it means."

"Thank you for that expression of confidence," Cass said gravely.

"I'm serious," Kahn answered. "If you two would see the implications of this story you wouldn't be sitting here so relaxed." He lifted the paper. " 'When called at his home late last night to comment on these recent events, Rabbi Winter said, "I see Braun's shooting of Martin as unfortunate and illegal, but less unfortunate and certainly more understandable than the ludicrous sentence the court imposed on the killer. Martin came to Donna Braun's house and slowly and deliberately strangled the life out of her because she refused to date him again. It seems to me a crime like that should be a capital offense." As regards yesterday morning's slaying of Leonard Goode, the rabbi reiterated his belief in Dr. Braun's innocence.' "

Kahn flung the paper down. The two other men shifted nervously in their deep leather chairs. *"Genug,"* Kahn said—the Yiddish word for "enough"—"I want Winter *out."*

"The question then is how," Sohn said, loosening his tie. "Try to fire him now, and we'll catch hell all over the Jewish community. Everybody will say we fired him just because he exercised his right of free speech."

"I don't care what they say," Kahn barked. "I gave him a direct order last night to shut his big mouth about this case. And what does he do? He goes right home and blabs to the papers about it."

Sohn got up and began pacing the room. He pointed a finger at Kahn. "We're all upset. But if the board dumps Winter over this issue, we're the ones who'll come out looking like the villains, not him."

"You have a better idea?"

"Until now the rabbi's been hogging the spotlight, and we've been reacting to him. We've got to change that. We have to take some actions and start making *him* react."

"I'm listening," Kahn said sourly.

"I think a board censure might be the way to start," Sohn said. "How about we propose a motion in the executive committee?" Sohn grabbed a memorandum pad out of his suit pocket and, slapping it down on Kahn's desk, started writing furiously. "The board of Congregation B'nai Zion," he read after a few minutes, "expresses its profound regret and disapproval over the recent activities of Rabbi Daniel Winter on behalf—"

A wave of Kahn's long hand halted him. "Sam Bornstein will be there, and he's the rabbi's puppet. He'll get a few other puppets to follow him. A resolution like that will only get under the rabbi's skin if it's virtually unanimous."

"Not necessarily," Sohn said. "You know the old joke? A rabbi has a heart attack—"

"It's sounding funny already," Kahn said.

"The president comes to visit him in the hospital and tells him, 'The board met last night, Rabbi, and voted a resolution wishing you a speedy recovery. It passed twenty to sixteen.' "

The three men laughed heartily, Sohn enjoying his own joke most of all.

"Great story," Kahn said, "now what good does it do us?"

"You think the rabbi with the heart attack looked forward to going back to work after that resolution? Even if Bornstein and a few other dupes oppose the motion, we could still get it passed. That alone might be enough to get him to resign."

"I don't know if I would chance it," Cass said. "That young rabbi has more clout than you give him credit for."

"Bullshit." Kahn again waved his hand in the air.

"I took him head-on at the board meeting Thursday night. And afterwards," he said, snapping his fingers, "they tossed Braun off the board like that."

"It's one thing to ignore what the rabbi said about Braun. But to humiliate him directly . . ." Cass shook his head. "I'm not so sure most of 'em would go along."

"Forget most of 'em. Would you?"

Cass fixed his eyes on the gray-blue carpeting. "I'm just thinking about the hell I'll catch from Stuie."

"Your son?" Sohn asked in astonishment.

Reluctantly, Cass nodded.

Kahn's large eyes were dangerously close to bulging. "Isn't this a case of the tail wagging the dog?"

Cass shrugged. "Stuie was fourteen when the rabbi came here, and he was becoming impossible for his mother and me to handle. He had quit Hebrew School after his bar-mitzvah party. Said he'd had enough of advanced spitball-shooting. A few weeks later Esther and I found melted-cheese scrapings in the broiler along with some meat. The little *mamzer* had decided to make himself a cheeseburger. Made our whole stove unkosher."

"This is, of course, very fascinating, Sidney," Kahn said, "but if this story has a point, Don and I would love to hear it."

"The first year the rabbi came here, Stuie came to *shul* with us on Yom Kippur. Acted like he was doing us the biggest favor in the world. But the next day he said this was the first rabbi he'd ever heard who made sense to him. Next thing we knew, he was going to *shul* every Shabbat, taking classes, the works. Now he yells at Lyn and me for not being religious enough."

"Aha," Kahn said, his brown eyes alert. "That's exactly my point. Instead of bringing a family together like a rabbi should, Winter's been causing tension between you and your son.''

Cass removed his glasses and stared at Kahn. "Don't twist things, Russell. I'm very proud of how Stuie's turned out. And he's not the only one here who loves the rabbi. And the people who don't, at least respect him. So when you go around bad-mouthing—''

"I'm not bad-mouthing," Kahn said with disgust.

"Okay, *criticizing* him—''

"For your information, Mr. Treasurer"—Kahn stabbed his gold pen directly at Cass—"your reading of the congregation is a hundred percent off. I've expressed my reservations about Winter to more than a few people here, and very few have ever disagreed with me.''

"Nobody likes arguing when somebody expresses a passionate opinion, so they humor you, nodding along politely." The treasurer smiled. "Don't delude yourself, Russell. You're not exactly the sweetest person in the world to argue with.''

"You seem to be doing okay," Kahn countered grudgingly.

"I don't want to see you make a fool of yourself. In the crunch, plenty of people who stayed politely quiet while you ranted against the rabbi are not going to follow you in giving him a public slap in the face.''

Kahn brooded for a few moments. The other two men were silent. Kahn pressed a button on his desk and ordered his secretary to bring in three coffees. He covered his mouth with the palm of one hand, then ran his fingers across his upper lip. He leaned forward, his dark eyes on Sohn. "You agree with what Sidney's saying?''

"I think if we try for too much immediately, we'll probably lose. That's why all of this is going to depend on orchestration. Orchestrate it right, and something that seems inappropriate today can seem very appropriate in two weeks. You know Chekhov's line on drama?''

"Which Chekhow? We don't have any Chekhows in the congregation.'' Kahn was impatient.

"Chekhov,'' Sohn corrected. "The great Russian playwright. I was asking if you know his great line about drama?''

"Of course,'' Kahn said gruffly. "I was just quoting it to Joyce this morning.''

Sohn ignored the sarcasm. "If you show a gun on stage in Act One you better make sure it goes off in Act Three.''

"That line makes him a great playwright?'' Kahn asked.

"The point is, we can't just go straight into Act Three and force the rabbi out. We've got to orchestrate it. Set the stage. Get people used to criticizing him a little more each time.'' Sohn got up and lifted the *Times* from Kahn's desk. "The rabbi doesn't have to be the only dramatist here generating newspaper publicity. We can turn this paper into our weapon, too.''

"Okay, Daniel,'' Cerezzi was saying. "I want you to try and convince me your friend Braun is innocent. And please, no emotions. If I'm going to go anywhere with this, I need tangible arguments, things I can use.''

Daniel nodded. He was seated now on the beat-up sofa that lined the wall opposite Cerezzi's desk. "There's no one fact I can point to, Joe, and say this is the non-smoking gun—the proof Jerry is innocent. There are too many little incongruities. Starting with the fact that when Jerry killed Martin he did it out in the open. With two police officers as witnesses. Right?''

Cerezzi nodded at him to continue.

"So why then deny killing Goode?" Daniel asked. "It would all be part of the same vendetta, wouldn't it?"

Cerezzi's black fountain pen tapped against his desktop. "Braun might have figured he could beat the rap on the Martin killing. Or at least get off with a negligible sentence—a jury would have to have hearts of stone not to be sympathetic. But for two killings—sympathetic or not—they'd put him away for a long time."

"And what about the way," Daniel went on, undaunted, "the two murders were performed? So differently. What do you call it, modus—"

"M.O.," Cerezzi said. "Modus operandi."

"Right. Martin was killed with a gun, and Goode was knifed. Isn't it unusual for a killer to use two such different methods?"

"We confiscated Braun's gun. Goode was stabbed with a knife taken off his kitchen rack. We—"

"Exactly," Daniel interrupted. "Which means he came to Goode's house without a knife. Doesn't that mean he wasn't planning to kill him?"

"Even if I grant you that, Daniel, it doesn't help you much."

"Why not?"

"Braun hated Goode," Cerezzi said. "Right?"

Daniel nodded.

"Maybe he really did come to bury the hatchet, or at least quiet things down. But Goode was an infuriating man—who knows that better than you? Who knows what he said to Braun?—and next thing he knew Braun picked up that very convenient butcher knife from the kitchen rack and buried all eight inches of it in Goode's chest."

Daniel was shaking his head vigorously.

"You have some arguments," Cerezzi asked, "to accompany the gestures?"

"You have no signs of forced entry at Goode's house, do you?"

"No."

"Then you tell me, Joe, how did Jerry Braun get in?"

"Probably by ringing the bell."

"That's ridiculous, Joe. When I was in court, I heard the way Goode spoke against Jerry. If Goode had seen him at his front door, he would have bolted it and called the cops. He wouldn't have invited him into his kitchen. But let me take this a step further. What do you, and the guys in forensics, assume Goode was doing just before he was murdered?"

"It's all conjecture, Daniel."

"So?" Daniel said, drawing out the word in Talmudic singsong. "Conjecture."

Cerezzi sighed. "The widow told us that Goode often worked very early. Used to say his brain was clearest at dawn. I would guess, in fact, he was working at the kitchen table from no later than five."

"If you're basing that on the time his alarm clock was set—"

Cerezzi's eyes narrowed. "I'm not talking about when he got up, I'm telling you when I think he started working."

"How could you possibly know that?"

"Elementary." Cerezzi went to his desk, picked up a heavy glass ashtray sheathed in plastic, and brought it to Daniel. "There are twelve cigarettes in this ashtray," he said. "Look at 'em."

"Mind if I remove the plastic?"

"No problem. It's all been inspected already. Matter of fact," he said, as Daniel took the ashtray, "I can even tell you the one Goode was smoking when the murderer came to his house."

"When did you start doing magic tricks?"

"Ever smoke, Daniel?"

He shook his head.

"I smoked for thirty years," Cerezzi said. "Compulsively." He pointed to the ashtray. "See how Goode put out his cigarettes? He flicked the tips off. Before he'd smoked half of the cigarette. Probably didn't want his fingertips to stink."

"I'm still not sure I'm following you."

"The way I see it," Cerezzi said, "Goode was at the table and something happened that surprised him. Possibly a sudden intruder or someone suddenly turning violent, but more likely someone ringing the doorbell. Look at this one"—with his pen he gently guided one of the butts away from the others—"this one he really smashed. It practically has the thickness of a penny. If only that cigarette could speak."

Daniel waved off the comment. "For all we know, Joe, these cigarettes could be from the night before. It's seductive, your reasoning, but in the yeshiva we used to call it *pilpul,* building one supposition on top of another, even though the whole underlying premise has never been proved."

"Well, if *pilpul*'s the same as circumstantial evidence, Daniel, you should know I'm a big believer in it."

"You have no basis—"

"Both Goode's widow and his secretary claim the guy was compulsively neat. Used to clean up his office, *after* his secretary. Said she'd be willing to swear these cigarettes could only have been there from that morning."

"Even if I grant you that, what does it have to do with Jerry Braun?"

"Let me tell you the scenario that I'll give you ten-to-one the prosecutor's going to offer in court. Braun got into the house somehow and startled Goode. That's when Goode crushed the butt in his ashtray and jumped up—"

"I tell you," Daniel interrupted, "this all sounds like a neat little package, but I'm just not sold. Whoever murdered Goode knew full well that the police were not going to conduct a normal investigation."

"What are you talking about?" Cerezzi growled.

"You know exactly what I'm talking about. Wasn't your first reaction when you heard Goode was dead to look for Jerry Braun?"

"One of my first."

"Of course. I have no argument with that. You did what made sense. The whole world knew Goode was claiming Jerry wanted to kill him. So Braun's showing up at the house made it almost impossible to think it was anybody else. What a stroke of good luck for the killer." *Unless,* Daniel suddenly thought, *it was someone who knew Braun was going to be at Goode's. In which case it wasn't luck at all.*

Cerezzi took the ashtray from Daniel and returned it to his desk. "How confident are you of what you're saying?"

"Of every detail, or that Jerry Braun is innocent?"

"That he's innocent?"

"Very."

"Then how come you can't convince your own wife?"

Daniel's cheeks puffed, then he blew out wearily. "Brenda feels responsible because of what happened at the bail hearing."

"She told me."

"And I think her guilt about that is making it impossible for her to think straight. Nobody seems to be thinking straight on this case. That's exactly what the killer's relying on."

"Have any thoughts of your own, Sherlock, as to who that killer is?"

Daniel raised his palms. "I barely knew Leonard Goode. I certainly don't know who his enemies or his associates are. The one who can find that out, Joe, is you, not me."

"In theory, yes, in practice, no."

"Meaning?"

"For one, the DA—"

"He speaks well of me."

"Which reminds me." Cerezzi eyed the cigarette stubs in Goode's ashtray almost wistfully. "You, my good friend, are Rabbi Persona Non Grata in this building. All I need is to have someone tell Captain Grier they saw us in conference together. The DA and Grier are Siamese twins on this one. The mayor is yapping that Braun should be kept in jail for the rest of his natural life. Grier told me this afternoon he wants to close down any other investigations on the killing."

"And you're unhappy he did that?" Daniel asked, a glimmer of hope in his voice.

Cerezzi sighed heavily and sat down. "I've never liked early closure in my life. But Grier's order puts me in a bind. Oh, I can continue asking around a few questions on my own, but I can't assign any of my people to follow other leads, at least not unless it's something very concrete." He pointed out to the street. "Otherwise, Grier will have my ass hanging out this window to dry."

"But you agree there's something to what I said?"

"You're a total amateur, but not without some talent." Daniel smiled. He knew that was as big a compliment as he was ever going to hear from Cerezzi. The lieutenant was rifling his desk drawer for his spare roll of Lifesavers. "Listen, right now this case is dead in the water, but I have an idea." He smiled ruefully. "I don't see what it can cost me, except maybe my job. But first, Rabbi, you got to promise me something."

"What?"

"That whatever I tell or show you is kept absolutely private. As God is your witness, Daniel, do you promise?"

"I give you my word."

Cerezzi scanned him skeptically. "Is there some sort of difference between the two?"

"In the Bible, oaths are always in God's name. Therefore, any deviation from the truth—even the slightest—and even if it's unintentional, is a terrible crime against God, because it associates God's name with a lie. I give you my word, Joe. I won't tell a soul."

"That means Brenda too."

Daniel was silent.

"I mean it, Daniel. This is totally unprofessional. I can't run any risks on this thing."

Daniel looked at him intently. "Brenda too."

"Then we're in business." Cerezzi extracted several manila folders from inside his top desk drawer. "I'm going to share with you what I came up with before Grier closed down the investigation."

For the next thirty minutes, Daniel sat quietly reading, then rereading the two documents in the top folder: Cerezzi's account of his meeting with Jason D. Perkins, and his visit to Goode's widow, Philipa.

"There's more," Cerezzi said, when Daniel finally looked up. "Sweet little Philipa wasn't the only one depositing her body in forbidden beds. Goode was too."

"But most affairs," Daniel said, "don't lead to murder?"

"Most affairs aren't with John the Gent's wife."

"John the Gent?"

"Vieto," Cerezzi said. "John Vieto."

"The mobster?"

"Goode was well connected to that world. Probably eighty percent of his income came from drug dealers and the mob. Think about it. How many honest people can afford to shell out two, three hundred dollars an hour for an attorney? It's organized crime, not the Ron Martins of this world, that kept Leonard Goode in those two-thousand-dollar suits from Bijon."

Daniel nodded slowly.

"But in spite of lawyers like Goode," Cerezzi resumed, "every once in a while, justice prevails. About three months ago, we got John the Gent sent up for a nice long stretch."

Cerezzi opened another folder, pulled out a color photo of a woman in her twenties, and handed it to Daniel. The sexy blonde was wearing a bikini and seemed to be ninety percent legs. "Mrs. John the Gent," Cerezzi informed him. "Varda Vieto. Goode's sleeping partner."

"How do you know?"

"An informant."

"I want to speak to him."

"Believe me, Daniel, you *don't* want to speak to him."

"Make up a story about me, Joe, anything, at least let me go in with you." The shake of Cerezzi's head was slow but very decisive. Daniel knew better than to argue. "Will you at least let me be there when you speak with Mrs. Vieto."

"We don't know where that lady is ourselves. Her building's super tells us she left yesterday with a small suitcase. Told him she was going to Hawaii. But she wasn't on any of the flights."

"Which means that she left right after Goode was murdered?"

Cerezzi allowed himself a small smile. "Our source also says Goode broke off with her very recently, and it was not a clean break. She was plenty mad."

"How mad?"

"Maybe mad enough, if that's what you're thinking. Her husband, I suspect, was even madder."

"He knows?"

Cerezzi smiled grimly at his friend's naïveté. "If we know, he knows."

Abruptly, Daniel stood up from the couch. Hands clasped behind his back, he began pacing the narrow office. "It's absurd that they've closed down the investigation. Look at all the people with grudges against Goode. Do you think it might help, Joe, if I spoke to Captain Grier?"

"Sure. In fact, while you're up in his office, I'll fly off to Jerusalem and ask the chief rabbi to declare ham kosher. As a personal favor to me."

Daniel's cheeks reddened. "Okay, okay."

Cerezzi pulled out a *Herald* from under a pile. He squinted at some words that had been underlined in black. "Now what can you tell me, Daniel, about Sara Levin's *get?*"

"Wh . . . What?"

Cerezzi smiled at Daniel's discomfiture. "Did I say *get* wrong?"

Daniel swallowed. "No. It's pronounced just like

the English g-e-t. I'm just surprised you knew the word."

Cerezzi passed over the paper, with David Hanks's report of the Tzedek demonstration outside Leonard Goode's office: RELIGIOUS GROUP DENOUNCES LAWYER'S REFUSAL TO "FREE HIS CHAINED WIFE." "It's in this article. I spoke with Hanks. He told me that Sara Levin mentioned your name to him."

"Sara Levin is in my congregation."

"Hanks also spoke to her boyfriend."

"Evan Singer?"

Cerezzi's eyes narrowed. "You approve of him, Rabbi?"

"He's not my type of person exactly," Daniel said, picking his words carefully. "Then again, Sara's the one marrying him, not me."

"Singer's a jailbird, Daniel."

"I know that. And what he did was terrible, I don't want to excuse it, but he didn't know there was a baby near the window. His act was political more than criminal."

"A lot of good that distinction would do a dead baby. That crowd he was running with, Rabbi Ring and the Vengeance Squad, did plenty of damage in New York."

"I know."

"Do you, Daniel? I wonder how much you really know about them."

"They harassed Soviet and Arab diplomats. Would show up at anti-Israel demonstrations and start fistfights. Things like that."

"Like what?"

"Like . . ." Daniel stopped. "What are you getting at, Joe?"

Cerezzi lifted another folder off his desk and

opened to a stapled report. He fanned the report against his desktop. "Eight years ago in New York, a pro-PLO spokesman was stabbed to death. One knife wound straight to the heart. There was no trial, but the NYPD are certain Ring's group was behind it."

"What does certain mean?"

"An informant. How do you think they caught up with your friend Sara Levin's playmate?"

"So why didn't they take it to court?"

"The government ordered the prosecutor's office not to. They were more concerned with not blowing the informant's cover." Amusement glinted in Cerezzi's dark eyes. "Don't look so glum, Rabbi. I just handed you another suspect. All nicely gift-wrapped."

"Joe, I truly believe Evan Singer has reformed."

Cerezzi did an imitation of a street-corner musician picking at a violin. "You're starting to sound like Father O'Brien."

"Somehow I get the feeling you don't mean that as a compliment."

"I'm serious, Daniel."

"Look, Evan never killed anybody."

"Only because he's a damn lucky son-of-a-bitch."

"All he did was throw a rock. He—"

"He has a temper, I gather. That much you'll concede, I hope?"

Daniel thought back to Sara's restraining comments at the Shabbat table. "He has a temper."

"And based on this *get* business, he—and Sara Levin too, for that matter—has a motive. You Jews don't have annulments like we do, do you?"

"As a rule not."

Cerezzi laughed sourly. "This is becoming a TV melodrama. Everybody a suspect. Goode's wife and her lover. The gangster client and his wife. Now the ex—or according to Jewish law, the non-ex-wife, and her boy-friend. Oh, I have no trouble agreeing with you, Daniel. There's no reason to assume Braun did it. For that matter, who says it's even one of these six?"

"Who are you thinking of?"

Cerezzi looked at Daniel squarely. "You had no love lost for the guy yourself, did you?"

Daniel stopped pacing. "Are you crazy?"

"Don't get excited, pal. I hated him too. More than one cop-killer walked because of Leonard Goode." Cerezzi turned and lifted a small framed photograph off the windowsill behind him. It showed a thin black man in a patrolman's uniform. "Eddie Johnson," he said, handing the photo to Daniel, "was the sort of guy who when they show him on a TV cop show, everyone thinks they're romanticizing the profession. Then along came a cocaine dealer named Snow-White Jenkins who had Eddie shot and dumped in a garbage can. We picked Jenkins up, all right. And he took his *mucho dinero* to Goode, who got him off."

"Jenkins was definitely guilty?"

Cerezzi's face darkened. "He was bragging all over town about it. What does that have to do with Goode getting him off? There was some goddamned fuck-up —excuse me, Rabbi—in the procedure by the arresting officer." Cerezzi snorted. "Eddie Johnson left a wife and two kids." Cerezzi jerked open his bottom desk drawer and pulled out a well-worn article. " 'In 1981,' " he read, " 'ninety-one police officers were killed—six by people who had previously committed murder.' " He slammed the report down on his desk. "These bleeding hearts go around telling everybody there's no proof capital punishment deters. Of course it does. If those six killers had been executed, six police officers would be alive today. Oh, don't doubt it for a moment, my friend. A lot of people—plenty of them very good people—hated Leonard Goode."

"But who hated him enough?"

Cerezzi shrugged.

Had someone told Daniel that morning that Cerezzi would concede that Braun might well be innocent, he would have considered the meeting a stunning success. But now, riding home, he realized that the lieutenant's concession seemed less relevant than his inability to offer any concrete help. Again and again, Daniel reviewed everything he knew about the six other suspects. Let him start his investigation with them. Singer and Sara he would have no trouble getting to. He even had a thought about how he would see Philipa. But what about Max Reiss? And Vieto? How could he get to them? When he thought of the mob man, the only association that came to mind was a garbage can. With Eddie Johnson inside.

18

Wednesday

She pulled up to a coffee shop, automatically checked her makeup and lipstick in the Chevy's rearview mirror, and jumped out. Two newspaper racks stood in front of the restaurant. She offered a silent prayer that one might be the *New York Times* national edition. No luck. She pushed in some coins and pulled out the Alexandria, Louisiana, *Daily Town Talk*.

Inside, she dawdled over her coffee and perused the paper carefully. Every time she turned a page she steeled herself to see a picture of Leonard's sprawled and bloody body. But there was no photo, and only one story was datelined LA. If Leonard's demise had set off any shock waves, they certainly hadn't traveled east. He had always bragged to her about what a big man he was. Not in Alexandria, she thought with satisfaction.

A hand came down on her shoulder. She jumped. Her left hand struck out, and scratched the intruder's face with her half-inch nails.

"Ouch," the man yelled, as a drop of red trickled down his cheek. She backed away, her two hands guarding her face.

"Varda," the man said hoarsely. He was tall, his body muscular. "Don't you recognize me?"

She stared at him, mute with shock.

"It's me, Bobby Kapp."

She dropped her hands, and her face relaxed. Bobby Kapp. Bobby had taken her to the eighth grade prom, given her a dozen yellow roses and her first kiss. Years later she heard he had married her best friend, Marcy Roon. "My God, Bobby. Why'd you go and jump on me like that for? I was scared to death."

"Lordy," Kapp said, his hand brushing at his cheek, "it's dangerous to be your friend."

Varda giggled, and the tips of her fingers gently soothed the scratch on his cheek. "Sorry about that."

"I didn't even know you were back home."

"Just passing through."

"Marcy and I were just talking about you."

"Talking about what?" Her voice became guarded.

"Nothing special. We were at one of them Hollywood pictures, and I said to Marcy, 'Maybe Varda'll be in it?' "

"Oh, that's so sweet, Bobby."

The man coughed. "You know, I think Marcy's a teeny bit hurt, the way you—"

"I know what you're gonna say," Varda interrupted, "and I'm real sorry. It's a bad trait of mine. Whenever I leave a place, I don't stay in touch. I suppose it hurts too much to think about the people I'm leaving, so I just sort of focus on the new place and people I'm going to."

"That's just what I told her," Bobby said eagerly. "I knew it was nothing personal. Anyway, what are you up to? Your ma's so close-mouthed whenever we ask." He looked at the ringless finger on her left hand. "Hard to believe a girl as pretty as you isn't married."

She jerked her head to one side and flung the curls off her forehead. "I'm getting divorced, Bobby."

"That guy must be the world's biggest chump."

Varda smiled tenderly. She had heard many terms applied to Johnny Vieto over the years, but "chump" had not been one of them.

"Hey, now that you're in town," Bobby exclaimed with enthusiasm, "come by and visit. We have two little girls, eleven and nine, and it'd be a real thrill for them to meet a glamorous lady like you."

She wrote down his number and promised to call.

She took a back road home, driving aimlessly past her dad's weekend farm, then alongside the route where she used to go horseback riding. Two hours had elapsed before she headed back to her parents' house on Park Place.

Her mother was standing outdoors, a large bouquet of yellow roses in her hand.

"You'll never believe it, darling. Mr. Hennessey just dropped them off. Said he got a call at the florist shop from a man calling himself a secret admirer."

Varda inhaled the sweet scent and smiled. It was so darling of Bobby, yellow roses just like the school prom. He had always been stuck on her, she knew. Maybe she really would go and see him and Marcy. She took the roses from her mother and brought them to her face.

"Was there a card?" she asked.

"You bet." The woman pulled a sealed envelope out of her apron pocket. "I don't know how much longer I could have waited," her mother prattled on. "A few more minutes, and I probably would have opened it myself."

"Well, then, open it now," Varda commanded. Her mother unsealed the envelope very carefully and passed it to her.

FOR LISA LEMON, it read.

The card and flowers dropped out of her hands.

The opening salvo in the *Los Angeles Times*'s letter section began:

> *The undersigned wish to express our great shame at the comments attributed in yesterday's paper to our synagogue's spiritual leader. Unlike Rabbi Daniel Winter, we deplore the revenge killing of Ron Martin by Gerald Braun and see this bloodletting as a continuation of the tragedy set in motion by the slaying of Dr. Braun's daughter last year. Our entire congregation is puzzled and stunned that our rabbi could be quoted as justifying any killing at any time, and because he did so in a public forum, we feel morally obligated to respond in that forum. While Rabbi Winter is, of course, free to express his views, we do not wish the congregational affiliation that followed his name to mislead your readers into supposing that B'nai Zion's members support vigilantism, revenge killings, and breaking of the law.*
>
> *Russell Kahn, President*
> *Donald Sohn, First Vice President*

A second letter, from Rabbi John Lerner of Tarzana, followed:

When rabbis speak as rabbis, they represent not only themselves, but also the Jewish people and tradition. It is therefore horrifying that Rabbi Daniel Winter has chosen to represent our religion in the vengeful eye-for-an-eye manner that one might better expect from one who has no respect for Judaism at all. Winter's protestations to the contrary, Judaism does not endorse capital punishment. The rabbis of the Talmud—the most important compendium of Jewish law—enacted numerous restrictions severely limiting executions. For an offense to be capital, there had to be at least two witnesses, who first had to warn the perpetrator that they saw what he was about to do. In addition, the perpetrator had to acknowledge that he had heard the warning, knew that he was committing a capital offense, and didn't care. Clearly, any criminal who went ahead with his act under such circumstances would have been spared the death penalty if only because he was insane. While capital punishment was never technically abolished, the Talmud notes that a Jewish high court that carried out more than one execution every seven years (and some texts read every seventy years) was a bloodthirsty court. Two of the greatest Talmudic rabbis, Rabbi Akiva and Rabbi Tarfon, stated: "Were we in the Sanhedrin [the Jewish high court] no man would ever have been killed." In light of these numerous and prevailing citations, if Rabbi Daniel Winter wishes to assert his privilege to support legalized murder by the state (a dubious privilege at that) let him do so as Daniel Winter, *and not as* Rabbi *Daniel Winter."*

Ken Levy entered the office of Irving Fein, president and CEO of National Life. There was no trace of his usual flashy grin, no toothy smile, not even a cordial hello. "Sit down, Mr. Levy," he commanded.

Levy eased his large frame into the armchair as unobtrusively as possible.

"I've been speaking to your supervisor," the president began grimly. "Am I to understand, Mr. Levy, that on at least three occasions in the last year you had personally heard threatening comments directed against Goode?"

"You see—"

"Yes or no?"

Levy gulped. "Yes."

"And it was only *after* Mr. Goode's murder that it dawned on you that it might possibly be relevant to share this information with us?"

"I was thinking—"

Fein's icy blue eyes halted him in mid-sentence. *"You were thinking?"* Fein pushed himself up from his desk and glared down at Levy. "If you had been thinking, Mr. Levy, we wouldn't be holding this two-million-dollar policy now, would we?"

Levy gulped, and his hands clenched.

The explosion seemed to have emptied Fein like a punctured balloon. He fell back on his chair and sat quietly for a few minutes.

"It might have been suicide," Levy suggested haltingly. Fein watched him warily. "You see, I was speaking to this pathologist I know, a Dr. Samson, over at Cedar Sinai. He told me the angle of the wound could possibly have been self-inflicted. Maybe we should hold off on payment for a while. I was thinking—"

"Hold off payment, eh?"

"Yes, you see—"

"Even though the police definitely say it's murder. Mr. Thinker, Mr. *Deep* Thinker, what sort of publicity do you think National Life would get if we deny payment to the family of a murdered policyholder? Worse, slander the dead man's name by claiming he committed suicide?"

"I'm not saying not to pay. I'm talking about holding off, sir. I was thinking—"

"Before you share with me any more of your *thinking*, Levy, I'm going to make you a proposition. If you can bring in proof, not fancy theories, but *proof* that Leonard Goode either committed suicide or was murdered by his beneficiaries, then I have some very wonderful news for you. Your office will remain yours, your fancy walnut desk will remain yours, and I will personally invite you up here again and present you with a box of Havana cigars. Highly illegal and highly delicious. If you can't come in with that proof, however, then the invitation to my office is withdrawn, the invitation to your office is withdrawn, and the walnut desk as well, for that matter."

The president stood up and indicated the door. "Good day, sir."

"Did you hate my father?"

The question startled Daniel, though he immediately realized it shouldn't have. He had been dreading making this *shiva* call—this mourner's visit. Yet he had been given no choice. Sara Levin had been very insistent that he come visit Debby.

"Don't speak to the rabbi like that," her mother said sharply.

The girl's cheeks flushed. "You shouldn't even be here, Mommy. You hated Daddy. Everyone knows that. And if the rabbi hated him, he shouldn't be here either."

Sara Levin raised both hands towards Daniel in a pleading gesture. She turned back to the girl. "I didn't hate your—"

"*You're happy he's dead, aren't you?* Now you can marry Evan."

Sara gasped. Her face crumpled.

"Do you think your mother is wrong for wanting to marry again?" Daniel asked.

The girl regarded him with brooding eyes. "She never loved my father. Only I loved my father."

"Of course you did," Daniel said. He took the girl's hand, but she yanked it away. "He was very good to you, wasn't he?"

"Uh-huh," Debby said, her voice low.

"Do you think he loved your mother?"

Debby shook her head, her face averted from Sara.

"So it wasn't wrong of your mother to want to re-marry, was it?"

"Yeah, but she also wanted him dead."

"I did not want him dead!" Sara Levin's voice rang out. Daniel was grateful that they had been given a room in the library upstairs, away from the other mourners and guests.

"I heard you speaking to Evan last night," Debby said. "How maybe it was all God's will. You're happy he's dead. Why don't you admit it?"

"Debby," Daniel said, "did you—"

"And you didn't answer my question, Rabbi. Tell me the truth. Did you hate my father too?"

He paused, his mind a jumble of thoughts. Had he hated Leonard Goode? Honestly? Yes, he had. The man had callously smeared Donna Braun's name just to help get her murderer off. Then blackmailed Sara by refusing to give her a *get*. And those were only his latest cruelties. Part of Daniel was irritated with Debby, though he knew the feeling was immature. *What exactly was it about your father that you loved?* he wanted to ask her. *That he was heartless to other people, but nice to you? Are we all supposed to love him because of that?*

But he could see the child's pain. And he knew that whatever face Leonard Goode had shown the rest of the world, the face his daughter had seen had been a kinder one. So what then? Give her the truthful answer she claimed to want? *Yes, Debby, I despised your father. In the battle between good and evil, he used his brilliance to help evil. The world is a better place without him.* Would anyone advise him to tell such a truth? Kant would have, he knew. The great German philosopher regarded all lies as wrong, no matter what the motivation. If someone runs past you, Kant had written, and then another person with a raised knife asks you in what direction the first person has fled, you must answer truthfully. Daniel had studied the passage in a university philosophy class. It was one of the reasons he never had become a Kantian. Judaism's attitude was more pragmatic. Where human feelings—let alone human life—are at stake, you can lie. When singing at a wedding, Rabbi Hillel had taught, always describe the bride as "beautiful and virtuous." Hillel's rabbinic opponent had been horrified. "No," he insisted, "describe the bride accurately, as she is." But the rabbis ruled with Hillel.

"Your father and I did not agree on many things, Debby. Don't you think it's possible to disagree with someone without hating them?"

"But you're friends with that man who killed him?"

"I don't believe Gerald Braun killed your father. I think the evidence against Mr. Braun is misleading."

There was a weary silence. Debby stared at the carpet and then lifted a tear-streaked face.

"If, God forbid, it was your mother who had died," Daniel asked, "would you have been half as angry with your father for how he had treated her?"

The tears now had turned to sobs.

"Your mother loves you with all her heart. Don't be angry with her. She suffered terribly also. She still is. Do you realize how much it hurts her to see you suffering like this? Thank God you have such a loving mother. Don't you know she would do anything in the world for you? Don't you know this, Debby?"

When he finally stepped out of the room, mother and daughter were locked in a weeping embrace.

Her heart was still pounding, but at least she was closer to freedom now. No one had been watching her at the airport, she was sure of that. And the plane seemed to have been safe—she'd been up and down the aisle three times. And this time she hadn't taken any stupid risks. No travel agents. Just paid her money and got on the airplane.

She was back in LA now. She'd drive her car straight to San Francisco, get a good twelve, fifteen thou on it from some dealer, and at least have a stake —a chance to start over.

Mom had been so panicky when she'd left. It was so sudden, not even waiting for Dad to come home. She slowed down now at the sight of the telephone booth on Overland. *Give Mom a quick ring,* she thought, *a few reassuring words. Even if those bastards have a tap on, they won't have enough time to trace it.*

She turned her back to the cars and spoke on the phone for no more than a minute. Quickly, she headed back to the cream-colored Seville, the key in her hand. She was reaching over to the ignition when a large hand clamped over her wrist. Another closed over her mouth.

"I plan trips too," Angelo Vieto's hoarse voice announced from the back seat. "And I have a very cozy one-way trip planned out for you, Varda baby."

Daniel was walking past the living room, about to exit the Goode house, when he heard his name being called. Or rather, "Rabbi." Rabbis—he knew—except when speaking to close friends, relatives, and other rabbis, didn't have personal names. But when Daniel turned around, the eyes of the people were focused elsewhere, on the red-headed Rabbi John Lerner.

"Daniel," Rabbi Lerner now called out.

Daniel stepped in cautiously. His eyes rapidly scanned the room, wondering which one was Leonard Goode's second wife, Philipa. The guests were chattering in hushed voices, each with a drink in their hand. Some were seated on the white sunken sectional, others were lounging in comfortable armchairs.

Daniel walked over to Lerner, his feet sinking into the plush peach carpet, and extended a hand.

Lerner grasped it lightly. "I would not have expected to see you here."

"I came to see Debby," Daniel explained, motioning vaguely towards the library. "Excuse me," he asked Lerner, "is one of the women here Mrs. Goode?"

"Philipa's stepped out," Lerner answered. "Why don't you sit down? She'll be back soon."

For a moment Daniel almost broke into a run. As if he'd been given a reprieve. But what choice did he really have? He had to meet her, get a measure of who she was.

He sat on the opposite end of the sofa from Lerner. The rabbi introduced him to the others, and fortunately, Daniel thought, none of them seemed to recognize his name.

"You know, I'm the one who performed Philipa

and Leonard's marriage," Lerner said. Daniel remembered his comments a few days earlier at the rabbinic meeting. How Lerner had scolded him, telling Daniel to send him Sara Levin and Evan Singer, and he'd perform their wedding. "By the way, Daniel, I'm sorry if my letter in this morning's *Times* came out a little harsher than I intended. To tell you the truth, I must admit I was a little ticked-off at you."

"I'd never have guessed," Daniel said with a small smile. "I was only surprised at how traditionalist you sounded."

A brunette with thick eyeglasses laughed. "Rabbi Lerner has never said anything traditional in his life. Whatever are you talking about?"

"Rabbi Lerner," Daniel resumed, in a neutral voice, "published a letter in which he seemed to be basing his opposition to capital punishment on the Talmud."

"The *Talmood?*" the woman asked, as the other guests on the sofa perked up.

"The Jewish oral law," Lerner answered, his wary eyes focused on Daniel. "It's a much later work than the Bible, but Orthodox and Conservative Jews still use it to determine Jewish law."

"But you're Reform, Rabbi Lerner?" an elderly woman in a lavender suit asked.

"Of course." He turned towards the woman. "As Reform Jews we don't regard the Talmud as a legal code. We see it rather as a repository of sometimes wonderful advice and wisdom. On many subjects. Capital punishment being one of them." His eyes returned to Daniel. "Sorry if I punctured your arguments, Daniel. My citations were all quite accurate, you know."

"A halber emes iz a gantser lign."

"What!"

"A half-truth," Daniel translated from the Yiddish, "can be a whole lie."

"What the hell is that supposed to mean?" Lerner snapped. "Rabbi Akiva *didn't* say he would never have allowed a murderer to be executed?"

The room fell into an embarrassed hush, and the other guests looked towards the sofa. Daniel responded in a soft voice: "Of course he said it. Only the same page of the Talmud contains Rabbi Shimon's response to him—'In that case, you would have multiplied spillers of blood in Israel.'"

"Right, Daniel. In a letter to the editor, I should have put down a whole treatise on Jewish law and capital punishment. The thrust of my letter was completely accurate, as you perfectly well know. The rabbis demanded two eyewitnesses, did they not, a warning, and an acknowledgment of the warning? If that wasn't intended to eliminate executions, then maybe you can explain to all of us less scholarly Jews what it was intended to achieve."

"You left out a few other relevant items in your letter, John."

Lerner rolled his eyes towards the ceiling and made sure that everyone saw the gesture.

"Like the fact," Daniel continued, "that all those discussions of the rabbis were theoretical. Written when Jewish courts no longer had jurisdiction to mete out criminal punishments."

"So what are they doing there?"

"Likely as not, as a protest against the Romans. The Romans controlled Palestine then, and executed whomever they wanted. On the flimsiest evidence." Daniel turned to the other people in the room, who were now eavesdropping unabashedly. "The world might know only about the case of Jesus, but between

fifty and one hundred thousand other Jews were crucified by the Romans in the first century. By demanding
extreme and impossible standards, the rabbis were expressing their protest at Roman barbarity.''

"Speculation," Lerner sneered. "I offer concrete
evidence, and you hand back farfetched theories."

"You left out something else, John."

"Equally crucial, I'm sure."

"Maybe. Though I happen to think it's the proof
that I'm right."

"What is it?" the nearsighted woman asked.

"The rabbis realized that they were insisting upon
standards that were virtually impossible to establish,
that would have paralyzed courts attempting to punish
violent crimes. So they added two further clauses. In
times of emergency, these extreme precautionary provisions could be suspended—"

"And you're the one, I assume," Lerner broke in,
"qualified to declare our current age a time of emergency."

"Right now, John, the average American in a large
city has a better chance of being murdered than the
average American soldier had of being killed in com-
bat during World War II. I'll be more precise. One out
of every hundred and thirty-three Americans will end
his life murdered. Maybe you consider that par for the
course. I consider it an emergency . . . Oh, one last
thing. The Talmud ruled that if it was clear to the court
that the defendant had committed the murder, but
one of the technical factors had not been fulfilled—
maybe the two witnesses hadn't delivered the warning,
maybe the defendant hadn't acknowledged it—they
locked up the murderer and fed him on barley and
water until his belly burst."

"Are you mad, Daniel?" Lerner shouted. "Even

you wouldn't have wanted me to put that in the LA *Times*. It's positively barbaric."

"So," said Daniel coldly, "is murder."

"But murder's the act of an individual. The individual alone is responsible. But when the state murders someone, all citizens of the state are responsible. And guilty."

"Was Israel wrong in executing Eichmann?"

A vein was throbbing now on Lerner's neck. "I'm not going to fall for your demagogic tricks. No, Israel was not wrong. Eichmann—"

"Then you agree with me, John, that capital punishment is sometimes justified. We're just arguing over when."

"When you murder six million people, that's when."

"That, my friend, is not a Jewish argument."

The elderly woman protested in a husky voice. "The Holocaust is not a Jewish argument?"

Daniel turned to her. "According to the Talmud, the reason God originally created the world with just one person, Adam, was to teach us that each person is a whole world, 'Whoever destroys one life, it's as if he destroyed an entire world. Whoever saves one life, it's as if he saved an entire world.' From that perspective, that each human life has infinite value, six million infinites are worth no more than one infinite."

The woman's brow furrowed. The man next to her interjected, "Judaism doesn't see mass murder as worse than killing just one person?"

"Any murder of any innocent person is the worst thing you can do. And most murderers, in any case," Daniel said, "are mass murderers. When Cain murdered Abel, God called out to him, 'Your brother's blood cries out to me from the earth.' The word that

God uses, though, is *d'mai*, the plural form, which means 'bloods.' "

"That makes no sense," the nearsighted woman objected.

"Exactly. So the rabbis ask: 'Why does it say your brother's *bloods?*' And they answer: 'His blood and the blood of all his descendants who will never be born.' " Daniel turned back to John Lerner. "It wasn't just Donna Braun whom Ron Martin murdered. What about her unborn children and their descendants?"

"That is demagogic . . ."

At that moment, both Daniel and Lerner turned, suddenly conscious of another presence in the room. A blond woman was regarding them gravely, as if she had been listening for several minutes.

"Philipa," John Lerner said, "this is Rabbi Daniel Winter."

The woman stood motionless.

Daniel rose slowly and self-consciously. The two studied one another, but neither spoke.

"Philipa, the rabbi came here to see Debby. I saw him passing by—"

"Mrs. Goode—" Daniel began.

"I would appreciate a word with you in private, Rabbi." She turned her back on the guests and walked towards the entrance. Daniel followed her. When they passed through the thick oak doors into the hallway, she turned abruptly and faced him. Inside, the guests were leaning forward and watching them. Her eyes stared intently into his, and the voice was very low.

"I never want you to dare enter this house again. Never come here. Never poison Debby's mind with your twisted ideas. And don't teach us how good murder is. I hope you heard me loud and clear. Every word. I'm trying not to make a scene, *Rabbi*. You don't deserve the title."

A thought passed through Daniel's mind. Did she deserve the title "wife"? Should he ask Philipa about her affair with Max Reiss? He was sorely tempted. But his eyes were fixed on her beautifully manicured hands. *It would not be hard,* he thought, *to imagine those hands picking up a knife and plunging it hard into her husband's chest.*

Only two questions had to be answered now. Was Philipa Goode the killer and, if so, how could he prove it?

"Good day, Mrs. Goode," he finally said. "And if I caused you any unnecessary pain, please forgive me."

With all the earmarks of a macabre joke, the call came in to 911 at 9:11. A teenage cyclist on Topanga Canyon, over near the Pacific Coast Highway, had seen a foot sticking out of a bush. The patrol car was there by 9:20.

The legs protruding from the short skirt were sensational. Patrolman Robert Kemp broke through the thick undergrowth to the face. There was a bullet hole through each of the two eyes. But that wasn't the worst. The entire tongue had been cut out and placed very carefully over the dead woman's mouth. At 9:26, Patrolman Kemp vomited.

19

One week later
—Wednesday

Sara Levin and Evan Singer came into Daniel's office a few minutes before 11:00 a.m.

"I just must tell you, Rabbi, how wonderful you were last week with Debby," the woman gushed.

Daniel was far from certain he deserved the compliment. "How is Debby doing?"

"That week of mourning really helped. Even the bad times, when she was crying or yelling at me—it forced everything out into the open. I think she finally started realizing that the issue wasn't really anger, just hurt. She needed to trust my love for her, just what you were telling her. It will take time, but Debby's going to be okay. I really think so."

"Is that your impression too, Evan?"

Singer sat forward in the black armchair, his fingers laced into each other. "You know my dad also died when I was twelve. He was a fine, decent man, no Leonard Goode. So I know what Debby's going through. That feeling that you're sinking fast—as if the floor's suddenly been pulled out from under you. It's a shock that takes months and months to ever start to heal. A kid cannot imagine that anyone could love you like that again. Look, we've got to give him that much, ol' Lenny really loved Debby. If you call that sort of love worth anything. My mom never remarried. But Debby's going to have a full-time dad. I know this will make a big difference."

"That's very good to hear, Evan."

"So can you guess why we're here, Rabbi?" Sara said.

Daniel's face creased into a smile. "I have a sneaking suspicion you want to set a wedding date?"

Singer raised his thumb in a gesture of victory.

Daniel started leafing through his calendar. "I also have a suspicion," he said, glancing up, "that you want to get married as soon as possible."

They nodded.

Daniel made a quick calculation, and his finger came down on a date. "How about June 27?"

"We were thinking like in a week," Singer said.

"That's almost three months," Sara wailed.

Daniel stroked at his chin. "Which is exactly why I picked it," he answered. "It'll be ninety-one days since Leonard Goode died."

"Who cares about ninety-one days?" Singer said. "Sara's a widow now. No more divorced, not divorced. A widow. So what's the problem?"

"There's a Jewish law," Daniel said, "that—"

"Oh, come on, Rabbi," Singer interrupted.

Sara put a restraining hand on the man's arm.
"Let's hear the law, Evan."

Daniel went over to a bookcase and drew out a
thick volume of the Shulkhan Arukh, the Code of Jewish Law. He brought it back to his desk, consulted it for
a few moments, then looked up. "In case the newly
married woman gives birth prematurely," he explained, "the rabbis didn't want any mix-up about who
the father was. So they established that a minimum of
three months pass after the divorce or death of the
husband before a second marriage takes place."

"But doesn't that only make sense," Sara asked,
"where the woman was living with the first husband up
to the day of the divorce or death?"

"It does," Daniel conceded.

"So then it shouldn't apply here?"

Daniel blew out slowly. "I wish it were that simple."
He looked down again into the book, scanning the
commentaries, though he was quite sure of what he
would find. Sara Levin was, after all, not the first person to raise this eminently logical objection. He had
raised it himself at the yeshiva. Unfortunately, though,
the commentaries surrounding the text seemed to be
in uniform agreement. Once the principle of three
months was established, the law was to be applied in all
cases, even when the first husband had been in a far-
away land or in jail. They cited the Talmudic principle
of *lo ploog*—"no exceptions"—lest everyone try to
prove that they are entitled to the exception.

"Listen, Rabbi," Singer said, "I hope you're not
trying to imply that any funny business might have
been going on between Sara and Leonard?"

"Of course not."

"Well, that's what this law's making it sound like."

"Rabbi," Sara said, "what if Evan and I agreed not

to even try to have a child for the first few months we were married? That way, by the time I become pregnant, God willing, there could never be any question about who the father is."

"I'm delighted that you and Evan want to have children," Daniel said.

"Of course we do," Singer said.

"So I'd hardly want to encourage you to delay the process of trying."

"But that's exactly what you are doing," Singer said. "You're delaying us three months."

"Fair-enough point," Daniel said. "Let me think a little." He looked down into the large volume again, though his thoughts weren't really there. He just wanted to be able to look away from the couple and their imploring eyes. Their basic argument was a hundred percent valid. There was no question in this case of paternity. When he died, Leonard Goode had been married to Philipa five years. And that whole time, he and Sara Levin had barely had a civil, let alone a conjugal, relationship. To impose this rule on them seemed to make no sense at all. On the other hand, the rabbis had made it clear they didn't care about exceptions. But then again, the very word for law in Hebrew, *halakha,* didn't really mean law at all. It meant, rather, "the way"—by which the rabbis meant the way to perfection. Sara and Evan had been waiting so long, trying so hard to abide by God's rules, despite the difficulties it had caused them. And all they wanted was to be together. Now. Not in three months. Who knows what could happen in three months? Donna Braun must have thought she had at least fifty years to live the evening Ron Martin ended her life. Sara and Evan had a right to be together. Marriage was one of the few subjects on which the Torah itself waxed romantic.

"Therefore," Genesis said, "let a man leave his mother and father and cling to his wife and they shall be one flesh." The first thing in the Bible God declared "not good" was aloneness. "It is not good for man to be alone," God said of Adam. "Let me make him a helpmate."

"Okay," Daniel said, looking up. "I think I have a solution. I'm a little embarrassed, Sara, asking this of you, but it seems to me it'll cover the demands of Jewish law. You see, when this law was formulated, doctors could only tell if a woman was pregnant much later in the pregnancy. But now, of course, they know much sooner. I want you to go to a gynecologist and have him give you a pregnancy test. When that comes back negative, I'll marry you immediately."

"I find that request very offensive," Singer said. "Do you really—"

"It's okay, Evan," Sara interrupted him, patting his hand.

"It's not okay," he said, shaking her off. "The very implication of not accepting your word, of having you examined by a doctor—"

"I think we both need a little perspective, darling. Two weeks ago we were wondering when, if ever, we'd be able to get married. If Rabbi Winter had told us then that the only thing required was that I take a pregnancy test, you would have jumped at the chance. I know I would have." Sara turned to Daniel. "Of course I'll go to the doctor. Today. And I want to set a date for the marriage right now."

Daniel consulted his calendar. "How's in eleven days," he asked, "a week from Sunday?"

"What time?" Sara said.

"There's an executive committee meeting of the

board here at eleven a.m. Is two in the afternoon good?"

Sara beamed. Singer nodded sullenly.

"Evan," Daniel said, "I understand you're upset, but I think this is one of those times when ends matter more than means."

He extended a hand and, after a pause, Singer took it. "I'm not blaming you, Rabbi. It just seems like there will never be an end to this maze we're in. Always another big hurdle."

"You and Sara," Daniel answered, "are finally getting married. So there's nothing to be upset about. Congratulations! From the bottom of my heart, mazel tov!"

Ken Levy watched from his car as the couple separated without touching. But he noticed the man softly kissed his own fingertips and then blew the kiss to her. The woman winked behind a wide-brimmed hat, as her lips curled in a slight smile.

The young insurance agent decided to tail Max Reiss's beat-up Skylark. Four days now, Levy had been trailing Philipa Goode, and this was the second time she had met this man on the street. *Did it mean anything? Probably not.* But Levy continued following. Better than waiting at home for unemployment checks.

Reiss turned left on Westwood and Pico, heading for the Mall. Levy found a nearby spot in the parking lot. He followed Reiss through the entrance and up an escalator into Broadway's. Reiss asked a salesman a question, then headed for the kitchen appliance section.

Levy hung back a little, in men's underwear. Philipa and Reiss hadn't spotted him, he was sure, but then again why crowd the guy? A little more caution in the past and he wouldn't have to be playing gumshoe now. He watched Reiss approach a saleswoman. Levy hastily started checking out some tight new Perry Ellis briefs. When he looked up next, Reiss was gone. Levy's eyes panned the whole appliance section, then the rest of the floor. He let out a soft string of vicious curses and headed over to the saleswoman Reiss had talked to.

"May I help you?" she asked with a pleasant smile. Her nametag said "Kathy."

"That tall fellow who was just here, with the dark blue sweater, you were waiting on him, weren't you?"

The woman's face was blank.

"I just saw you with him," Levy said.

"When exactly was this, sir?"

"Two, three minutes ago. You were standing here waiting on him."

"Carol," the woman called out. A chunkier replica of Kathy came out from behind a door. "You might be confusing me with my sister," Kathy said, smiling. Then to Carol, "Were you waiting on a tall gentleman a few minutes ago, wearing a blue sweater?"

"Uh-huh."

"Did he purchase anything?" Levy asked.

"He bought a— Excuse me, sir, why do you want to know?"

"Oh, he's my cousin. Max. I was supposed to meet him here, but I got held up in traffic, and Max must have just left without me."

"Yes?" Carol said.

"Well, you see, I was supposed to buy exactly what Max bought. That's what he told me to do."

"Exactly?" the woman asked.

"Exactly."

"That's very peculiar."

"Oh, no. That's what he told me. To get exactly what he got."

"Very well, then." The woman did an about-face and led him into cutlery, to a large rack filled with knives. She pulled out a long one, with a black handle, and handed it to Levy. "Your cousin's knife had gotten dented and ruined his set," she said. "Why ever would you want to buy the same knife?"

But Levy no longer heard her. He had seen the pictures from the homicide scene. The knife he was now holding seemed to be a replica of the one that had murdered Leonard Goode.

"Why would you want to buy the same knife?" Carol asked again.

Levy paid her no attention. "How much does this cost?" he asked.

"$21.40, with tax," Carol answered. "Just the same as it cost him."

She rang up the sale. Levy put a twenty and a five down on the counter. "Keep the change," he said, and hurried off.

"Strange one, wasn't he?" Carol said when her sister Kathy came over. "What do you think, sis?"

"Gay guys, Carol, bet your dinner on it. You know how fussy those people are. Exact same utensils. Oh, they're gay boys, you mark my words."

"You owe me a major mazel tov, Rabbi," Sam Bornstein announced, stepping inside Daniel's office. The synagogue's immediate past president and current chairman of the board, Bornstein was, as always, in a hand-tailored suit and immaculate. He was the only man Daniel knew who had his hands manicured twice a week.

"Should I give you the mazel tov first, Sam, or are

you going to tell me what I'm congratulating you about?''

Bornstein slapped a palm on Daniel's desk. "I sold the Samborn development out in Chatsworth, the whole thing.''

Daniel stood up and shook Bornstein's hand vigorously. "That's great, really great, Sam.''

"It's more than great. Twenty-five point two, that's what it is,'' Bornstein said.

"What?''

"That's what they're paying me. Twenty-five point two million.''

Though the enormous sum seemed incomprehensible, Daniel felt genuinely pleased. Bornstein had always been a good friend, and the only president who'd consistently supported his work in the congregation.

"So what does the Talmud say, Rabbi?'' Bornstein asked with a jovial smile, pulling a cigar out of his suit's inner pocket. "Any special insights there about a sudden windfall?''

"*Aizeh hu ashir,*'' Daniel began, citing a proverb from the *Ethics of the Father.* "Who is rich? He who is happy with what he has.''

The man chuckled, lit the cigar, and took an unhurried puff. "Uh-oh,'' he said, as he rested it in the ashtray. "I might not be as rich as I thought.''

"Meaning?''

"I've already been thinking about how I could double it . . . What about you, Rabbi? Are you happy with what you have?''

"Money-wise or in life?''

"Both.''

"Money-wise, no complaints. Look, I'm no ascetic, Sam. If God revealed the lottery numbers to me in a dream tonight, I'd be out there buying a ticket tomorrow. But I'd be back here the next day, maybe two days later, doing the same work I'm doing now. I love my wife, I love teaching Torah, bringing some people to Judaism. I'm pretty rich, Sam. At least in the Talmudic sense."

"So you're happy at B'nai Zion, Daniel?"

"Most of the time."

"Kahn wants you out."

Daniel nodded slowly. "I think he's made it pretty obvious."

"It's becoming an obsession with him."

"Has he talked to you directly?"

"He wouldn't dare!" Bornstein crossed his two forefingers. "He knows where you and I stand. But I hear reports from the boys. He's going to pull something at that executive committee meeting, Daniel. I feel it in my bones."

"Any suggestions?"

"Any hope you could back off on this Braun business, maybe take Kahn out for dinner? You're such a good diplomat when you want to be, Daniel. It's no sin to let him see that side of you."

"Of course I'll take him out to dinner if you think it'll help."

"And drop the Braun business."

"Sam, do you want Daniel Winter to be the rabbi of this congregation?"

"What kind of stupid question is that? You think I came here today for my health? Of course that's what I want."

"Well, if I deserted Jerry Braun just to keep my job, I wouldn't be the same person anymore. I don't want to sound like some self-righteous prig, and I might even be all wrong on this. But it's more important that I like and respect me than that Russell Kahn likes me."

"Isn't peace also a value in Judaism, Daniel?"

"Not at Russell Kahn's price. You want to be there with me, Sam, when I tell Jerry Braun that I'm skipping town? That it's just not expedient for me to associate with him anymore?"

Bornstein smiled. "I figured you'd say that."

"Do you agree with me?"

"I'm not sure, Rabbi. But I'd rather be wrong with you than right with Russell Kahn."

"Thanks, Sam. I suppose that's about as much as I can expect. The question is, how many more people on the executive committee do you think feel like you do?"

"Plenty. Only they don't all know it yet."

20

Eleven days later

—Sunday

Brenda poured coffee into two cups and handed one to Daniel. "Funny they want me at the wedding," she said. She sat down opposite him at the wooden block kitchen table.

"Sara was very insistent. Said she felt the two of you could really become close."

"Good thing she didn't overhear my analysis of her and Evan that Friday night."

Daniel cleared his throat. "If human beings overheard everything that other human beings said about them, all friendships would dissolve."

Brenda lifted her cup toward Daniel and bowed her head. "Thank you, Rabbi, for sharing those words of wisdom with us." They sipped their coffee in silence for a few minutes, yet Brenda studied him intently. "Your mind's been a million miles away the whole morning, Daniel. Does it look so grim with Kahn?"

"I think it's going to be bad."

"It's a good thing he's not a dictator, or it would be off with your head. How many people will go along with him?"

"Sam says he can't tell."

"And the board people you've spoken to?"

Daniel shook his head. "I haven't spoken to anyone."

Her green eyes narrowed. "That's not like you."

"I've been here four years, Brenda, and I haven't exactly been a wallflower. So there's no sense in my calling up Henry or Frank or Leo—what do I have to tell them that they don't already know?"

Brenda set her cup down with such force that coffee spilled into the saucer. "That you're here, Daniel. That you want to stay here."

"Not if they don't want me."

"Kahn just has everyone panting like dogs after his money. They're confused as to what they want."

"It's not just the money, it's the whole Braun business."

"For Kahn it's all a pretext," she snorted, "a power play. He ordered you to back off, and you disobeyed him."

Daniel shook his head. "Don't underestimate his sincerity. Look how upset *you* were with me over how I acted."

"Exactly. I thought you were wrong in testifying for Gerald Braun and I still do. I really think you made a monumental error and, worse, forced me into one. With very terrible consequences. I'm not happy about it, but I go on to other things. Because I love you,

Daniel. But he doesn't. Kahn figures he caught you in a mistake, and now he'll just keep exploiting it until he can get rid of you and find some more malleable rabbi."

Daniel's blue eyes hardened. "And if the others are willing just to sit back and let him do it, *then let him do it*. If it comes to that, I'll have to find another pulpit."

Brenda slammed her spoon against the tabletop. "Listen, Mr.-too-proud-to-fight, this isn't about your getting another pulpit. You're the most brilliant man I know, Daniel Winter, and I believe you can get whatever position you want. It's your passivity that's worrying me. Forget Kahn and the executive committee. There are hundreds of people in this congregation who love you, whose lives you've changed and enriched. Look at all the people who've moved into the neighborhood just to be near this synagogue. If you want to be passive about your own interests, fine. But you owe *them* something too."

For the first time, his mouth formed a smile. "Okay, coach, what do you think I should do?"

"Get off your rear end, *Rabbi*. If that means going public and confronting Kahn, then go public. Better than sitting around morbid and passive . . . Are you listening to me, Daniel?"

"If I had a hearing aid, I might turn it—"

"Daniel—"

"I heard every word you said."

She came over and brushed a crumb off his cheek. "I also think—"

"No more political discussions," he said. "I know what I have to do, Brenda. Enough. Don't worry." He pulled her onto his lap. "You smell delicious this morning, copper." He started nuzzling the back of her neck, and his hand reached under her blouse and massaged her back. "If we adjourn this discussion to upstairs, I promise you, I won't be passive there."

She laughed and drew away a few inches. "I adore you, Daniel, and I personally don't give a damn if we have to leave B'nai Zion. What did Ruth say to Naomi, 'Where you go, I will go?' That's where I stand. But if you saw Russell Kahn doing to somebody else what he's doing to you, you'd fight him. I just want you to fight as hard for yourself."

"I am going to listen to what you said. I really am. Can we adjourn now and go upstairs?"

Brenda smiled. "For as long as you want, Rabbi."

"We have a wedding at two."

"Then we still have a good two hours. Are you going to go out there," she whispered in a husky Mae West twang, "and fight for your rights?"

He squeezed her tightly to him. "It's a good thing they're not letting me into that meeting."

"Oooh . . . Why's that?"

"Because when I'm with Russell Kahn, I think about Russell Kahn." He kissed her. "And it's a lot nicer to think about you."

Ira Rich started the executive committee session with a twenty-minute report on the status of the new traffic light the mayor's office had promised the synagogue two years earlier. Then Sidney Cass, speaking for the employee's compensation committee, distributed three sheets breaking down the forthcoming pension plan. A few other routine items were raised and voted on, with almost no discussion.

"Any other business or good and welfare?" Kahn asked.

No hands went up.

He straightened the gold clasp on his red silk tie

and cleared his throat. Kahn's whole upper body stiffened as he looked around the table into the eyes of everyone present. "In that case, I feel it incumbent upon me as your leader to share a few thoughts with you. I know you're all aware of the recent tension between Rabbi Winter and myself." Kahn consulted the yellow legal pad in front of him. "Motivated I'm sure by the best intentions, the rabbi has, nevertheless, caused our synagogue's good name to become an object of public ridicule. Instead of being regarded as a spiritual center, B'nai Zion is increasingly identified as the synagogue whose rabbi supports murders that he personally deems appropriate. Such a reputation makes a mockery of the ambitious plans we have so excitedly developed to expand this synagogue into the premier Jewish congregation in Los Angeles. For that reason, I must announce at this time the suspension of the one-million-dollar pledge I was planning to announce for the Myron Kahn Community Center. I stress that this suspension is temporary, and the pledge will be reinstated when a change has come to the congregation that will make it feasible to think again in terms of expansion."

"And when's that going to be?" Rena Raditz called out, breaking the stunned silence.

"When once again," the president said, "we have a unified rabbinic and lay leadership—both acting in conjunction for the best interests of the synagogue. Vice president Donald Sohn has likewise asked me to announce at this time the suspension of his $250,000 pledge until a more opportune period."

"Are you saying the million and a quarter is off until the rabbi is out?" Joe Aaronson asked.

Again Kahn's eyes wandered from face to face

around the table. His expression was stern. "That's not a decision I alone can make."

"But that's what you want?"

"The rabbi has, in my—and I think many, many people's—opinion, been obstinate, selfish, totally unwilling to be a team player, and in general a fool." The calm manner had disappeared and now he was scowling. "Don't pin it all on me. Do any of you think it brings honor to us when the city's district attorney denounces our spiritual leader at a press conference? What conclusions do you draw about Rabbi Winter's behavior?"

"You want conclusions?" Sam Bornstein bellowed, forcefully setting down his cigar. "I'll tell you conclusions."

"We can all hear at normal decibel levels, Sam," Kahn said. "What do you want to say?"

"The reason," Bornstein began, "that this synagogue stands ready to become, in your words, Mr. President, the premier congregation in LA is not because we're going to put up the Myron Kahn Community Center, and maybe make the rest of the *shul* a little prettier. It's because everybody knows we have a rabbi who teaches and touches people in his sermons, who's not afraid to make demands of us, who's willing to take risks for us, who tries—and I think pretty damn successfully—to be a *mensch,* and to make all of us a little more decent. Don't any of you kid yourselves—that's why our membership has doubled in the four years the rabbi's been here. Nobody chooses this *shul* because Russell Kahn is president or Sam Bornstein is chairman of the board. They come because of the rabbi. Of course, when you're president, you'd like the rabbi to do what you say and never argue back. But that's not a rabbi, that's a hired hand. And Daniel Winter is nobody's hired hand. He answers to one boss, God—or at least God as he understands Him. And there'll always be times some of us will disagree with the rabbi's direction and be angry with him. But if he leaves, who are Russell and the search committee going to bring in? A hired hand they can control. Inside of a year we'll have the prettiest synagogue in LA, and an empty Community Center and an empty sanctuary." Bornstein raised a stubby forefinger and pointed it around the table. "Over the last few days, it's occurred to me that all this is really a fight about the Golden Rule. Rabbi Winter's golden rule is the one he always likes to quote from the Talmud: 'What's hateful unto you, don't do unto your neighbor.' Right or wrong, that's how he wants us to act towards Jerry Braun. Russell's golden rule is a little different. 'He who has the gold makes the rules.' "

"I resent that, Sam—" Kahn broke in.

"Not more than I resent your calling *my* rabbi a fool." Bornstein turned back to the others. "I'm sure we're all shocked by Russell and Donald's withdrawal of their million and a quarter in pledges. The way they coordinated that announcement, I assume they intended to shock us into passing some insulting resolution that would force the rabbi to leave. But an issue as important as this must be decided on the basis of merit, not money. So before we continue this discussion let me at least take the sting out of this shock. Two weeks ago, as I suppose most of you have heard, I finalized the sale of the Samborn development. The rabbi always taught me that Jewish law says that those who are able to should give at least ten percent of their earnings to charity. I would therefore like to announce a contribution of $2,000,000 to our building fund." A buzz started around the table. Kahn's whole body seemed rigid, but his lower lip was moving involuntarily. "But," Bornstein interrupted, "at a time when so many people are taking potshots at our Rabbi, all I ask is for a resolution *before the end of today's meeting* acknowledging the board's pride in having Daniel Winter, *whose presence and teaching stimulated the gift*—and I want those words in—as our rabbi."

Precisely forty-one minutes later, the resolution passed the executive committee by a vote of 7–2. Within seconds, Russell Kahn and Donald Sohn, the two dissenting voices, announced their resignations from the B'nai Zion board.

"I'll find places where my money and my work are appreciated," were Russell Kahn's departing words.

Sam Bornstein, cigar in hand, offered a resolution thanking the two men for their years of service to the congregation. It passed unanimously. Whereupon Sidney Cass moved to reintroduce the resolution acknowledging Bornstein's gift. This time, without any discussion, it passed 7–0.

Joyce Kahn had once predicted that her husband wouldn't last two months as president. She was wrong. He lasted two months and ten days.

The groom's room at B'nai Zion was actually the synagogue's austere conference room: stark white walls lined with portraits of the congregation's former presidents and rabbis. A massive oak table and chairs were its only furnishings. But Luther Johnson, the *shul's* janitor, had an uncanny ability to transform the room's spirit. White streamers twisted and curled from the ceiling, while a large sponge cake dominated the head of the table flanked by bottles of the finest whiskeys and wines. Laughter filled the room.

When Daniel entered, carrying a long cardboard cylinder, Cantor Shlomo Bloch raised a shot glass towards him. "Mazel tov, Rabbi!" he called out. Daniel wasn't sure if Bloch was referring to the wedding, or if the outcome of the board meeting had already become public knowledge.

He returned the cantor's engaging smile, though he shook off the man's offer of a brandy. "Don't you worry about drinking, Shlomo, before you have to sing?"

The robust cantor laughed heartily, *"Ah-de-rabbah—* just the opposite. The more 777 I drink, the sweeter I sing."

At the rate the cantor was imbibing, Daniel thought, it looked like the singing under the canopy would be very sweet indeed. He worked his way through the gathering crowd towards the head of the table.

"Mazel tov, Evan."

The groom clasped both of Daniel's hands and squeezed them tightly. Evan's lean face was flushed with happiness and excitement.

Daniel sat down and laid the cylinder on the table. As he pulled out and unfurled the document inside, some of the surrounding guests ohed and ahed.

"It's a beauty!" one man called out, noting the painted doves and gazelles surrounding the folio's hand-lettered text.

"What is that exactly, Rabbi?" a nearby man asked.

"The *ketubah.*" Daniel turned to him. "The Jewish marriage contract." He held up the sheepskin sheet so everyone could see it. "This document outlines Evan's obligations to Sara."

"What about hers to him?" the same man asked.

Daniel smiled. "Evan's the only one making promises today."

Cantor Bloch began humming a familiar tune. The

guests slowly joined in. Soon the room filled with the haunting sounds of an ancient Hebrew chant. Daniel and Evan swayed with the song.

As the singing died down, Daniel turned to the groom. "Shall we do the *ketubah* signing now?"

"Anything you say, Rabbi."

"Who'll be signing?"

"Very funny, Rabbi. Me."

"That *would* seem to make the most sense, wouldn't it? Actually, two witnesses sign the *ketubah*, certifying that they saw you assume its responsibilities. Are there any people in particular you would like to designate as witnesses?"

"Uncle Billy, Uncle Sidney," Evan called to the back of the room.

The sounds of talking and clinking glasses stopped. "Relatives are excluded as witnesses," Daniel said. He saw the puzzled look on Evan's face. "Because they might someday have to testify about the document they are signing," he explained, "the rabbis were afraid their testimony would not be trustworthy. They might favor whichever party they were related to."

"Can you and the cantor do it?"

"We'd be honored."

Daniel reviewed the contractual provisions of the *ketubah*, most notably Evan's obligation to provide his wife with food, clothing, necessities, even sexual relations. The rabbis assumed women were too shy to initiate sex, so they listed it as an obligation of the husband. This was particularly important in ancient Jewish society, which allowed polygamy, and where the older or less attractive wife might otherwise find herself ignored. In accordance with Judaism's legal and generally nonromantic character, the *ketubah*, Daniel explained, also spelled out the husband's financial obligations in the event of divorce.

"Could you give me the pre-nuptial agreement now?" he asked Evan.

"Sara has it."

"Okay, I'll get it from her when she signs the civil papers."

Recently Daniel had started to insist that, at all weddings he performed, the couple sign a pre-nuptial agreement. "In the unfortunate event that our marriage be terminated by a court of competent jurisdiction," the contract read, "each of us consents to promptly take such steps as will effect the termination of our marriage by the giving and acceptance of a divorce, a *get* . . ." Judges, he knew, regarded the agreement as enforceable by the state's courts, and it meant that never again could a Sara Levin be victimized by a Leonard Goode.

Daniel gave a last look at the *ketubah,* then pulled a long, freshly laundered handkerchief from his pocket.

"Do you undertake, Evan, to fulfill all of the provisions in this *ketubah?*"

"I do."

Daniel held up the kerchief and instructed Evan to grasp the opposite end. "This physical act hereby certifies your acceptance of the *ketubah.*"

He called over the cantor, who took out an old-fashioned fountain pen and wrote his name, Shlomo ben Yosef, on the bottom of the document. A minute later Daniel affixed his Hebrew signature right under it. "Mazel tov," he said to the groom.

Evan's Uncle Billy came over and crushed the smiling groom in a bear hug. Spontaneously the crowd burst into a spirited rendition of *Od Yee-shama,* Jeremiah's 2,600-year-old prophecy to the Jews being exiled from the destroyed city of Jerusalem: "Again there shall be heard in this place . . . the sound of mirth and gladness, the voice of bridegroom and bride . . ."

Daniel got up from his seat. "Give me maybe ten minutes," he said in a low voice to Cantor Bloch, "before you bring Evan over to Sara."

He headed to the bride's room. Sara was there with her daughter Debby, and two good friends, Amy and Fran. She wore an ivory silk dress, and French braids framed her face.

"Mazel tov! Mazel tov!" Daniel sang out when he came in. Excitedly, the two friends signed as witnesses to the civil document, and Daniel collected the prenuptial agreement from Sara.

"It's almost time for the *bedekin*," Daniel said.

"The what?" Fran asked.

"The veiling," Daniel answered. "The groom veils the bride before the wedding. Ever since Jacob was promised Rachel as a bride, and his father-in-law substituted her veiled sister Leah, all grooms veil the bride before the wedding. That's to make sure they know whom they're marrying."

Sara laughed nervously at the explanation. She rested her bouquet of white roses in front of the mirror, checked her veil, and pinched her cheeks for added color. "Rabbi," she said, "how much time do we have?"

"Four, five minutes."

She lifted a half-empty pack of cigarettes off the vanity table and pulled one out. "I'm going to sit down and just try and relax."

"Hey, Sara," Fran said devilishly, "let me slip your veil on my face and see what Evan does."

"I'm not sure Evan will appreciate that," Amy said.

The girls all laughed.

"Mommy, you promised Evan," Debby said petulantly as her mother smoked. "This is your last one. I don't want my mom to die too."

"Oh, my poor darling," Sara called to the girl. "Of course I made that promise! And I will absolutely keep it. This is my last cigarette. Rabbi, you are a witness."

Debby beamed and threw her arms around her mother. Sara took a last reluctant drag, forcefully crunched the butt into the ashtray, kissed her daughter, and gathered up her roses. Fran adjusted the beads on her veil, and they eagerly left the room.

The wedding ceremony that followed the *bedekin* was brief. A violinist played as the guests filed into the sanctuary. The cantor chanted verses from the Bible as the wedding party marched down the aisle. After reciting the first blessings, Daniel read the *ketubah* aloud, while Evan and Sara stood together under the canopy. Evan then placed a plain gold band on Sara's finger, and Daniel recited the *sheva brakhot*—the seven blessings. Then Evan crushed a small glass with his foot, and the guests broke out in a chorus of "Mazel tov." The couple was immediately escorted by two witnesses back to the conference room where the *ketubah* had earlier been signed. They were to be alone there for a short while, symbolically indicating their togetherness as a couple.

"What now, Rabbi of mine?" Brenda asked Daniel teasingly as he stepped down from the raised canopy. "That was really quite beautiful."

"We'll stay for a while," he said. "I want to dance at Sara's wedding." They started moving towards the banquet hall. "A lovely soivice," a white-haired woman called out to him as they passed.

Daniel bowed his head in acknowledgment and

then snapped his fingers in the air. "The pre-nuptial agreement," he said. "I left it in the bridal room."

Brenda walked back with him to get it. The paper was lying on the counter in front of the mirror. As he reached over to lift it, he froze. His hand was on the agreement, but his eyes were on the ashtray.

"This has been some day," Brenda was saying. "First, that board meeting. I can't get over Sam's gift. You know, it occurred to me— Daniel, you're pale. Are you okay?"

"I think," he said, his hand rising to his throat, "I'm going to be sick."

Daniel entered the wedding hall and surveyed the scene. A small circle of men were spinning in the center of the room; others stood by clapping and singing. He headed straight towards Sara and Evan's table.

"I must speak to you, Sara," he said, leaning close to the bride's ear.

Her sparkling eyes regarded him curiously.

"Certainly, Rabbi."

"Now."

She broke into Evan's conversation with his uncle. "I'll be back in a minute, darling."

"You're certainly acting mysterious, Rabbi," Sara giggled as her heels echoed off the marble floors. Daniel did not reply. In silence, he led Sara to the bridal room.

Sara sat down on the leather chair, adjusting the ivory folds of her dress. Daniel perched on the counter by the mirror. "Okay, Rabbi, what's the big secret?"

"Does Evan know?" he asked.

"What?"

"Does Evan know?" Daniel's tone was stern.

Sara said nothing.

"Don't either of you even care what Jerry Braun is going through?"

She stared at him, her lips parted.

Daniel nudged the ashtray. "Is this your usual way of putting out your cigarettes?"

Sara continued watching him, mute.

"Smokers tend to put out their cigarettes in their own individual way. You know that. Every cigarette. Every time."

Sara's eyes dropped to the ashtray, but she kept her head still. The knuckles of her hand whitened.

Daniel waited. The room was so quiet he could hear his own quick, hard breathing. "There were twelve cigarettes found in Goode's ashtray," he continued. "All the same brand. All of them half-smoked and flicked off at the tip. Except for one." He prodded the butt in the ashtray. "That one looked exactly like this, crushed—how did Cerezzi put it—until it had the thickness of a penny."

Sara slumped in her chair. The fine silk dress suddenly looked creased and misshapened.

"Cerezzi was convinced," Daniel continued softly, "that Goode had been startled that morning and that he quickly stamped the cigarette out like this because the doorbell rang or there had been a surprise visitor. And, of course, everyone assumed it was Jerry Braun. But that surprise visitor was not entirely welcome, was she? Or should I say, the *two* visitors?" Daniel got to his feet. His face was ashen with misery. Sara was now shaking her head to and fro, and covering her ears.

"That was the cigarette *you* smoked, wasn't it?"

Sara did not lift her head or take her hands away from her ears.

For a few moments he stared at the back of Sara's head. Her thick braided hair was so feminine, so refined, he could hardly believe what he was saying. "Everyone was obsessed with one question: How did Jerry get into the house? Goode would certainly never have opened the door for him. How did you do it? Debby must have had a key to her father's house. Did you copy it, or did he just let you in? But if you came with Evan, you must have had a key."

Daniel stopped speaking. The sounds of dancing and *klezmer* music wafted through the halls. He rested one hand on her silken shoulder. Finally she let her hands drop from her ears. Without lifting her head, she began to speak, her voice clear and monotone.

"I didn't go there with this plan, and I didn't go with Evan. Evan doesn't know a thing about this. I went there that day to beg, like a dog with its tail dragging. I knew Leonard was always up early, and I figured I had my best chance seeing him at the house instead of the office. He let me right in. I told him straight out, 'Let's not fight anymore. All I want is the *get.*' For the first few minutes he was actually pleasant. He invited me to sit down, offered me a cigarette. I began to feel that there was hope, maybe he'd finally be human with me. But he was just playing his nasty power games. A minute later he turned. He always turned. He began laughing at me. Called me a little fool, and mocked Evan. 'What's a little sin of adultery for that jailbird boyfriend of yours?' I panicked. He was frightening me with that laugh. I realized the whole visit had been a bad mistake. I put out the cigarette and was about to run out the door. I swear this to you, Rabbi, all I wanted was to run right out. But he struck at my weakest spot. He always knew the spot. 'Be a good girl,' he called after me. 'Be a good, foolish little girl.' He always cut me down. During our marriage he always cut me down, humiliated me. It was that snide, mocking tone in his voice. 'Be a good girl and give me custody of Debby, and just maybe, if you're real good, I'll give you occasional visiting rights.' I got a buzz in my ear. Honest to God, it was so loud, all I could hear was the buzzing. His words made me so wild with rage I lost all control. I became like an animal. Almost without thinking I grabbed one of the knives. I tore him and cut him just like he was trying to tear and cut me." There was a savage fire in her eyes. "I tore at him. I tore . . . cut . . ." Suddenly her voice trailed off. "He wanted to destroy me, only I destroyed him first."

For a long moment Sara's last words rang in Daniel's ears. *Self-defense,* he thought. He was quite sure that had a defendant come to Goode with Sara Levin's story he would have gone into court, and more likely than not got the defendant acquitted. Goode, after all, had offered Sara a sadistically inhuman choice: never marry the man she loved, or give up her daughter forever. Leonard Goode's career, his life, had been devoted to getting murderers with much weaker cases acquitted. Daniel looked at Sara's slumped figure in the mirror. Would it be so unreasonable this time if his murderer got off?

The hum from the fluorescent lights buzzed unpleasantly in his ears. A terrible weariness had now overtaken him. He longed to just walk out of the room and pretend he never heard a word of hers. But he *had* heard it, and as profound as his compassion for Sara was, he also knew what had to be done.

"Your life was not threatened," was what he finally said.

"Neither was Gerald Braun's when he killed Ron Martin."

"But Martin had murdered Donna."

"And Leonard was *killing* me. It was an eye for an eye, like you quoted from the Torah, Rabbi."

Daniel stared a long time at the worn carpet. Then he said softly, "Leonard Goode was a vile, disgusting human being. And still you had no right to murder him. Sara, you must not deceive yourself."

"I haven't slept a whole night through ever since. Please, Rabbi—"

In the distance, Daniel heard footsteps advancing.

"Do you believe in God, Sara?"

"Of course."

"You know the right thing to do, don't you?"

In silence, she lowered her head.

Evan was at the door, his black tuxedo in disarray, sweat pouring down his forehead. "They're going wild out there." He laughed. "They want to lift the two of us up on chairs." He looked from Sara to Daniel. "What's going on here?"

With infinite fatigue, Daniel crossed the room and sat down on a low stool by the window. He turned to Evan. "I think, my friend, you and Sara have to speak."

21

One week later

—Sunday

Sam Bornstein lifted a champagne flute. "In honor of the rabbi and our congregation's future," he called out. *"L'chayyim!"*

"L'chayyim," the fifty guests at Bornstein's house shouted back.

L'chayyim, Daniel thought. *To life.* Donna Braun was dead. Ron Martin was dead. Leonard Goode was dead. And the man leading the toast, Sam Bornstein, was the only survivor of a family of nine. *L'chayyim,* to life.

The chairman of the board put his glass down and descended on Daniel, thumping him heartily on the back. "So you got your synagogue back," he said with a huge grin. "Anything else you want, rich man?"

"Just a quiet room, Sam. I need to make a call."

In the relative peace of Bornstein's bedroom, Daniel punched out the numbers. The call was picked up on the third ring.

"Hello."

"It's Daniel Winter, Joyce."

Her voice became immediately guarded. "What is it?"

"I want to speak to your husband."

"I don't think—"

"Please, Joyce. It's very important."

He heard her feet pattering away.

"Yes," a deep masculine voice came on a moment later. "So now that Sara Levin's confessed, you must be gloating, Rabbi?"

"Hardly . . . I'm unhappy about our fight, Russell."

"Mmm."

"I want peace."

"You got what you want, Rabbi. I'm out of your hair."

"I'd like you back in it."

"I'm sure."

Two verses from the Torah ran through Daniel's mind—"An eye for an eye" and "Do not take revenge or bear a grudge." Many people claimed the verses were contradictory, but Daniel knew their inconsistency was apparent, not real. Justice was one thing, revenge another. It might not always be easy to distinguish them, but they definitely were not the same. And keeping grudges going was not justice.

"We're family, Russell."

"No sermons, Rabbi."

"Had the Nazis gotten hold of us, Russell, they would have shoved us in the same crematorium. Is it only in their eyes that we're family?"

The man was quiet.

"I want you to think about rejoining the synagogue."

"You're still not getting the million dollars, Rabbi."

"Fine. Now, what about your coming back?"

"You're serious?"

"I am."

"I'll think about it."

When he returned to the parlor, Bornstein was speaking with Brenda.

"You look, my sweet," Brenda told him, "like you just swallowed a canary."

"They're not kosher." They laughed, and Daniel quickly filled them in on the conversation with Kahn.

"Think he'll come back, Rabbi?"

Daniel gave a satisfied nod.

Bornstein's features tightened. "And that makes you happy?"

"Very much."

"Your husband's a maniac, Rebbetzin. It just cost me two million dollars to get Russell Kahn off his back." He turned to Daniel. "I don't have any more Samborn developments up my sleeve, Rabbi."

"It's okay," Daniel answered.

"You're very lucky I have such a sweet disposition," Bornstein grumbled. His wife, Hilda, called out to him from across the room, and a minute later he drifted away.

Brenda's green eyes met Daniel's. It was their first moment alone since they'd arrived at the party. "Anything else you want, rich man?"

He lifted her chin. "Why don't you tell me what *you* want?"

She looked at him lovingly but didn't answer. Her eyes sparkled.

"Hmm?" Daniel asked, his finger tickling her chin.

"A baby," she whispered.

Daniel's face softened. He reached for two champagne glasses from the table behind him and handed her one. "Would it be okay if our baby has your green eyes?" They clinked their glasses together. *"L'chayyim,* copper," he said. To life.

22

Epilogue

On October 31, Sara Levin Singer was convicted of voluntary manslaughter in the death of Leonard Goode. She was sentenced to six years imprisonment. At the time of her conviction, she was two months pregnant. In an interview in the next day's *Los Angeles Times,* Evan Singer announced that he would raise the child alone until Sara's release. When the reporter asked if it bothered him that his child's mother was a murderer, Singer said: "If Leonard Goode were alive, Sara and I would still not be married and would have no prospect of ever marrying. The price Sara has paid is a stiff and unfair one, but we are together now and always will be."

•   •   •

Three months later, Daniel Winter took his seat beside
Brenda in the front row of Los Angeles Superior Court
to hear the sentencing in the case of The People vs.
Gerald Braun. Several weeks earlier Braun had
pleaded guilty to the voluntary manslaughter of Ron
Martin. "I have agonized long and hard," Judge
Klinger began, "over this particularly unhappy case.
This court has received no fewer than one hundred
and twenty-nine letters and character statements from
relatives, friends, and acquaintances of the defendant.
While the letters generally set out to convince me that
Dr. Braun is a saint unequaled on this planet since
Mahatma Gandhi, they did indeed convey to me that
he is a man who has done immense good and, most
significantly, has saved numerous lives through his
medical work. This alone, of course, does not mitigate
his crime, but it enables me to see him and consider
his punishment in a broader perspective. In addition, I
feel that there were significant, unusual, and extenuat-
ing circumstances in this unfortunate death, most notably the terrible, terrible stress under which the
defendant was operating at the time of the crime."
Klinger squinted down at the typed sheets he was holding. "The report submitted at my request concerning
Dr. Braun shows him to have no prior record of criminal activity; indeed, he has been an exemplary citizen.
I feel quite safe in saying that he is no danger to society
at this time." The judge asked Braun to rise. "I am,
therefore, sentencing you, Dr. Braun, to probation. As
a condition of felony probation, you will be required to
offer one thousand free hours of medical examinations
to indigent individuals not otherwise covered by welfare. You will report to a probation officer within the
next five days and keep him continuously informed of
your whereabouts for the duration of your probation,

which will extend for five years. You are not to own any guns. You will also pay a restitution fine of one hundred dollars as provided for by law.''

The judge paused and stared sternly at the defendant. ''I hope I never have occasion to see you again in this courtroom.'' The gavel descended, and the courtroom erupted. Almost in unison, several rows of spectators stood up and gave the jury a standing ovation. Enid Gurney, Donna Braun's friend, cupped her mouth and started chanting triumphantly, ''Justice for Donna, justice for Donna.'' For long minutes the judge made no effort to quiet the pandemonium. Gerald and Roberta Braun collapsed in each other's arms, her worn face streaked with tears of joy and relief. Braun turned to Daniel. ''Come with us out the back exit,'' he urged. ''It'll be a madhouse out there. I can't deal with the press.''

The moment they stepped outside, Daniel grasped both of Gerald's shoulders and drew him close. Brenda stood by, her head bowed. In a choked voice—his eyes moist—Daniel asked Gerald to repeat after him the *gomel* blessing: *''Barukh ata*—Blessed are You, Lord our God, King of the Universe, Who bestows favor on the undeserving, for having shown me every goodness.''

Gerald said the words haltingly, and Daniel added on the traditional Hebrew response to the blessing: *''Me she-ge-malkha*—May He Who bestowed every goodness upon you continue to bestow every goodness upon you forever.''

''Amen,'' Roberta whispered. Daniel opened one arm to her, and they huddled together in silence.

The Brauns then slipped into the back seat of Daniel's Cutlass Supreme. ''Would you mind taking us to the cemetery?'' Gerald asked.

Thirty minutes later they drove through the gates

of Mount Sinai. It was a bitter January day, yet the sun was shining. The expansive grounds were lush and peaceful. The four walked without speaking.

Daniel recited the twenty-third Psalm, "The Lord is my shepherd." Then he, Brenda, and Roberta lifted up small stones and rested them on the tombstone, a sign they had visited the deceased. They started off.

"I'll join you in a minute," Gerald called after them.

He bent down over the memorial stone, his lips kissing the cold rock. "Whatever I did, Donna, I did for you. I love you, sweetheart. Good-bye."

Excerpts from Daniel Winter's Article,
"An Eye for an Eye:
Some Twentieth-Century Reflections"

The conflict between Judaism's priorities and those of American criminal law is a fundamental one. For Judaism, the principal goal of life and of its legal system is the same: justice. As the Torah ordains: "Justice, justice you shall pursue" (Deuteronomy 16:20). Compare the passion of the Bible's verse with the cold logic of one of America's greatest jurists, Oliver Wendell Holmes: "I have said to my brethren many times that I hate justice, which means that I know if a man begins to talk about that, for one reason or another he is shirking thinking in legal terms" (Letter to Dr. John Wu, July 1, 1929).

"Legal terms"—as Holmes styles it—is apparently the concept which liberates American courts from the biblical obsession with justice. This attitude, Judaism cannot countenance. Though the Torah demanded, for example, "an eye for an eye," the rabbis ruled early on that the assailant must pay a fine rather than have his own eye extracted. Why? Because of the demands of justice. As the Talmud expressed it: "Now if you assume that actual retaliation is intended, it could sometimes happen that both eye and life would be taken [in payment for the] eye, as, for instance, if the offender died as he was being blinded" (Bava Kamma 83B-84A). So even though one who intentionally blinds another deserves to be blinded, in practice the assailant pays compensation, lest the court commit the greater injustice of killing as well as blinding him.

In the case of premeditated murder, however, no such scruples apply. In this instance, justice not only allows for capital punishment, it demands it. The Torah repeatedly reiterates this demand:

1. "Whoever sheds the blood of man, by man shall his

blood be shed, for in His image did God make man'' (Genesis 9:6).

2. "He who fatally strikes a man shall be put to death." That the law clearly restricts itself to premeditated murder, is indicated by the following verse: "If he did not do it by design . . . I will assign you a place to which [the killer] can flee" (Exodus 21:12–13).

3. "And you shall not take reparations for the soul of a murderer who deserves to die, but he shall be put to death" (Numbers 35:31).

The biblical rationale for executing murderers seems to be twofold. First, "That people shall see and be afraid" (Deuteronomy 19:20)—in other words, to deter other would-be killers. A society which does not severely punish evil in effect publicly announces that there is no *pragmatic* reason not to commit evil. Today almost everyone, with the exception of liberal criminologists, accepts this commonsensical assertion. As former U.S. Solicitor General Robert Bork has noted: "The assertion [by liberal criminologists] that punishment does not deter runs contrary to the common sense of the common man and is, perhaps, for that reason a tenet fiercely held by a number of social scientists."

Despite this ongoing debate over whether or not capital punishment deters murders, two things are clear:

A. Since the widespread suspension of capital punishment in the United States since the 1960s, homicides against strangers—precisely the murders most susceptible to deterrence—have more than doubled. At least one reason for this is that without a death sentence, criminals have fewer compunctions about murdering potential eyewitnesses.

B. If nothing else, capital punishment ensures that the murderers themselves never kill again.

The second biblical rationale is: "And you shall burn

the evil out from your midst" (Deuteronomy 19:19 and 24:7).

The Bible obligates us to hate and destroy evil. In the final analysis, the reason the Allies hanged the Nazi leaders at Nuremberg and the reason Israel hanged Eichmann had little to do with deterrence or with the fear that these people might kill again if released. It was the feeling rather that the evil done by the Nazis was so enormous that it deserved an enormous punishment, in the words of the rabbis, *middah ke-negged middah*, measure for measure.

And lest one argue that capital punishment, therefore, would be appropriate punishment only for mass murderers, Jewish teachings insist that every innocent human life is of infinite value. Hence, the murder of one innocent person is the ultimate evil; the murder of ten more innocents increases the magnitude, not the evil.

About the Author

JOSEPH TELUSHKIN, a well-known national lecturer, holds a rabbinic degree from Yeshiva University and a graduate degree in history from Columbia University. From 1977 to 1983, he was education director of the Brandeis-Bardin Institute in California. He is the author of *The Nine Questions People Ask About Judaism* and *Why the Jews?* (both with Dennis Prager), as well as *Jewish Literacy* and two earlier Rabbi Daniel Winter mysteries, *The Unorthodox Murder of Rabbi Wahl* and *The Final Analysis of Dr. Stark.*

BANTAM MYSTERY COLLECTION